# FORGOTTEN MAGIC

EDEN BUTLER

CITY OWL
PRESS

FORGOTTEN MAGIC
Crimson Cove, Book 1

CITY OWL PRESS
www.cityowlpress.com

Cover Design by Mibl Art. All stock photos licensed appropriately.

Edited by Yelena Casale.

For information on subsidiary rights, please contact the publisher at info@cityowlpress.com.

Print Edition ISBN: 978-1-949090-89-5

Digital Edition ISBN: 978-1-949090-88-8

Printed in the United States of America

# PRAISE FOR EDEN BUTLER

"Butler's tantalizing fantasy romance, originally self-published as *Crimson Cove*, burns slow and hot...The magical elements are electric and the chemistry between Bane and Janiver is delicious. Butler builds the tension slowly, carefully pulling story threads to a satisfying but open ended climax. Readers will be eager to return to Crimson Cove." - *Publishers Weekly*

"Butler's LUSH descriptions evoke the love and terror the past couples feel as they face violence that threatens their relationships and lives. The complex structure crystallizes into an impressive resolution that ties up loose threads hidden in the very first pages. This SPLENDID story is destined for many a keeper shelf." - *Publishers Weekly Starred Review*

"I am so overwhelmed by the quality of [Eden Butler's] writing. I am getting emotional just thinking about it." - *Natasha Is A Book Junkie*

"Beautifully written, skillfully interwoven, a wonder of a tale. It's not often that I am truly impressed, but Eden Butler has blown me away." - *New York Times & USA Today Bestselling author Amy Harmon*

"Infinite Us is a gripping story of the roots that define us, the hardships that test us, and the healing power of love and acceptance. It's a testament to how far we've come and how very far we have to go." - *J.A. DeRouen, Bestselling Author of Low Over High*

"Eden is a masterful storyteller who takes mere words and turns them into magic. She takes you on an intoxicating journey that refuses to let go. Infinite Us is an unforgettable story that'll leave you breathless." - *Cassie Graham, Bestselling Author of Who Needs Air*

"Simultaneously commercial and literary—a thinking person's romance." - *Christopher Ledbetter, Author of The Sky Throne Series*

"Butler shines again in this emotionally moving tale of love, despite life and its trials and tribulations. The writing is crisp, lyrical and the flat out FEELS between the characters leak from the pages straight into your heart. You WILL be moved." - *Trish F. Leger, Author of the Amber Druid Series*

*To the old guy who rolled his eyes*
*when he read about the kissing bits in this book:*
*I'm smiling at you in southern.*
*Bless your heart.*

*The sound of a kiss is not so loud as that of a cannon, but its echo lasts a great deal longer.*
*— Oliver Wendell Holmes, Sr.*

# ONE

Magic is elemental. It's a full-bodied thread in all that we are. To me, to all my folk—witches and wizards of every make and the other supernatural creatures that co-exist in our ley line-loving world—magic simply *is*.

It was magic that lived deep inside me, hidden beneath the wretch of who I'd been, of what I'd done ten years ago at age eighteen. My father would call me a hypocrite— if we were still talking. He'd tell me that keeping myself from the covens in New York and from my family back in Crimson Cove, keeping myself from the life he taught me to be proud of, was a coward's way.

I was a witch only when it served my purposes.

Like now, slipping inside the dreams of such a talented writer. My client, Ivanna Ride (pseudonym, of course), was the hottest thing in erotic romance. She outsold and out published even the most popular authors and she did it on her own. There was no major house working behind her. Just Ivanna, her clever English-nerd husband, and me, Janiver Benoit, graphic artist extraordinaire. Well, that might be pushing it. It was magic that made me extraordinary and it was my gifts that helped me slip inside Ivanna's mind and discover the theme, the vibe, the truly disturbing imagery she saw when she dreamt of her characters.

This time around it was Kjel, the 1050 A.D. Viking warrior in love with an enemy clan leader's daughter. Blood and war and lots of sex. That's what I had to make come to life on the cover of her book.

Walking inside Ivanna's mind was like taking a stroll through a Renaissance Fair—on acid. The mist around me as I stepped into her dream was thick, a clotting smell that stuck in the back of my throat and choked me with the heavy scent of lavender. It hung in my sinuses, made my dry mouth collect with saliva. But on the back of that scent was something I recognized only vaguely as sweat. In Ivanna's dreams, there was sex. It became apparent that's what she had in mind, literally, when her REM cycle kicked into high gear.

Kjel—or who I took for Kjel—stood barefoot atop a bear skin rug in a rugged stone hut, glaring down at some whimpering, silly girl who looked more turned on than frightened. She was the enemy's daughter knocking on the door of womanhood, looking at Kjel like she wanted him to guide her way through it.

With a shudder of sound and the shift of light, the scene changed and the small room with its dirt floor became a boudoir with fine, cerise linens and a massive four-poster bed. The girl's face transformed to mimic something like Ivanna's. At least, how she'd looked this afternoon when I listened to her babble on and on about the pending Kjel series and her vision for the rest of her books, her promo graphics, and the blog tours she wanted to organize.

I'd listened to her politely, nodding where appropriate as this mid-forties woman tucked strands of curly brown hair behind her ear. Damn. Was it petty of me to notice that there was gray flirting in those strands near her temples? She guzzled on an iced coffee as she talked, never once asking for my opinion or curious about what ideas might have come to me when I'd read the manuscript. That didn't bother me, though, not really. My clients typically didn't want to know what I thought. They just wanted to make sure I made magic happen on their covers and their promo materials.

Funny how close that was to the truth.

I'd listened to Ivanna for nearly an hour, sipping my own Venti

English Breakfast Tea, more interested in the chipping black paint on my fingernails and the wadded napkin Ivanna had used to wipe her mouth. That would be the souvenir I'd take to give me access to her dreams.

Magic, no matter what fantasy authors or Renaissance vendors tell you, is just an old school name for the things mortals want proof of to believe. Everything we do has to be logical, must have an explanation.

It is true that there has to be basis for every spell or hex. There has to be something elemental that connects our target or, in my case, client, to the magic we twist. It isn't simply supernatural. It's dependent on the natural. Magic elevates it. That's why I needed Ivanna's napkin. It was something she'd held, something that she'd left a bit of herself behind on, and it was the element I needed to slip into her dreams.

But I didn't like doing it—dreamwalking. Not like this. It was an invasion that made me feel cheap and simple. Intruding into someone else's private dreams? Seeing the things they'd never freely admit to desiring? I was like some kind of perv trying to make my clients happy by copying their own imaginations.

Still, it paid the bills. So I stalked in the shadows in my client's dreamworld. Kjel and dream Ivanna were starting to go at it. Bleaching my eyeballs was the first order of business when I woke up, which needed to happen right now. I had work to do.

I started that slow awakening, the controlled transition that would bring me out of Ivanna's mind and back to the "real" world. It was a simple enough process—a little focus on my breathing, on the things around me. I drew upon a picture in my mind's eye of my tiny apartment, of myself lying in only a black tank and red boy shorts, my dark hair covering my face, tattoos and runes dotting around my ankles, thighs, up the side of one bicep. The black ink was shaped in ancient languages, looping around my arm, connected to a black and gray rose on my left shoulder.

Things were calm, my mind working effortlessly to bring me back safely, away from Ivanna's Viking wet dream and her saccharine world. I was nearly there, watching myself sleep, turn beneath my white sheets, knocking over an empty tumbler on my bedside table—not the bourbon, thank God—and then, the alert of a video chat on my laptop blasted across the room.

*Jani! Jani!* The alarming scream of my brother's voice shot through the slow retreat my mind made. Sam's voice became a grating, loud yelp that made my chest constrict as my heart sped.

*Jani! Jani, for the gods' sake, wake up!*

And I did, jerking from my sheets, sending my pillows shooting onto the floor and the thick gasp of air in my lungs coming out like a yelp.

"Shit!"

The bell alert from my laptop lying on the floor next to my bed kept ringing, that low, constant loop that announced an incoming video call. Sam hadn't actually spoken to me, but still had a way of scaring the hell out me, nineteen hundred miles away. My brother could call to me, unannounced, whenever he wanted, but especially when I was unconscious. The annoying sibling connection was a nuisance I'd never be rid of.

"Stupid, intrusive..." My laptop flopped against the mattress when I picked it up and jammed my finger on the surface to accept the call. I didn't bother letting my big brother explain a damn thing. "You asshole, I was in someone's dream."

"Well hey to you too, little sister."

A quick glance at my cell phone to cut off the insistent text I knew Sam had sent me and I caught the time. Shit, someone was probably dead.

"Who died?" My brother's small chuckle was the only thing that made me relax enough to leave the bed and tug on my jeans.

"No one yet, though I'm pretty close to killing your brother-in-law." My brother always blamed me when shit hit the fan, and from his tone, I'd guessed that this time the shit had slammed into the proverbial fan in buckets.

Still, that wasn't my fault. "Ronan is your brother-in-law too, Samedi."

"Yeah." The frustration was heavy in his voice at my using his full name. "Well Mai is your twin, *Janiver*, and since it's her husband that started all this shit, it should be you that gets us out of it."

Mai was younger than me by only four minutes, but somehow we were years apart. I always picked up the pieces when she let her world fall apart—like it was now, with her in the middle of a bad breakup with her lazy, perpetually cheating husband. Still, it wasn't my fight.

"You've got the wrong twin."

I cut Sam off from whatever excuse I knew he was going to use when he cleared his throat by shaking my head and reaching out to grab the bottle of bourbon that had been sitting on the table beside my bed. I took a deep pull on the bottle, despite the glare my brother gave me. "Ask Mai to work out this mess."

"She can't. She's gone off the rails."

That meant trouble. It was habit, something my twin did when she couldn't handle the messes she'd made for herself.

"What..." A small exhale and I readied for the bad news I suspected was coming. "What do you mean?"

"She's back at Papa's and won't come out of her room."

"*Circe help us.*"

The bourbon didn't burn when it went down, despite the long swig I took. My throat had grown numb to the sting of liquor a long damn time ago, and the small little noise of judgment Sam made got completely ignored. When you numb yourself in order to forget, something that had become one of my more practiced habits, you tend to get used to both the bite and the judgment, no matter where they come from.

Mai's hiding away—my twin's way of forgetting—wasn't the worst of the situation. Not by a long damn shot.

"She caught him with that same stripper from last year."

"The one with the pixie cut?"

"Yeah, whatever, but this time he didn't bother begging Mai not to kick him out." Sam leaned on his arm, rubbing the back of his neck. His complexion was darker than mine or Mai's, taking on more of our mother's Haitian creole features than our blue-eyed father's French, but like both me and Mai, Sam had full lips and hazel eyes. We were all a good mix of both our parents. "Papa thought giving Ronan a job would maybe keep that asshole from running off for weeks at a time." Sam looked tired, like he hadn't bothered with sleep in days. My stomach tightened at the thought, and I couldn't quite ignore the weight in my chest that settled there. My brother had enough to deal with. He didn't need Mai's jackass of a husband doubling up his anxiety.

"Bet that was pointless."

"You got no idea." Sam released one long exhale and scrubbed a hand against his fade at the back of his head. He'd abandoned the short afro he'd grown out the last time I saw him and looked more like himself. "He totally fucked us over."

"What do you mean? What happened?"

"If Papa hadn't let Ronan take care of so many clients when they came calling, none of this would have happened. He just botched up too many jobs, was too sloppy, and I was too busy to notice that his haplessness had become a serious problem."

The whole time he had been talking to me, Sam had kept looking at his cell phone. It wasn't like him to let a text distract him. The string of beeps coming from his phone was odd, but the expression on his face was almost funny. *Almost.*

"The whole damn town is talking about it. Papa says if we can't pull in a big client, our name will be ruined." Another heavy sigh and Sam threw down his cell. "Not to mention all the damn attention we've been getting from the mortals."

Watching Sam, seeing the tension bunching up his features, I suddenly realized that this conversation was the longest we'd had in a year. In the past, we simply fought all the time. Even after our mother died five years ago, we hadn't managed a civil conversation. But then last summer, his wife, Adele, and their unborn child died in a car crash. The kid that killed them had been confused, barely legal, and since their deaths Sam and my conversations had simply become short and to the point. But this was different.

"Has Ivy or his men been snooping around?" I'd held my breath after asking that question. Ivy Beckerman was Crimson Cove's chief of police. We all suspected he wouldn't blink twice if he caught any weres shifting into their animal forms or spirits haunting the edge of the cemetery, never mind any chance encounters with a wizard doing something beyond human comprehension. There was something about the man that made him different from the other mortals. They only saw what they wanted. But Ivy was smart, observant; he saw things that the others didn't. So far, though, he'd kept his questions to himself.

"No, not so much," Sam said, once again focusing on his phone when it beeped, offering only a glance my way when he spoke, "but he did come by asking who busted in the store window." Sam waited for that to make an impact.

"What the hell happened to the store window?"

"Some asshole pissed off that we hadn't done our best to hide whatever bullshit they didn't want the mortals to see, we think. Thanks to Ronan, we got a sledgehammer through the front window."

That was unnerving. My father had managed to keep up the façade of running a respectable antiques store for decades. It was a decent way to front his real business—making sure the mortals never caught wind that a good majority of the Cove's residents weren't mortal at all; Papa was what the supernatural community called a "fixer."

"How bad is it really, Sam?" That question came in front of a small, silent prayer that I could help my family from the comfort of my fifth-floor walkup in Brooklyn.

I should have known better.

Another of Sam's exhales came out slow, this one with a labored drag of frustration, maybe the small hint of defeat. "Carter Grant has pulled his coven's contract with us. He doesn't want to be involved in any accidents we can't quite cover up."

"Shit." That revelation warranted another swig and another disapproving shake of my brother's head. If the Grants, a founding family and one of the oldest covens—and the one family our ancestors had pledged fealty to generations before—cut ties with us, then things were about as bad as they could get.

"We've asked a couple of the other Finders to help out, Jani, but none are as good as you. Papa says you're our last resort."

Whatever I was ten years ago—Finder of Lost Things, twin of a mighty healer, daughter to a man who swept our lives away from mortal eyes—I'd packed up in a steamer trunk my father swindled from a Tulsa antiques dealer and hopped a bus to New York. I'd been eighteen and thought Crimson Cove had seen the back of me. I hated being wrong.

It probably was tearing Papa up to know Sam was going to ask me to come home. He'd always maintained that once you left, that was it. No need to drag up the past with a trip down memory lane. Besides, he'd always told me "nothing but heartache for you here, Janiver." But after the bomb my brother dropped, I had little choice.

"I'll take the red eye."

"About that, Jani..." Another alert. This time Sam read the message then immediately snapped his gaze back up to the screen. "You don't need to worry about getting a ticket." My brother swallowed, shifting his attention away from the camera like he'd rather do anything than explain himself.

*Damn it.* This definitely required more bourbon.

"Thing is, someone is coming for you."

"Who?"

"In a few minutes, actually."

"Samedi, who?"

"Should be there. Now."

"Son of a bitch."

*Please don't let it be him, I prayed.*

I wanted to handle this issue my family had and be done with it. I had no intention of *reconnecting.*

*Please, please, don't let it be him.*

"He was already in the city."

"What are you talking about, Sam?"

"Look, Jani, something happened, with the Elam."

The Elam? The talisman through which all the magic in Crimson Cove converged, which kept us hidden from mortal eyes and in check?

"Someone attacked and took it..." Someone had *stolen* it?

"You don't lead with *that?* My God, Sam..."

"I know...it's just... Look...we really, well, we tried finding anyone else to help find it, but shit, sis, you're the best and there is so little time and he was there in New York and..."

"Balls..." I said, already knowing what point my brother was skirting around.

This was bad. Very bad. No wonder my family was on the edge of panic. I emptied the bottle but kept it between my legs as Sam tried and failed to explain himself.

"I just hope you don't—"

Three loud drums of a knock on my door had me almost jumping out of my skin. The temperature in the room suddenly shifted, and on the other side of the door I picked up two signatures: elemental magic that identifies a witch or wizard like a thumbprint. Unbidden, my pulse started racing, and I found it hard to breathe.

"Jani..." Sam's warning was too little and way too late. Nothing would save him from the shit storm I'd level at him as soon as I landed back home.

"Not another damn word, big brother."

One of the bodies out in the hallway radiated heat and a familiar spicy, rich smell that made my mouth water.

"Jani...let me explain."

Sam's voice was rushed, muddled as I left the bed and stood in front of my door, my hand hovering over the handle. I didn't need to look through the peep hole to know who stood out in the hallway.

"Whoever stole the Elam used old magic. They needed an old bloodline to make the hex work." I squinted, looking over my shoulder toward the laptop as I twisted the handle, then didn't blink or breathe at all as my gaze lifted to see Bane Iles. He stood on the other side of the open door.

"Yeah," he said, as if he had been listening to our conversation. Just as shocking as his appearance at my door was the fact that his face was bruised, and there was a cut along his bottom lip —injuries that shouldn't be there at all. "And that blood was mine."

# TWO

BANE ILES HAD RUINED MY FAVORITE SUBJECT.

Senior year at Crimson Cove Regional, we'd started the semester with the Romantics—reading Shelley and Lord Byron, forgetting our town, the weird dichotomy of our lives among the mortals, by integrating into their schools. The language, the love of literature made me forget that I was the only girl in the small class of fifteen that wasn't mortal. Cherrie Miles, a bottle blonde who wore her t-shirts torn at the neck and frayed to her chest, always asked how I managed to keep my light brown skin free of any blemishes at all, while Samantha Riley gave too close a squint at the smooth flick of my eye liner. They weren't my friends, hadn't bothered to make me feel as if they wanted to be, but even back then, at eighteen, I'd known the importance of tolerating their daily examination of my make-up and outfits. That took less effort than diverting the lewd cat calls I got from the boys the second I walked through the doors of that school my senior year.

Ricky Morris had no problem grunting at me like a wolf when I passed him in the hall. Evan Ames liked to call after me, mutter my name in a way that seemed somehow disgraceful and inappropriate.

But all that stopped when Bane came down the hall after me; one glance and an angry glare sent the mortal boys scattering.

We were meant to mingle, to fit in. We were supposed to act like them, disappear within a crowd of them to pull attention away from ourselves. But mortals and magic did not mesh. Ever.

Percy Bysshe Shelley distracted me from those curious stares. Lord Byron annoyed me just enough that I was too worked up over his personal history to notice how often Cherrie and Samantha gawked at me or how Ricky and Evan kept silent around me, ducking Bane's gaze when he caught them watching whenever he happened to pass by. The first few days, I thought the material would keep my focus from all the curious stares. And it had. I'd barely noticed the shrewd, critical—or leering—looks. Then, with one schedule change, that beautiful bastard walked right into the classroom and my attention on Romantic literature went the way of land lines and printed phone books.

The moment he stepped into the classroom, days into the beginning of the semester, Bane held the attention of every person sitting stoically still at his approach. One step, two more, and with each tousle of his thick, dark hair, with every click of his boots against the tile floor, the air seemed to evaporate a bit more. The room had gone soundless and cold like the wind stilling before a storm, readying for a torrential onslaught that flirts in the heavy clouds far above. Bane entered that room ten years ago with a casualness I'd never seen anyone else repeat. He'd been a boy too grown for his body, with limbs and muscle threatening to break through all that taut skin, as though another creature pulsed beneath his bones, something fiercer that would rattle everything boring and mundane about Crimson Cove. Just like the hurricanes that disturbed the Cove and broke the pines and maples from their root beds, Bane Iles came into my world ready to rip it apart.

He did that with one slow look my way.

And now he was doing that yet again as I stared at him standing outside of my big city door.

"Janiver Benoit."

It wasn't a greeting, not something Bane uttered to make me feel welcome. He spoke my name like a forgotten memory. One that maybe he should feel guilty about recalling but enjoyed too damn much to let that guilt settle in. At least, those cool, steel eyes, that not-really-there smirk, said that's what my name off his tongue meant.

It was like seeing a beautiful caged animal behind bars; one that wasn't really trapped, like it had sorted out just how to escape and wanted to toy a little with his keeper. But I had never kept Bane Iles. I doubted anyone could.

Bane had been beautiful—a silent, grumpy heap of maleness that made others back away whenever they caught sight of him. Girls ignored their schoolwork or the attention of any other boy whenever Bane walked down the hallway. He turned heads because he was massive, well over six feet tall. He kept those heads turned because he was beautiful. Bane and his younger cousins that had been sent to live with his uncle in their higher coven territory were like most of the Grants—handsome and hard. Rugged, but still refined. Bane, though, was darker, his complexion deeper, like the color of a tawny hawk's feather, but his eyes were the palest blue I'd ever seen. They almost looked like bright silver. They'd shone like crystal whenever he slipped into our English Lit class just seconds before the tardy bell rang.

Still, that easy calm that he'd pulled off as a kid—his face turned toward whatever lecture Mr. Matthews was giving yet his eyes slanted down at me—had strengthened with time, had leveled into something so smooth and effortless, I would have sworn it was instinctual. His limbs were too relaxed. His fat, tempting bottom lip dented just slightly in the center as though he couldn't keep from tucking it just a bit between his teeth was just too perfect.

Everything about him—the mammoth arms barely concealed beneath that brown leather jacket, the long, slim fingers and thick veins along the backs of his hands, the endless stretch of his legs in those dark jeans and the relaxed cast of his body, the threat of violence pulsing behind his crystal eyes—was a giant contradiction of strength, violence, and sensuality.

"Ah, excuse me, sir, but the plane is waiting." A smooth glance at the guard standing next to him and Bane nodded. *Right.* There was a second signature. I almost forgot.

"You packed?" he asked me, moving to step over the threshold until

I stopped him. Bane wasn't a wizard accustomed to people getting in his way, and I, with my arm blocking him from entering my apartment, gave him just enough pause to glance down my body, that gaze lingering a bit too long at my braless chest and unbuttoned jeans. "Red?" He grinned, catching a glimpse of my underwear.

I refused to let it show that him just standing there, looking the way he did, evoking the memories and sensations he did in me had thrown me in the least. That way led to madness and chaos. I'd never recover from either. "This isn't the Cove. You don't get to come and go as you please."

He leaned against the door, ignoring his guard as the man nodded and walked toward the elevator at the end of the hall. "You know, Jani, I think you'd like how I come and go."

"Thanks, not interested." *Lie. Total and complete lie,* I told myself.

It took him exactly three seconds to smirk. It was more than a grin this time, but not an expression that a stranger would take as friendly. That's generally about all Bane could manage in the way of a friendly or even mildly flirty grin. "Pity," he said, still giving me the once-over.

"I've had about a two-minute warning that you'd be here. Give me twenty minutes."

"You gonna let me in?"

"Let the man in, Jani," I heard my brother call from the laptop. I had totally forgotten that he was still there. "He's taking you back in a private jet for free."

"Nothing is free," I tossed over my shoulder, deciding to don a defense of indifference, maybe mild rudeness where this wizard was concerned. I relented enough to not slam the door in Bane's face before I turned back into my apartment and slipped into my bedroom.

"Is this the part where we discuss your payment?" Bane asked, resting against the door leading into my bedroom as I tugged out my suitcase from the closet and started throwing clothes into a messy pile in the center of it.

"You mean you two haven't discussed that without me too?" One glance in his direction was all I offered, and I tried not to get too annoyed at the way he moved his gaze around my place, looking over his shoulder into the tiny kitchen and sparsely outfitted living area.

There was only one bathroom and one bedroom, and every wall in the place was a beige-gray with thick, pre-war molding, original lead paint and all. Only my bedside table held anything personal—a picture of me and my siblings two years ago, back before Sam lost his wife and Mai's marriage went into the toilet, and one of my mother before she left Haiti for New Orleans and met my father.

The barren landscape of my apartment was by choice. The sterile wall color and vintage appliances and bathroom fixtures weren't, but I usually only stayed here long enough to pass out or lock myself in my bedroom with my laptop in front of me as I worked.

"Would we do that, sis?" Sam asked, his voice a little too chipper for my liking.

"Plan on a conversation when I get there." He might have looked worried when my face popped up too close to the camera on my laptop. I wouldn't know since I hit the exit button and powered down the machine before he could argue.

"You'll be paid well if you can get the Elam back." Bane settled smoothly on my bed as I continued to move around the room gathering essentials, and he didn't bother looking away when I tugged off my tank to put on a bra behind the half-open closet door.

In the mirror on the back of the door I noticed Bane working his hands together, one of only a couple nervous ticks I knew he had. He had more runes on his skin than I remembered, peeking out beneath the cuff of his long gray t-shirt and others that became visible when he discarded his jacket.

Mortals thought those were only tribal-style tattoos. We let them think that. In fact, we didn't explain anything to the mortals, even if they happened upon our world. Generally, if they sorted out who and what we were, they were too terrified or too convinced their mind was playing tricks on them to understand the complexities of magic.

Bane defied explanation anyway. Mortals looking at him would see only what their eyes told them was true—that the rugged face likely came from a roughneck gene pool; that his stature was the result of hours spent honing and sharpening his physique, that his tattoos were clever designs some artist fashioned out of his imagination on slow shop nights. But none of that was true. No artist inked doodles into glyphs and forms at random. Every line, circle, and etching on his skin had meaning.

The marks were runes, ancient symbols that engendered power, fine art that resulted from study, from sacrifice so that Bane would become more than a gifted wizard. He knew spells that time had buried, rhymes and hexes that evoked power, terror that mages and clerics of every conceivable study had blown into the winds of time. They were literally etched on his body.

My gifts did not demand the sacrifice of blood and pain. I had studied, not to Bane's extent, but my runes were there—smaller, simpler, but still very much there.

Mortals would never know what the symbols meant, but that didn't mean their own instincts wouldn't keep them from the instinctual understanding they held to avoid underlying strangeness and possible danger. That much hadn't changed in ten years.

I shut the closet door with a kick of my boot and zipped my leather motorcycle jacket up with a noisy scratch. Bane gave me the once over again, his gaze shifting up my body before he moved it back to my face. Bane also did like the way I was put together. At least, he seemed to always watch me like he did. Every square inch of my skin warmed beneath that close examination, and I realized maybe going back with him wasn't the best idea.

I hadn't left Crimson Cove because of Bane Iles—I had left despite him. He was just the sort of man that could have easily kept me in that tiny town with his perfect not-a-smirk and the slow, hungry glances of his eyes.

I'd left before Bane had convinced me to stay.

I'd left because staying was all I'd wanted to do.

"You look good." That seemed a little too honest, something out of character for Bane to admit, and he seemed to regret it the moment he spoke. His frown, the heavy dip of his eyebrows made him look annoyed by his own honesty.

Years ago, when I leveled one soul-rattling kiss at him, after nine solid months of his silent stares, Bane had managed a handful of words —small promises I knew he didn't mean. I'd spent years unable to pull them from my thoughts. But I'd trained myself not to think fondly on those promises. They were pointless now and his just-uttered compliment didn't mean anything to me. Especially since I was there to do a job, not stroll down memory lane with him.

Still, I'd been a lying fool to deny what he already knew.

"Mr. Iles, so do you."

Time kept him frozen in my mind. Over the years I recalled the quick glances he'd give me when Mr. Matthews would drone on too long in class. The glances became longer, slower until we spoke wordlessly. A flick of his lashes, the hooded cast of his eyelids, my breath fanning over my teeth, my lips barely touching as I watched him—those silent moments spoke volumes, and now, letting him take me in, I wondered if it was the same for him. I wondered if Bane remembered how we were back then, silent and curious, longing and eager but held up by the confines of the classroom and the lives we lived outside of it.

"No one calls me Mr. Iles unless they're trying to get me to unload my wallet."

"Technically, I *am* trying to get you to unload your wallet."

He let that almost smile return, and I got the feeling he was fighting his humor. "For a service." That last word came out with the smallest hint of a growl, and I tried to ignore the sweet little ache in the pit of my stomach.

"Well, yeah," I said, standing straighter. The scent of his skin was thick, reminded me of the honeysuckle vines that lined the path around the town square. Blinking did not move my focus from that smell or what it did to my senses, so I concentrated instead on the small bruise under his left eye. It was crescent shaped and turning yellow. "That service." My voice came out in a rasp despite the jar in my throat when I cleared it. "Let's discuss that." He turned away from my finger when I pointed at his face. The scrape was a dull purple but was turning lighter at the edge. "When were you attacked?"

Bane let the humor leave his features and the frown he gave edged close to the scary side. "Two days ago."

"And you're still busted up?"

His cheeks pinkened, and I thought the temper that had always gotten Bane into trouble would surface, but he managed to keep himself in check. "I am *not* busted up."

Just like a wizard to get defensive. There was nothing worse than a man with a bruised ego along with a busted lip. Add that to a strong, connected wizard whose body should heal in hours, not days after an attack, and you've got the makings of some serious deflection and chest thumping.

"Sorry," I amended, ignoring the frown fracturing the beautiful contours of his face. "I just thought you would have healed by now."

"I know." Bane left the mattress with an ease that seemed practiced. A performance that reminded me of a peacock stretching his feathers, but I doubted he was the sort to grand stand for a woman. Least of all me. Instead, he closed my suitcase, snapping the lock before he pulled it from the mattress. "You done?"

"Yeah."

He watched me turn off my lights, that hard gaze following me as the apartment darkened and I tugged a scarf and my bag on. Bane stared at me, a bit longer than necessary, with his jaw working. "I suspect, as does the Oracle, that they used dark magic to inflict the injuries."

Dark magic to hurt him, blood magic to take the Elam. This sounded like someone who knew what they were doing—the spells and curses would have required more than what both the Oracle and the Crimson Cove covens allowed its practitioners to perform.

That had me thinking of the theft again, and my gift inched back to the Cove and the stolen Elam. Even from here, something was unsettled, like a sting against my conscience, some unknowable thing that niggled at my awareness. Eyes closed tight, I inhaled, stretching my mind back to what I knew of the Elam, of all the times I'd passed by the town square yet ignored the talisman set there as something customary and usual. My gift took over, sliding my awareness beyond my apartment, through the busy street outside my building, from Brooklyn, Manhattan, through the park, until I could no longer make out the New York landscape, until land and rivers flew past me, dropping me into New Orleans, past the bayou, past the marsh and right into Crimson Cove with its lush pecan groves and the lands split between the higher and lower covens.

In my mind I saw the Elam clearly—worn brass chains stretched out, imbedded into the wooden statue that made one column of the town square's gazebo. The chains connected out, layered underneath the wood awning, right beneath the earth, straight into the hum of energy that ran directly through the town, right into the ley lines that weaved around it. In the center of the Elam, concealed as the single eye of the statue's whittled, masculine face, was an amulet carved from turquoise, the color dulled by the decades, but power hummed from the center of its turtle-faced surface.

The relic was as common to wizards as Founder's Day was to the entire town. But as my mind prickled with the recall of the Elam's surface, the beautiful craftsmanship and magical ability it took to fashion something that would veil us from the humans' notice, that image became fractured. As I clamped my fingers into fists, trying to keep them from shaking, the Elam disappeared completely.

"*Damn.* If the Elam is gone..."

"You didn't see it?" Bane asked, voice even but clipped.

"I saw it, then didn't. Then...then there was blood."

"We've established that."

A breath released in a long sigh from my mouth. "If that's true, then whoever took the Elam used Grant blood to conceal the theft. The spell concealing it was formed by the founders. Since there were only Grant and Rivers kin left from those lines...well. It could only be someone from one of those two covens." The tension along my skull eased as I blinked my eyes open. A thought occurred to me. "The Oracle couldn't trace it?"

Bane's frown only deepened with my question, and I took his arched eyebrow as answer enough to know I shouldn't question him. As we walked down the hall and waited for the elevator, I realized that with Bane, one of the last sons of one of the founding covens being the one attacked, there surely would have been a full inquiry. Not only would the Oracle and his team investigate—that was coven protocol— but I assumed the Grants, Bane's family, would have spared no expense in finding out who'd bloodied his face and taken his blood.

"And they found nothing?"

He punched the *Down* button as though he had zero patience. There were several calluses across his knuckles, red with barely healed scabbing. "The *nothing* is why I'm fetching you, Janiver."

"Me?" A quick, humorless laugh lifted from my mouth when Bane didn't explain himself. "Listen, I've been away from the Cove for a long time. I'm rusty. My nexus is twisted, blocked."

I didn't like the way he watched me or how he kept his attention on me as I moved into the elevator. It wasn't a lie; I *was* blocked, stunted from the lines by years of city life. Yes, I could still find things. That would never change, but being separated from my roots, from the lines that fed my nexus—the one source of energy that connected me to the ley lines—made my abilities harder to control. It was one of the main reasons Sam's call had irritated me so much. I knew with that frantic call my family needed me, but I was completely out of balance, magically. And I hated the possibility of failing them because I had let myself go.

"The Oracle can center you." Bane sounded too confident, verging on smug. "Besides you don't look so twisted to me." The injected humor in his tone set me on edge. I'd never seen Bane laugh. Barely smile, in fact. But when that smirk reappeared and he stared down at me, his slow gaze whispering suggestions he should keep to himself, I got the distinct impression that he found me funny. He shrugged, bringing his gaze back to my face. "Sam told me about that little kidnapped girl you rescued in New Jersey, and the missing guy you found in the desert last summer."

"You and my brother. That's a dangerous partnership."

"Sam's my friend. Especially since he helped me with a job two winters ago." Bane rubbed his neck, the second nervous tick I'd seen from him. "This thing happened with the Elam, and Sam was at my door within the hour." Bane sighed, scrubbing the back of his neck. "You know what will happen if we don't find the Elam before the next full moon."

I hadn't been gone that long. The Elam obscured magic from the mortals and magical creatures from their notice. It wasn't foolproof, but it assured that most wouldn't notice our world. If that Elam remained gone, the ley lines couldn't be converged with the new moon and the town would be flooded with magic. There would be nothing channeling its power. Everything would be in plain view of the mortals.

"Of course I know."

The lines stretched all over the region, down the gulf coast, up to Mississippi and splintered into various lines throughout the country. But it was our territory and those of our neighbors that would be exposed should the Elam remain unfound. Packs, clans, and covens in surrounding states would be at risk. They'd want to be involved in the search, to strengthen any locator charms we used to identify who had been involved in the theft. Bane would need to call them all.

My chest was tight, and I moved against the back of the elevator, needing to keep space between us. Bane took up so much of it. Even his aura bubbled around the small confines of the car. I shook my head, still not convinced I was the right person for the job. "I'm not sure how I can help you."

"Your brother thought you'd be the best person for the job, and I wanted to help your family with a little cashflow since..."

"Since Ronan screwed us?"

A terse frown shadowed across his face and Bane shrugged, passing off my brazen description of my brother-in-law's behavior. "Since your family has always been willing to help mine."

He didn't seem to like the laugh I released or how I punched the *Down* button to make the car move faster.

"I'm speaking the truth," Bane said, his mouth tight.

"My family is honor bound to yours, Mr. Iles. If we refuse to help, we will be cursed. Nothing we do is done willingly."

The tightness around his mouth hardened, and Bane moved his hand into his pocket, retrieving his cell like he decided against the bother of looking directly at me. "Your father suggested we try getting someone else to help," he said, not looking up from his phone, "but I figure if anyone can find the Elam, it's you."

Bane was the type who was stingy with his compliments. One coming from him was something special. I should have been flattered, especially since that compliment came after I insulted him. I should have at least nodded, managed even a small smile, but Bane had always made me nervous enough that I forgot all the things I should have done. He was like a shot of whiskey that burns all the way down, the one you know you shouldn't take but can't seem to keep away from.

For a moment his flattery won me over. He even ignored his phone long enough to watch me again. I stared at him a little longer than I should have, brushing my hair off my shoulder to distract myself. "Yeah, Papa would resist coming to me." No need to elaborate. Bane didn't need to know what had kept me from the Cove all these years or why my father was fine with me staying away.

The elevator stopped at the lobby, and he ushered me through the open doors with his hand on my lower back. The static of his fingers was electric, and I managed to cover the quick shudder that ran down my spine at that touch. It wasn't the first time I'd caught this feeling or the first time the weight of his touch had me forgetting where and who I was.

"Miss Benoit!"

Damn. Not again. Two steps out of the elevator and old man Dinkens found me. That man was relentless, likely high, and had the worst timing in the world.

"Mr. Dinkens. What can I do for you?"

"The packages, Miss Benoit. There are three now. Are you sure you wouldn't like to open them?" The old man moved his long nails through his gray and white whiskers and stopped at my side when Bane glared at him. He reeked of three-day-old tuna and two-dollar beer. "They are chocolates, and that whiskey I know you favor."

"Mr. Dinkens, you're sweet, but I can't take gifts from you." Dinkens had been my downstairs neighbor for three years. You bring a lonely old man one Thanksgiving dinner from the shelter where you volunteer *once* and the attention doesn't stop.

"My dear, it's just a trifle, nothing at all but the return of your kindness."

"And still not appropriate." When the old man took hold of my hand, Bane stepped forward and the grip he held on my suitcase tightened. "Mr. Dinkens, this is a family friend from back home." Stepping next to Bane may have deflated the old man's gusto a bit, but Bane's size and presence also tamped down his enthusiasm. "I'll be going back to my hometown for a while. Would you mind telling the super to hold my mail until I can send him a forwarding address?"

Dinkens had wrinkles under his eyes and a bunch of severe dents over his forehead. Slipping his gaze from me to Bane and back again exaggerated the lines and made him look much older than his sixty years. "Going back?" He shuffled toward me at my nod, stopping only when Bane moved a half step in front of me. "To Louisiana?"

"Yes." A quick elbow in Bane's rib that Dinkens didn't seem to notice and the wizard's shoulders relaxed. "It's a family matter. Would you mind telling the super for me? It's a little last minute."

"Of...of course, my dear."

The old man watched Bane closely, looking worried, maybe a bit nervous until I took his hand again. "Here." He grabbed the card I'd slipped from my back pocket and offered to him. "This has my cell number on it." When Dinkens' eye lit up, excited, I pulled the card back. "It would be a hardship if my phone started ringing all the time. I'll be busy with my family's situation, so *please* only use this as a last resort if the super needs me. I'm trusting you to guard my privacy." The whiskers twitched with the old man's frown but then stilled as he nodded before I finally handed over the card. "Thank you. You..." I cleared my throat, not eager for Bane to overhear me. "You keep yourself fed and inside when the snow comes, okay?"

"Of course, my dear. Of course," he said, holding my card tight between his fingers. Mr. Dinkens watched us walk out of the lobby and remained there until I waved at him through the front doors.

"Boyfriend?" Bane asked, handing over my suitcase to his guard when the trunk popped.

"Yes, that's my thing now. Old drunks who forget to shower."

He opened the door, waving me into the warmth of the Mercedes' heated interior. October in New York was not cold by northern standards, but the Louisiana girl in me still caught a chill when temperatures dipped below fifty. It seemed Bane held the same cold-natured habits and had slipped on his jacket when he slid in next to me, folding his arms against the chill. The movement brought my attention back to the tempting scent of his skin and the warmth from his large frame that didn't come from the seat warmers under my ass.

"We have a plane ready at LaGuardia."

"Lovely."

That gaze was hot against my cheeks when he looked at me. "You'd rather deal with a commercial flight?"

"I'm not complaining, Mr. Iles."

"Jani…"

I jerked when he brushed his hand against my leg. It may have been accidental, but that didn't keep me from an instinctual desire to get out of that car. Hera only knew how I'd survive the four-hour flight alone with him on his family's plane.

I bristled when he leaned over me, his hand reaching for my cheek, like he'd pull me toward him. I wondered, for half a second, why he got so close, why I let him. Then Bane gripped the seatbelt, his sweet, warm breath fanning over my mouth as he pulled the belt across my lap. "Safety first," he said, gaze running all over my face, stopping on my mouth like he couldn't keep his attention clear of it.

"I…can…do it myself," I told him, my heartbeat thundering, my sinuses filled with his thick, rich scent. "It's a boujie Benz. Not a rocket. Seatbelts can't be that different than even middle-class rides."

His gaze lingered, but Bane shook his head, like he couldn't quite understand me and hated that he couldn't. "I forgot what a snob you were about money."

"I'm not a snob about money." My leg squeaked against the leather seats when I moved closer to the window. "In fact, I'm a fan."

"Just not higher coven money."

"No." The look I gave him likely wasn't one an employee should shoot at her boss, not if she wanted to keep her job. But I'd spent ten long years away from the Cove, away from the by-your-leave attitude given to the likes of the higher, wealthier covens. I'd stopped reserving my contempt for them the day I left. "Not the higher covens."

I never much liked any higher coven witches, especially Bane Iles.

But when we were ten, on the night of the biggest storm the Cove had ever seen, he'd saved me.

He nodded, moving his lips together as though he needed a second to think of something diplomatic to say. "And what does that say about your opinion of me?"

That was something I couldn't answer. Not even when he looked at me as though my opinion mattered. As though I did.

*I can't stop touching you,* I heard, recalling what hearing that same line had done to me ten years ago, when I was eighteen. Remembering that I'd wanted to hear him say things like that to me forever.

*I don't want to ever stop touching you.*

But he had stopped touching me, because I made him. And I had made him stop because it would not do to hold onto something I could never have. Not if he was going to lead his coven.

Just then, as he sat next to me, leaning closer, his knee and elbow edging toward me, I doubted he was even aware of how he always seemed to gravitate toward me. Although I had closed my eyes and rested my head against the window, it did little to keep him away and me off his radar. Just as he had years ago, he sat too close, and I wondered why he always did that. Even in school when those looks lingered for months, when the others shied away from him and he didn't notice, when I unconsciously leaned toward him, Bane would match me. He'd always invited himself into my personal space.

I knew why; I just hated to admit it to myself. The "why" is what I'd been running from all these years. From what had happened on that one day ten years ago, from that one decision to leave behind what I could have had with the boy who always watched my back. From that one afternoon in an empty classroom, when Bane learned everything there was to know of me.

And then I'd taken it all away.

He'd tasted sweet on that decade-past day, like mint and sugar, and I'd wondered if his skin was as delicious as it looked, and if it would be as sweet as his tongue. Would it give me a head rush? Or more?

I'd wanted to ask him a thousand things back then, in that empty classroom. I'd wanted Bane to know that I'd give anything to kiss him, that I had lain in bed some nights and thought about how he'd feel hovering over me, inside me, that sometimes those thoughts lasted all night, and I had to spell my room from any sound so that my parents wouldn't hear me crying out as I masturbated to thoughts of him.

But that day in Matthews' class I hadn't told him any of that. I couldn't, not with him stepping closer, with him backing me up against the wall next to the door. Not when he pulled the door closed with a flick of his finger and with his attention fixed on my face.

*"Gotta be honest. I'm not sure what you want..." he'd almost stammered.*

*"Just one thing." He'd looked confused when I said that, maybe a little taken aback that I wasn't like most of the other girls in the covens, the ones who were looking to make Bane Iles, and by extension his money and power, part of their Marry Well and Wealthy plan.*

*"Just one?" he'd asked, tilting his head like he knew there was a plot brewing behind my dark eyes. He hadn't seemed all that bothered that there might be.*

*Bane had come to me so easily that day—a tug on his face, my hand at the back of his neck, and he'd relaxed against me. He hadn't fought the touch of my fingers on his face or how I moved our positions so that he was the one against the wall. He hadn't moved when I brushed my fingers over that beautiful face because it couldn't be helped. His lips, those high and chiseled cheekbones, that jaw line—his features were symmetry in motion, classic, something that didn't seem to fit with a time of smart phones and email. That face seemed ancient, something that would have made even Michelangelo's David ache with envy.*

*And because I'd taken that now or never-ever moment like I'd owned it, just then, for just a moment, Bane belonged to me. A small brush of his mouth against mine, that smooth, slow movement of his jaw relaxing, his hands smoothing up my back, holding me still while I'd moved his face between my fingers. We'd become a rise and fall, breath full of so much potential, so much possibility that the sensation of it all had staggered me.*

*"Jani," he had whispered against my lips and, "Yes, Gods yes..." had become a prayer I hadn't thought Bane meant to speak aloud. But it hadn't been the heat collecting in the room or the soft echo of our moans, or our breaths becoming the only sound we'd heard as I'd deepened the kiss that froze us in that moment. It had been more. Much, much more, and I hadn't recognized what that more meant, not until it was too late to back away from it.*

I'd left the Cove behind. I had to. I'd buried Bane's memories, pretending to let him bury mine, but the truth lingered, always, even though it was now so deeply shut away. Whether I wanted to admit it to myself or not, I'd claimed him at eighteen and no matter how many men I let take me, no matter how many times I told myself I felt something more than attraction, deep down I knew I'd never be satisfied with anyone but Bane. We were bound together, connected.

He knew me. No one in my life, save my twin, could say that. Mai and Bane—one I could never have, the other I could never be rid of even if I wanted it—were the only ones who knew who I truly was.

But that had been ten years ago. Back when I was connected to the ley lines.

Back when they called to me.

When I had been as open to them as I had been to him.

Our nexus, the source of who we are individually, was connected directly to the ley lines, to that ancient energy part of us all. And sometimes, very rarely, our nexus is so open, so accepting of another's that the two powers collide; they meld, touch, and twine on their own, and you know undeniably that this person will be part of you.

For one brief moment Bane's and my nexuses melded, touched and tantalized when we'd claimed each other. But I'd concealed it, had taken it back from both of us, so why would he still gravitate toward me? The years since, among the mortals, skimming just outside the touch of magic, only flirting with it when it was needed, had taught me one thing: surround yourself with laughter and lust, humor and pleasure, but the faces would always be void, the friendships always forced. Loneliness doesn't come to us because we are alone. It comes because we never let anyone see who we really are.

One day, a long time ago, I'd let Bane see who I was and today, as I rested against the car window, trying my best not to let his warmth, his scent, his presence penetrate too deeply in my mind, I promised myself he would not see me like that again.

Not ever again.

# THREE

THERE IS A RHYTHM TO MAGIC. IT IS THE RAW THUD OF THE strongest, surest heartbeat. The same kind of beat that pumps beneath the earth. It is the one that each being alive on this planet echoes inside their bodies. And it was that beat drumming inside my skull as I lay sleeping.

I was dreaming. Logically, I knew that. Only in dreams does fog have weight and in this one, the iridescent sheen of sweat coated my body, my arms as I ran and ran. I was just another creature looking for an escape. Was it a fire? No, the air was too clear for that. My breath came in and out too easily. Not a fire then, but something that still chased us all...me, the animals, the weres, and creatures that scurried at my side from the forest, and...the light. The white, thick light that felt like fog—light I could see. Light I could feel.

It was everywhere, absolutely everywhere, and I knew, without reason, that it wasn't simply light. It wasn't energy. It was the ley lines, the magic flowing from the lines, pumping, rolling, coursing, screaming, filling my mind, my lungs, the forest floor, the fur and scales and feathers of the animals around me. It coursed, it flooded, it drowned us completely until I could only scream. Until my throat ached. Until that thick white light filled my lungs, suffocated my throat, stole my voice.

And then...I woke.

Alone.

Sweating.

Unsure where I was or how I got there.

My skin was cool, as though my body had just fought off a fever. My face wet, hands shaking. Where was I? And who the hell was yelling?

"...complete and utter bullshit and you know it!"

"You might want to remember who the hell you're screaming at, Cari."

"I know damn well..."

I tried to block out the noise. The woman's voice was shrill, made my ears ache, and from the deepening of Bane's angry growl, I understood that the sound wasn't all too pleasing for him either.

There was a soft rapping at my door, and I jerked up from where I had been sleeping, hair tangled in my face, knotted against my shoulders as I left the bed. I cracked the door open just an inch.

The guard peered through the small opening I had made, his eyes bright and alert. Even with the raised voices outside, he looked more relaxed than he had on the flight back to the Cove. The stoic, silent manner was mostly gone, and his smile came easier. I couldn't help but notice that he appeared to be in his early thirties with a handsome, slightly rugged face and a thin layer of ginger hair stubbled over his jaw.

"Miss Benoit, I'm sorry to bother you." His British accent was thicker than it had been during the brief one-word replies he'd given Bane on the trip home, and I detected a slight slowness to his words, as though he'd had a whiskey or two in the hours since.

"Not like I can sleep with all that racket." I moved my head toward the dark hallway where the screaming continued.

"Yes, about that," the guard said, pulling a silver chain from the pocket of his leather jacket. There was a small turquoise stone fastened at the end and the faint light from the den glinted on its surface. "I've taken the liberty of fashioning a silencing charm for you since Mr. Iles has warded the cabin against any spells save his own."

"Excuse me?" The guard, at least, looked embarrassed. He should. His boss had made it virtually impossible for me to protect myself with my own magic.

He frowned when Bane's cursing took on a few choice insults that had even my eyes widening. The guard shook his head. "I cautioned Mr. Iles that you might find his ward insulting."

"You don't say?"

"Well now," he continued, ignoring my attitude, "he is a bit..."

"Stubborn?"

"Ah, I was going to say overly cautious."

Another wave of shouting filtered down the hallway and I swung the door open, tired of straining to hear the guard over the noise. "Come in so I can actually understand what you're saying." He hesitated only for a moment before I grabbed his elbow and ushered him inside. "What's your name?"

"I apologize," he answered, giving me a quick bow that was more cursory nod. But his smile was warm, and despite the thick make of his frame and the intimidating stretch of his shoulders, I thought the wizard seemed friendly. "I'm called Prosper Lennon." He offered me his hand, which I took.

That accent seemed to exaggerate the more relaxed Lennon became, and I tilted my head, wondering why Bane would hire someone not local. "Obviously you're not native."

"No, Miss Benoit. I've only recently come to Crimson Cove a few years back." He didn't elaborate further, and I made a mental note to do a little recon on the wizard just to satisfy my own curiosity. "As to the charm...would you care for—"

"No, I'm fine." Rarely did I trust anyone else's spelling. I was perfectly capable of twisting my own craft. Besides, you could never be completely sure what you were getting when you used someone else's magic.

Actually, I was more than a little miffed that Bane had set a ward in the first place. Oh I got why—he had just been attacked with dark magic—but that didn't mean I was okay with him leaving me unable to protect myself. *I* hadn't attacked him.

Lennon lowered the offered hand and shoved the charm back into his pocket. That professional, friendly smile faltered a little with my rejection, but I wouldn't coddle the wizard. That wasn't in my job description.

Through the closed door the shrill female voice rose even higher, and for a second I contemplated changing my mind and using the charm, if for no other reason than securing a good night's sleep. But something about the entire situation niggled with me, something that made me a little cautious about accepting help from Lennon or Bane.

That didn't mean my *boss* wouldn't hear me doing a little screaming of my own when I saw him again. "Just so you know, I fully intend on having words with Mr. Iles about the wards. I don't like being unprotected."

"Mr. Iles would never allow any harm to come to you, Miss Benoit." He might be big and burly, but Lennon did come off as being slightly uptight. There was more than simple concern in his expression when he spoke; he was genuinely worried.

"Really, stop with the formalities." I wanted to put him at ease a bit, maybe distract him for the pending argument I was sure his disclosure had caused. "Call me Jani. And your boss has a funny way of showing his idea of protection. Why the hell would he ward his property against me?"

Lennon stretched his neck, adjusted the jacket he wore so that the sleeves bunched up. "If I'm not much mistaken, he wanted your protection to be his responsibility."

Control freak. Yeah, that fit. Bane had always been a little mean, but I thought that attitude had been reserved for the mortals in our school, not for magical folks and certainly not towards me. I guessed, though, in a situation like this, Bane wanted to exude control and composure regardless of who was watching. Or, more frustratingly, maybe he really did think I was pathetic and wanted to make sure I didn't get myself killed. That idea rankled.

"Because he didn't think I could take care of myself?"

"Because," Lennon said, stepping a bit closer; there were green flecks in his hazel eyes and his smile had turned friendly again. "He wanted to make sure you didn't have to, miss."

"Oh."

He didn't wait for the words to sink in completely. One curt nod and Lennon left my room, but not before I heard the sharp "Stop your screaming, Cari," spill out from the den. I blinked, shaking myself from my own imagination and impossible thoughts about why Bane would want to handle my security on his own or why the hell he'd insisted I stay here instead of with my family.

Cari, I thought, pulling a fluffy blanket from the bed to stand in front of the glass door that opened onto the patio. I'd bet two month's rent that "Cari" was Caridee Rivers, the witch Bane was supposed to marry. As the two oldest and highest-ranking families, it was the Rivers and the Grants who were responsible for maintaining the magical balance in Crimson Cove. They were the strongest covens. Naturally, they'd want to join their families. It was well known that Bane, being the eldest male descendant of Carter Grant, his uncle and current head of the Grant coven, would be married off to whoever the Rivers clan decided was best suited for an alliance. Small problem with that, as far as I could see: Caridee Rivers was a raging bitch. Always had been. I couldn't imagine Bane, no matter how much this town and his coven meant to him, settling for someone like Caridee.

But that wasn't my business. Finding the Elam was. That's all, nothing else.

Unfortunately, the screaming only got louder, and when Cari called Bane an "unemotional, robot bastard," I ducked outside and onto the patio. The screaming echoed in my head and I slipped my boots on over my knee-high wool socks, but not before pulling out the flask of bourbon that I had hidden inside one of them. When the insults got louder, became ruder, I tipped back the flask, not caring to hear any threats or insults to Bane's manhood. By how loud Cari's voice grew, I got the feeling manhood insults were next. I really didn't want to hear her criticizing any of his *abilities*.

The patio was still wet and a slow trickle of rainwater fell from the pitched roof onto the brick floor. It was early October and the chill of fall hadn't quite settled in, but the storm that had come through earlier still rustled in the wind and lowered the temperature.

The air smelled of wet leaves and that earthy, bitter scent that a storm leaves behind, but wild winds from earlier had finally quieted and the threat of the storm seemed to have passed.

Nostalgia never worked on me; it never made me itch to return home. Others may opine on thoughts of *home*, but in my mind, the pine needles in the Cove took ages to disappear from the ground, the sap always stained car roofs and windshields, and the gardenia blooms set off my allergies. The maples that circled the cove bled red leaves for months and were a curse on my memory. Their red and orange leaves, the bend of their brown barks were like some sort of silhouette stuck in my mind, a warning that the way to Crimson Cove led to tedium. I was far past picturing the place in even faintly romantic terms.

But there was always the quiet hum of magic. The air pulsed around me and held my attention, made me feel wanted. Being this close to the ley lines, which I could hear humming above the small orchestra of sounds around me, filling up the black forest—wolves, or shifters, howling up at the moon, owls hooting their steady refrain, and the throaty chorus of crickets singing back and forth, made my skin prickle and vibrate. I hadn't heard anything like it in so long.

Above the forest sounds, pulsing in the distance, I heard the lines, their steady thump swishing around the blackness, and even though my nexus was dim, twisted by the distance of the city, its raw, ancient power still pulled at my core. Magic called to me like a siren, weaving through the trees and the wet, dark earth until I could feel the tips of my fingers tingling from the lines' breath whispering into the night.

Just then, I knew it would not take long for the Oracle to sort out my block. I could already feel the hint of the lines around me, urging that quiet, primal voice in my head to rise up, to be who I would, to forget my mission, the client, and the family I meant to protect and just...become—with the lines, with the magic they held.

I knew it was a greedy, selfish voice that called to me, that the magic was always, at its heart, hungry and wanting. Yet the most basic part of who I was wanted to run from that cabin, from the still-arguing voices I could just make out behind the closed doors. It wanted me free from the life I loved and the one that could be mine if I succeeded in my task and found the Elam. All I had to do was step off of that brick and run toward the lines.

*It would be easy, that ancient voice told me. So easy to forget. Come. Just be.*

It wasn't the first time the song of the ley lines had sung to me. But it had been years, ages, since I had heard it so strongly, and just like that day in Matthews' classroom, that voice tickled against my mind, flirted with my heart. I'd wanted it then. I'd wanted what it promised could be mine. I'd wanted so much.

That day in Matthews' classroom, I knew only one thing: Bane Iles came from a family that was too powerful, too established to ever meld with a commoner like me. Even though friendship would never be enough, love would be too much to ask. It would be impossible. And yet...that's exactly what had happened. A melding. Unbidden, impossible, but unstoppable.

Until I made him forget.

Behind me, in the house, I heard glass shattering and the rage-filled scream of a woman beyond anger.

"Damn," I said, blinking fast before I squinted beyond the porch railings and into the inky forest that surrounded me. As if in answer, the wind blew a quick gust against my face, blowing the blanket from my grip—nature's kiss that made promises that would never be broken. It was in that moment that I understood what the missing Elam would mean not only for the humans, but for every magical creature hiding in plain sight. The ley lines held so much magic, so much pure energy that it had to be contained. Taking in too much of it, coming too close to it, listening too carefully to its song, you could be easily destroyed, consumed. Mortal and witch alike.

"Stupid, arrogant, blind idiot!"

I snuck a long swig from the flask, then shoved it down the front of my shirt and between my breasts when the glass doors swung open behind me and Caridee Rivers slammed onto the porch, still screaming at Bane. The woman was thin and pale, but her cheeks were bright with pink blotches and strands of flyaway hair were escaping her once perfectly coifed blonde bun. She wore a classic, casual dress and lush-looking leather boots that came up above her knees. Her look was one of both wealth and health—and high disgust that I was staring down at her. Two quick steps and Cari stood in front of me with a twist curling up her top lip.

"Leave her be, Cari." Bane had followed his fiancée out onto the porch. Despite all the hysterics coming from Cari, he wasn't frantic. I doubted he knew the meaning of the word, but the constant calm that kept his temper contained bristled around the edges, and I glanced at the fierce line wrinkling between his eyebrows. "You're being ridiculous," he told Cari, stepping behind her.

"Ridiculous? Please." Cari whipped her attention from me to Bane and back again. She stood less than a foot in front of me, face scrunched up in fury, that constant little twitch of her top lip verging toward a full sneer. Which, I'll be honest, approached hilarious considering she was only about four feet, six inches tall and I was pushing five-eight. The expression on her face was severe, angry, and those large doe eyes of hers would look fierce and threatening if she wasn't so petite.

"You," she said, and I pressed my lips together in a pathetic attempt not to laugh.

"Me?"

"Yes. You." Cari squared her shoulders, pushing up her chin. "Why the hell are you back?" She tilted her head and her desperate, not-remotely-threatening eyes blazed like wet glass. "What are you plotting?"

"Is she serious?" I asked Bane, glancing over the top of Cari's head.

"She's being a pain in my ass," he agreed, but there was something that bordered close to pleading in his expression. Eyebrows lifted, he kept shaking his head as though he needed a self-reminder that she was his fiancée, despite appearing more like a harpy than a witch.

"Quiet, Bane." Surprisingly, he listened to her, which seemed completely out of character for him. But hell, I really couldn't claim to know him at all anymore. Some things were bound to change in ten years.

But really, the witch was definitely inventing things in her mind. That much I could tell by the quick slip of her gaze between my face and Bane's. Most women are territorial, sure. But a witch with her eyes on property and power like Bane's? Yeah, anyone fool enough to threaten her advantageous marriage plans would be in for one hell of a fight.

Instead of antagonizing her, like I very much wanted to do, I decided to be the adult, try my hand at playing professional. "Listen, Caridee, I'm just here to do a job."

"Yeah, witch, I heard about the jobs you do." Another step toward me and she pointed one long, manicured nail in my direction. The nail was filed square and covered in fire engine red paint. "Find things? Please. You take off for ten years and then conveniently come back right when that dumbass brother-in-law of yours screws up and your father's business goes under?"

"His business hasn't gone under," I said, gritting my teeth and trying to loosen my fingers, which threatened to ball up tight into fists.

"May as well have." She stepped closer, pushing that nail into my shoulder. "I know why you're here. I know you think you can snake your way into beds you have no business being in."

"What?" She barely blinked when I brushed her hand away from me.

"You stay the hell away from Bane." She actually lifted her chin in some pathetic mimic of a threat. "He belongs to me."

"Have you lost your mind?" This was so ridiculous that I considered that maybe I was being pranked. I even glanced up at Bane again when the witch did not back down, getting further annoyed when he shook his head and rested against the porch railing.

"I know how you left, Janiver Benoit." Cari's voice was low, serious, and that anger in her features shifted to something that honestly did feel like a threat. She might be tiny, but that look told me she wasn't without a little fire in her gut. "I know what you tried to take from me back then."

"Back then? Back when? You mean him?" I nodded in Bane's direction.

"That's right."

The air around us cooled as I stared down at the petite woman. Professionalism was great when it was appreciated, but I damn sure wouldn't let this ridiculous witch throw out accusations when I'd only taken a job.

Or was it that some ancient part of myself raged against the entire situation? A voice echoed in my mind with constant refrain that Bane did not belong to Cari and he never would.

Some of that primal voice seeped out as I narrowed my eyes at her. "Seems like if you were so convinced he belonged to you, you wouldn't have to make threats." I stepped closer with my arms folded, forcing Caridee to retreat half a step. A quick pulse of magic seeped into my limbs, warming my skin with a barely distinguishable breeze. "Seems to me if he was yours and you were his then you'd have a hyphen on your name already. Funny how that hasn't happened yet."

"There are traditions, guidelines to follow. You damn well know that."

The smile I gave her wasn't warm, and as I tilted my head, inhaled deep as a small breeze pushed my hair from my shoulders, the pulse of anger mixed with that sweet rhythm that the lines pushed into my body. "Is that the excuse he gives you?"

"That's enough. Both of you." Bane pulled Cari back by her elbow and frowned at me like I'd gone ahead and cursed her. I wanted to, knew she deserved it, but Bane's frown took away some of the heat warming my limbs.

"I don't have to explain myself to you," he told Cari, ignoring her when she jerked out of his hold. "We aren't married yet and you damn well know it." She stepped back further, looking wounded, and Bane's shoulders fell. "Besides," he said, his voice a bit softer. "If we don't find the Elam, a marriage to reinforce the covens won't matter much, will it? Not if the lines flood the Cove. Jani is here to do a job, that's it. That's all. There's nothing..." He paused, shooting his gaze to me before he straightened his shoulders, head shaking like the entire explanation was pointless. "She's...she's just a temporary employee."

That hurt a little more than it should have, and I hated that he wouldn't look at me. I hated even more that I could feel his anger, his irritation, and that I wasn't sure who it was directed toward—Cari for the fuss she made or me for rising to her.

"Then why the hell is she sleeping here?"

I stepped back, watched as the small witch lost all her fight and took to fidgeting with the hem of her jacket. Her big eyes went wider still, as though she needed Bane's reassurance more than any denials he'd given her. It was actually sort of pathetic and for just a second, I was a little sorry for her, having to play such games.

"I don't need to explain shit to you, Cari. Now go home." He nodded toward the open door, pushing her hand off his wrist when she reached for him. "Jani and I have a lot of prepping to do for this search, and the other covens and dens will be here tomorrow afternoon. I don't have time for jealous fits." He looked up at me when he said the last and part of me wondered who it was meant for—the woman with the right to her anger, or me, the one who'd given up the right to feel anything for him at all.

# FOUR

THE HANDS WERE SURE, CERTAIN, WITH SMALL CALLUSES ON THE palms and at the tips of the fingers. With every touch, the liquid push of magic smoothed over my skin, through my limbs, wedged and held in the center of my torso.

"Just breathe, little one." There were years of whiskey, of pain and wisdom in each syllable he spoke. His was not a calm voice, not meant to settle, but to invoke, inspire.

He smelled of pipe tobacco and eucalyptus. Arthritis had taken root in his joints and the eucalyptus helped ease the pain. He smoked the pipe to annoy my twin when her boss was in the mood to hear her fussing. That, oddly, happened a lot.

"You have let that city eat into your mind. Its smog and traffic have noshed away at your nexus. I can hardly feel it inside you." The Oracle inhaled, rounding his chest so that his plump stomach brushed against my arms. "I hear the lines call to you, don't you?" My mind was too focused, too clotted by the hum of the lines beyond the walls around us and the sensation of Bane's signature battling with my father's on the other side of the closed door.

My father had wanted to observe, a request I shot down quickly. It didn't matter that the Oracle was his brother, Batty. It didn't matter that Batty had been clearing the blocked nexuses of every coven member in the Cove for generations, my father still insisted on tagging along. Mainly, I think he wanted to keep his eye on Bane. He'd never liked the wizard. But Batty had ordered both wizards to sit in the waiting room outside his office and slammed the door shut in their faces when the protests started.

I kind of loved him a little more for that alone.

"Yes, there," the Oracle said, pressing his rough palm on my stomach. "As rigid as a board, Janiver, and tight as a drum." He leaned closer and I could feel his smile against my cheek and hear the humor in his voice. "You need release. How long since you've been with a man?"

"None of your fucking business, you nosy pervert." I tapped his hand when he stilled. "Get on with it." And above his wheezing laughter, the Oracle squeezed against my stomach, filtering into my muscle, my organs a fire of sensation that left my nails curling into my palms. "Here we are," he said, swaying, and the crescendo of energy, of movement threatened to soak inside me, around me, until there was nothing at all but me and the magic pulsing, shifting, and away went the clot of life, of noise, of crowds, of all the everlasting reality. My gift crested, tingled in my synapses, brushed along my imagination as the Oracle whispered and chanted.

After a moment, minutes that could have bent time, crushed realization, I could not hear anything or sense anything at all. There was only me floating, shifting above the earth. I was energy and vibration, something born of fire and bathed in light. Something that could not be defined, that would not be labeled. I was lost and found and I heard myself crying out.

Just as quickly as that distance from reality had come upon me, it jerked free and I came back to myself, to that body, that skin, his hands upon me, that room around me. That grip holding, securing, whispering over and over that I would be fine.

But as I opened my eyes, blinking past the muddy blur of light and shapes, it was not the Oracle that stilled me. I did not smell tobacco and the burning scent of eucalyptus. Bane held me firm, and I lifted my head—though I did not recall resting it on his chest—and blinked again when his sweet breath warmed my face.

"You alright?" he asked, still holding me, pushing back a strand of loose hair out of my eyes. I couldn't answer, couldn't do more than watch him, trying to define the faint recollection of seeing the opened office door, my father watching from the threshold, hearing Bane when I'd moved away from myself. "Jani?" he said again, this time with the smallest shake against my arms.

"Yeah." He only released me when my father took me out of his reach and wrapped his arm around me.

"She's fine, Iles, don't worry over her," Papa told Bane.

But the dizziness in my head had me gripping Papa's sleeve and, despite my father's warning, Bane still reached for me. "I'm fine," I told him when he stepped close. "Really, I'm alright."

"You don't look it."

"I'd say she's just about in fighting shape." The Oracle patted my shoulder. There were small clusters of sunflower seeds stuck between two teeth when he smiled at me. "Give yourself a bit and you'll be squared away. And you," he said to Bane, moving his head so he could watch the bigger wizard at his side rather than having to look up at him. "She's got a rare gift. Best you mind paying her what she deserves."

"Batty." But the old man ignored my fussing, then winked down at me.

"You're my brother's girl, Janiver. What kind of kin would I be if I didn't stick up for you?"

I let Batty hold my hand, squeezing it once as I stepped away from all three wizards, then abruptly stumbled, only keeping upright when Bane looped an arm around my waist. "I'm..."

"Fine, yeah, you said." He straightened, glancing at my father when he cleared his throat. "Mr. Benoit?"

"Give me a moment with my daughter, Iles, if you don't mind." His normally lilting voice was like ice.

There was a hesitancy in Bane's stature, but he did leave the room, following Batty out before he shut the door.

"You need to be careful."

"I really don't think this is the time, Papa." He'd been cautioning me about the same thing my entire life, ever since I was ten and somehow managed to get lost in the forest with Bane.

"Janiver, I'm only trying to think of what's best for the Cove."

"Yes, Papa, I know you are. You *always* are."

There was a bite to my response, one my father must have caught, because his mouth went tight and he lifted his chin, as though he'd somehow taken offense to an insult I didn't speak. Both Papa and Bane's uncle had discovered us that day in the classroom, but it was my father's warning that convinced me to block Bane's memory of it.

*"Stay with him," he'd told me then, "and your life will not be your own."*

Staring at me now, I knew the same unwelcome warning was coming. Papa didn't want me associating with Bane. He wanted me to stay far away from the wizard.

"Papa, I'm here to do a job," I told him, walking toward the door.

"Just see that's all you're here to do, *mon petite bebe.*"

My father left the bar through the front room before I could argue any further with him. I found Bane leaning against the wall as my uncle continued to lecture him about my payment.

Batty cleared his throat, opening his mouth as though to fuss at Bane again, but the younger wizard waved his hand, silencing the old man with a flick of his fingers. "I know what she's worth. Don't worry about that."

Something caught my breath when Bane looked down at me, and I was reminded of that sensation from a few minutes earlier, of the feeling that though I'd moved beyond myself, I'd still heard Bane, sensed him near me. With him looking down at me, the air around us shifted and that familiar pulse, the taunting whisper of the lines told me to take what was mine.

That was impossible. I'd blocked Bane's memory of that day, and done away with mine. But just for a second I swore I saw something akin to recollection in Bane's eyes, as though a light that had been dimmed years before was starting to flicker to life.

"Jani..." His voice was low, and I let myself stare too long, let that ancient voice prick too sharply that this man belonged to me. "Jani...why do..."

"Fine," I interrupted, waving him off. "Feeling better already." My smile was forced and the energy I pretended to have did a good job of bypassing the small moment we'd just shared. For Bane at least.

As I nodded toward the door, allowing Bane to lead the way, my uncle hung back, stood close enough so that only I could hear him. "I saw that, little one."

"You didn't see a thing, old man."

"That right?" He stopped me, held me back while Bane slipped down the hallway. "Then why was that boy looking for all the world like you were something he'd misplaced and only just remembered he'd lost?"

"It's not like that at all, Batty." But the Oracle knew things that I didn't. He saw the truth no matter how deeply anyone tried to keep it hidden.

A twist of his lips and those scrutinizing, narrowed eyes watched me close. "I suppose you've your reasons for keeping things to yourself."

"I do." I couldn't shake that look or ignore altogether the way Batty tried to unravel the knot I'd made of my past. He was simply too observant, too aware. "It's not important."

"That's where you're wrong, *nièce*," Batty said, all the teasing, all the humor leaving his expression. "No matter what his folk lay before him, Iles has an obligation to the lines, the heartbeat beneath us. He has an obligation first to the one that claims him."

"Yeah and that's Cari, not me."

"Horse shit." Batty stepped closer, his eyes lit bright and a quick swirl of green edging around the irises. "There's only one who's claimed Bane Iles and we both know who that is. Don't we?"

But before I could answer, before my old uncle could finish his disapproving lecture, a crash sounded outside of the door and Bane's loud voice growled into the nearly empty bar beyond the office.

*"Circe and Hera,"* I grumbled, running from the office.

"What is it? Can you see?" His regular eyesight was horrible, but he seemed to pick up the screech of my twin sister's yell from across the bar. "Ah. It's that rotten Ronan come after Mai again."

"Good," I said, walking away from the Oracle. "I've got several choice words and one mean hex for my brother-in-law."

# FIVE

THE SECOND MAI BRAVED THE OUTSIDE OF HER BEDROOM, I KNEW about it. The plane hadn't been on the tarmac for more than ten minutes, and I could feel my sister shaking off what remained of her isolation caused by her husband's betrayal.

That had been two days ago, or so my brother had relayed, and since that time she'd tidied herself up, returned to work at Batty's bar, and spread the word around the Cove that she'd be selling the little bungalow she bought less than a year before. It seemed it was that particular decision that had hacked Ronan off. Seeing how he still happened to live in the place.

"You got no rights, Mai. None whatsoever." My brother-in-law tried using his size, his height to intimidate my twin, but it didn't work. She was over a foot shorter than him, but that glare, the snarl on her mouth made her seem a damn sight more vicious.

"Yeah, you rotten, dead-bolted scullion?" Mai smiled at that insult, seeming proud she'd reached back into the old coven slang to abuse her husband. "I got *every* right."

"It's my house!"

Her laugh was loud, mocking, and Ronan slammed his fist on the bar as though he didn't like hearing it. But Mai wasn't frightened of him. She wouldn't back down again, not like she'd done so often in her marriage just to keep the peace. After his repeated infidelities, the shoddy handling of my father's business had been the last straw. "Funny how my name is the only one on the mortgage. You're gonna move out or I'll have you kicked out!"

Mai was a romantic, given to quick bouts of lust and passion. Any combination of the two would suit her fine but put both inside a criminally handsome but lazy wizard like Ronan, and you've got the makings of a not-so-happy ending.

*"Isn't that the case?" she'd told me the night before when news of my return had my twin calling my cell at four a.m. I was still a little drunk and prone to blunt honesty.*

*"What's that?"*

*"It's always the good-looking ones. They've the biggest heels to stomp your hearts."*

*"Then maybe, little sister, next time you should pick an ugly man."*

But I doubted an ugly man was the answer, and just then, with Mai letting loose her fury at her soon-to-be ex sauntering into Batty's and demanding that she take the bungalow off the market, I realized the glass mugs and array of dishes being flung right at his head was the sort of catharsis my sister needed.

Bane, however, didn't seem to agree.

"Aren't you gonna do something?" There was still cool calm in his tone but beneath his crystal eyes was the clear swell of irritation.

"I am." I pulled Bane out of the line of a flying mug. "I'm staying out of the way. You might want to do the same." I wasn't worried about any real damage those two might cause. They couldn't hex or spell each other. That was a funny little aside to a coven marriage—witches and wizards were bound from hurting one another with magic. But damn if Mai didn't know how to fling a glass or toss a plate right across the room. I almost felt sorry for Ronan, but just almost.

"Damn Benoit women." I heard Bane's mutter, caught that disbelieving head, shake but only had to glare at him before he noticed my frown. "What?"

"You wanna repeat that?"

"Not if it's gonna keep that look on your face." We ducked again and when a third mug flew too near my head, Bane pulled me behind the bar. "This is fucking stupid." He grunted, seeming annoyed when I rolled my eyes at him. "Busting up Batty's place isn't going to do anyone any favors."

"Sure it will." I edged around the side of the bar, smiling when the plate Mai leveled at her husband zinged him in the shoulder. "It'll make her feel better."

"Come on. We've got shit to do." He pulled me back, grabbing my shirt in his fist until we were nearly nose to nose. One slip of my eyebrow arching and Bane exhaled, following my glance at my shirt crumpled between his fingers, and released me. "Your nex is all sorted. The dens and outer covens will be in town soon. There's shit to settle before we begin our search."

Behind us, Mai continued to scream, and I rubbed my temples, wondering how much energy, how much rage she needed to release before she was sated. If my twin was anything like me—and God knew she was—then her little catharsis could go on and on. I wouldn't begrudge her the release of the anger she had pent up for months, but Bane did have a point. Still, I wasn't worried that we'd lose trace of the Elam. I had a feeling that with my nexus centered again and the lines being unhindered, my abilities would be wide open and very sensitive.

"The trail isn't going to go cold, Bane, and my sister is only defending what is hers."

The bell from the front door opened, blunting the flinging of dishes, and I peeked to stare out over the counter, my eyes rounding when I spotted Freya Douglas ducking as she moved through the opening.

"Mai Benoit, is this shit necessary?"

"Ah," Bane said next to me. "The damn calvary."

"You wish." Freya straightened, her hardened features and world-weary expression years working for the mortal police department had given her softening when she turned at my approach. "She's exorcising the demon."

"Holy shit." Ignoring my twin and her bickering husband, Freya adjusted the gun at her hip and marched toward me, her pale skin brightened pink at the cheeks. "Never thought you'd *ever* land back in the cove again, Jani."

"Never wanted to."

It was a quiet look we shared, one that probably would have said a lot if we let it. There was nothing to say. Time and many late-night phone calls had taken care of the apologies I owed her. But Freya had been my best friend when I was eighteen. She knew everything about me and, by the look she gave Bane when he stood at my side, my guess was she was recalling all the secrets she knew about how much I'd wanted him. And, Gods, I had.

I'd wanted Bane and the life the ley line had promised could be ours. Who we were, how we found our center, the source of power, the link to life was a very tangible thing. Like a war cry or a school chant in the middle of the big game, finding that center, that link, which bound us together and that coursed through every magical creature—witch, wizard, were, whoever they were—with a sudden, sometimes blissful effect, was a tantalizing and at times almost overwhelming pull.

The melding. It always came back to that moment. To that promise I had to break.

The one Bane knew nothing about.

"Well, whatever the reason." Freya moved her gaze from Bane, not bothering to hide the smirk on her heart-shaped face before she looked at me. "I'm happy you're back." Then, like it hadn't been ten years since she'd seen me, like she forgot I'd left her behind too, my friend pulled me in for a hug. "Damn, I've missed you." Her thick, auburn braid brushed against my cheek when she squeezed me, and by how easily I got my arms around her, I could tell Freya had finally managed to gain the ten pounds of muscle she'd been shooting for our last year of high school.

"Yeah," I told her, smiling when the hint of lilacs and clove cigarettes hit me. She hadn't given up the habit, it seemed, or stopped using the lotion her mother made for her.

"Now, this particular demon..." Freya turned, wincing when Mai managed to clock Ronan with a bottle to the back of the head and the fool jumped behind a table. "Batty called me in case any of the other mortal shop owners in town heard the ruckus. Can't have Ivy or anybody else patrolling catching wind of this."

"She's winding down," I told Freya, moving my head to my twin when she leaned against the bar. My sister wobbled, wiping her forehead with the back of her hand, then looked down at her fingers and something caught her attention. Likely, the small diamond Ronan had somehow managed to give her. It seemed to piss Mai off and she caught a second wind, pushing away from the bar, darting right toward the cowering man who hid behind a table.

"Oh, *Circe,*" Freya said, stepping in time with me, likely ready to help me when I lunged toward my sister, but Bane moved faster.

He let out a quick, "To hell with this," and had his hand whooshing through the air in a wave before Freya or I could reach Mai. Ronan jumped up from his crouch, his expression hard and angry, a mug shooting from his fingers, but both he and Mai froze in their spots, captured in Bane's suspension spell that made their movements slow and disjointed.

His spell had caught Mai in mid-wince, just as Ronan's released mug split her bottom lip. "Son of a bitch!" I yelled. All I saw was the pain scrunching my sister's face, her brown complexion paling as the spell and pain worked through her, and the wild glee of pleasure that lit up Ronan's features. Bane caught me before I could get my hands on my brother-in-law, with his large arm pinning down my hands.

"Jani, no." He held me back, strong arms barely loosening as I moved against them. "You wanna end up in front of the board of covens for attacking a spelled wizard? Calm down."

Mai and Ronan fell in slow movements, their bodies, their reactions distilled by Bane's release of magic, and I nodded, let him move me away from Ronan as my brother-in-law slowly fell to the floor. Freya stood over him, holding her hand toward his head, a nasty hex ready, I was sure, anticipating the catch she'd have to make once the spell broke.

I reached Mai, threw the immobile mug away from her face and caught her around the middle before she fell, my touch completely ending Bane's spell, and we both landed on the floor in a whoosh of breath.

"Shit, that hurt." Frowning, Mai cupped her bottom lip and I tugged the rag from her apron, holding it against her mouth in an attempt to get the bleeding to slow. Her wild mess of curly hair fell in her face and I twisted it up, securing it in a knot at the back of her head. It was natural and thick, like our mother's, but where mine had grown straight and long, Mai's was a mass of ringlet curls she never seemed quite able to tame.

"Hey, asshole," Bane said, bringing both our attention across the room as he knelt in front of Ronan. Freya shoved him back down when the jerk tried jumping off the floor. "What's it gonna take to get you out of that house?" Ronan looked around the room, glaring over at Mai, then back at Bane. "Answer me."

Again Ronan tried to move off the floor and Freya pulled him down, gripping his shoulder until he went still. He shot a glare at the woman but reserved all his venom for Bane. "You can't throw money at this shit, asshole."

"Pretty sure I can."

There was a heavy feeling in the pit of my stomach, one that reminded me of the time Sam roughed up Michael Little after he and his friends threw spitballs at me in Miss Deaton's PE class. I hadn't needed Sam scaring off anyone. Not Michael anyway, since he spent the next week with a chronic case of chicken pox, and my mother made me clean out the attic and rearrange her canning equipment when she realized I'd spelled a mortal. Point being, I could handle myself despite the consequences I faced. I could handle this, as well, if Mai couldn't get through to Ronan. Benoits settle their own debts. Bane had no business speaking for us.

Patting Mai's shoulder, I left her on the floor and stood next to Bane. "What are you doing?"

He didn't look at me when I spoke and that only annoyed me further. "There's a problem that's keeping your attention." Finally Bane glanced at me, his face expressionless and that same fire making his eyes appear gray and glowing. "I need all of your attention, Jani. Hence me throwing money at said problem."

"We don't need you to fight our battles." I wouldn't budge on that one. He didn't know me anymore, but he knew my brother. He knew my father, and if Bane had spent more than a few hours with either of them, he'd have sorted out that the stubborn streak was evident in everyone in my family.

Still, a quick look at Mai's bloody mouth, and whatever Bane's experience with my family seemed irrelevant. He certainly didn't look altogether fussed about me being annoyed. "Maybe not, but as I've already said, we don't have time for this." He looked at Ronan again, then to Freya, the muscles around his jaw flexing when she shook her head, but spoke to me. "Bastards like this don't care about anyone. They get by on their connections, their looks, and when that don't work anymore, they resort to blackmail, sabotage."

The subtle pop of Bane's knee sounded when he stood and fit his hands into his pockets. His face had cleared a bit more since yesterday, but it was still slow to heal. Whatever dark magic his attackers had used on him, it worked perfectly to keep him roughed up, and I assumed his injured leg still needed more time to heal.

But watching him glower at my brother-in-law like he was pathetic, nothing but a nuisance, with that cool, scary calm keeping his features even, I realized that Bane would be intimidating no matter how injured he was. Hell, the bruises likely helped that menacing air along.

"Ronan here thought that your sister was weak. He thought that your father was stupid."

"You got no clue what I thought, Iles," Ronan said, spitting out a line of bloody spittle when Bane refused to look at him.

The wizard shook his head and looked as though he fought to keep a smile from twitching across his mouth. "It'd be very easy to be rid of him, but I'm not a murderer. Neither are you," he said, glancing at Freya as an afterthought. This wasn't mortal business, and while she stood in this bar, watching what was happening, hearing what was said, she wasn't a Crimson Cove cop. She was the witch we knew we could count on to hold our confidence.

Bane continued, finally looking at me squarely. "So we have to resort to basics for a very basic wizard." The doorway creaked behind us and I thought maybe Batty had exited the building, likely not eager to see what Bane would do in his bar, but then I smelled the familiar scent of Lennon's cologne and another new scent, this one like pine needles. Looking around, I saw that Lennon had been joined by another wizard who rivaled Bane's height and stature.

They weren't here to usher us back to Bane's territory. From the slow movement of their eyes around the room, then back at their boss, I understood that they were there to handle whatever it was Bane needed. At that moment, Ronan needed handling.

"He wants money so he doesn't actually have to work for a living. That's why he latched onto your sister and, if memory serves, to Widow Aldridge when we were in high school. Remember that, asshole?"

"Bullshit," my brother-in-law argued, fighting against Freya when she pulled him to his feet. Ronan flashed his gaze at the two guards and tried to put as much space between himself and the threat that loomed, but Freya didn't let him move more than an arm's length away from her.

"Bled her dry and the poor thing ended up in the mortal homeless shelter until she died." Bane reminded me of a tiger, pacing around Ronan with a relaxed, calm expression on his face. He looked almost bored, a little unsettled, but I think that cool demeanor made him even more threatening. Ronan would not take his gaze off of Bane, not when he walked around him, not when that blank expression twisted into a smile that was not friendly at all. "So, the best bet is to send him someplace where he can't return."

"I thought you said you weren't a murderer?" Ronan shouted, turning to face Freya. "Aren't you supposed to serve and protect? Damn, woman..."

"The innocent, asshole," she said. "And you know damn well I'm not a woman. I'm a witch."

"You don't deserve an easy death." Bane still kept his hands inside his pockets and tilted his head, looking at Ronan as though staring would make the ideas and possibilities in his mind arrange themselves into a logical solution. "And you're right, I'm not a murderer, but you damn sure won't be staying in the Cove."

"You...you can't do that." Ronan didn't sound convinced. "You don't own the Cove."

"Yeah," Bane said, laughing, moving his shoulder into a shrug. "I kind of do." He nodded and the guards cornered Ronan, but Freya didn't let him go.

Instead, she glanced at me, like she wanted me to tell her what I wanted to be done with Ronan. She knew me, still. She had to sense the irritation I felt. I stepped forward, in front of Ronan, shook my head, and Freya moved him back to her side.

Bane's coven was large, and he was in line to lead them when his uncle Carter passed away. So yes, Bane did, in effect, own the Cove. The Grant coven's reach and Bane's acquired power may have silenced my sister while he threatened her husband. It was definitely the very reason Ronan's arguing had silenced and why that wild, open fear collected in his eyes. But it meant nothing to me. No matter who he'd been to me once upon a time, no matter the guilt I had felt and how it had sent me fleeing and, on the worst days, climbing into a bottle, I no longer cowered to the social order in the Cove. I was free of that.

"You own the Cove, Mr. Iles, not my family," I said evenly.

Ronan glared at me when I approached, but his fear seemed to ease as I looked into his undeniably handsome face. Poor jackass. He was too stupid to worry about me, too arrogant to fear me, and he didn't even blink, didn't shy away when I rested my fingers along his forehead and whispered, "*Awendan,*" so only he could hear me. The hex shifted his features, made him stare at nothing, eyes unfocused and glassy.

"You will go to Easton Williams. Try working a grift on those Nevada witches. Their graves are deep and their deserts are endless. You will fail, Ronan, and will leave the Cove and my sister alone."

I didn't like Ronan. Never had. Hell, since he was a kid he'd been a pain in most everyone's ass, and if I was being honest, I wasn't sad to see Freya finally hand him off to Bane's guards and escort him out of Batty's and out of our lives forever. I didn't care.

Bane didn't watch his guards escorting Ronan out of the bar. He seemed more interested in my profile. But when I glanced at him, expecting a reprimand, maybe a reminder that I was expected to abide by that shitty social order, Bane kept silent, giving me a nod and the slightest hint of approval with the dip of his chin.

"Now that you've handled that," he said, clearing his throat, "can we get back to business and prepare for the arriving covens?"

"Jani," Mai said, her voice muffled against Freya's shoulder as my friend helped her stand. When I reached her, I realized that her bottom lip had swollen, and the cut still bled.

"Here." My twin didn't fight me when I dug a balm out of my bag and dabbed a bit of it onto her lip.

"Wouldn't it be faster to just work a charm on her?" Bane asked.

"It would, but Mai is a healer. They're the hardest to treat." I barely glanced at Bane when he grunted and met my sister's worried eyes. "It'll be gone in the morning."

"Papa will still worry." Mai adjusted herself onto a barstool as I rubbed more balm into her split lip. "And you know, with his heart... Damn, Jani I shouldn't go home."

"Don't you have a house?" Bane asked, his frustration evident in that clipped tone. He glanced at Freya when she cleared her throat, but quickly looked back at me.

"Hey," I told him, "this isn't your business. None of it."

Grunting, Bane glared at me, squaring his shoulders so that his shadow stretched over mine. "It is when I hire someone to do a job and they're too distracted by family drama to do the work they're being paid to do."

That famous Grant temper was still in place, clearly. None of this was my fault, but that didn't seem to matter to Bane. Aside from his uncle and cousins, he didn't have much family to speak of—no siblings, no parents left alive—so I guessed all that isolation, especially when you'd been left to be raised by your wealthy distant family, had made him a little less understanding of familial bonds. Especially when it came to siblings. Still, I didn't care about how rough his childhood was. That didn't entitle him to be an asshole.

Freya took the balm from me and tended to Mai's lip as I stepped in front of Bane. "I haven't seen the first dime on this job, and besides, you're the one stepping in and trying to take over. Trying to work out our problems, warding your property so I can't even protect myself."

Mouth dropping, that temper heightened, and his eyes went steely. "I was protecting you."

"And did I ask you to do that?"

"Jani, it's fine," Mai said, but I kept my attention on the beast glaring down at me. "Bane's right, I can go back to my house and..."

"Didn't you tell me when I got here that you'd had the power cut off so Ronan would leave?" I interrupted, glancing at my sister.

"Yeah, but..."

"No buts. You can't stay there with no electricity and you can't stay with Papa with a busted lip." Tilting my head, I crossed my arms. Bane would simply have to understand. "He'll worry too much."

"I'd offer my place," Freya started, "but you know how crazy it is there."

She wasn't wrong. Freya still lived with her mother and five sisters. They were all close and would never move out of her family home at the center of town. It had been handed down for generations and one day it would be hers.

"It's no problem, Frey," I told her.

"Fine," Bane said, voice loud, exasperated. "We'll take your sister back with us. Lennon can watch over her while we search for the Elam."

"Fine," I mimicked him, not liking him doling out orders, but not willing to put Mai in a situation that was bad for her. "Then let's go."

I ignored his low oath of "Finally" and helped Mai off the stool, leading her and Freya out of the bar, not waiting for Bane to follow us.

# SIX

"LANDON LUCAS. YEAR THREE. YOU LET HIM TOUCH YOUR..."

"I do *not* recall that." Freya's face was red, a clear sign the witch was lying. She also took a three-second swig from the whiskey bottle rather than her usual two. Another indication that she was deflecting. "If you remember, Landon Lucas was touchy with everyone. Including Mai when..."

"Hollow-eyed wretch! You besmirch your family's name!" That exaggerated coven insult earned a snort from my friend and the bottle, which I gladly took. It wasn't the same quality that I generally used to fill my flask, but it did so remind me of the dozens of nights lying out on our roof with Freya and Mai, sneaking mortal wine and cigarettes Sam had bought for us.

"Well," Freya amended, waving her hand to deflect. "In my defense he was pretty. And the pretty boys..."

"Are a load of shit!" Mai called from the bed before she turned over, already drunk and seeming ready to get more so before I pulled the half-empty glass from where she'd wedged it between her elbow and one of Bane's luxurious guest pillows.

"She'll be out in about ten minutes."

"Bless her." Freya inclined toward the bed, her smile thin as we both waited for Mai's soft snores to start. She'd untwisted her braid and her thick, curly hair spilled out in a heavy auburn mass. "She always was a lightweight."

"That's the truth." There were dark circles under my sister's eyes and her already-thin face looked gaunt. Sam had promised he'd watch over her, but from the look of her, he'd done a piss-poor job. Her usually light brown skin was pale and ashen, and she hadn't bothered to keep herself together, something that was well out of Mai's norm. When she grumbled in her sleep, I caught Freya's attention and nodded toward the door. "Come on. She's out for the night."

My friend followed me, navigating through the massive hallways of Bane's large home with her hand on my arm and the bottle tucked in her grip.

"Are you drunk?" I whispered, not sure why I was.

Bane's house was so large—a mammoth Acadian-style number that had to be well over ten-thousand square feet. He'd disappeared into his den after lowering the wards around his property at my insistence when we'd returned with Mai's bag and a stash Freya had brought with her from Anderson's Market. He claimed there was a lot of planning to do before the covens and dens made their arrivals.

"*Madame*, please," she said, not hiding her laugh. "I am an officer of the mortal law. I can hold my liquor."

"Uh huh. So that's a yes." I reached behind me, holding out a hand, and grinned when Freya grunted but still deposited the bottle of whiskey in my palm. "Some things never change."

"Like you and Bane?"

I felt seventeen again, laughing with my friend, her wearing my sweater because, like when we were kids, she forgot hers, as we moved through the hallways and out onto the back deck that overlooked the lake.

"You are much misinformed, Officer Douglas."

Freya's chair scratched against the wood decking when she sat, and if I wasn't mistaken, I thought I spotted a hint of disappointment glinting in her eyes. "Then that's sad."

"Is this where you start recounting impossible fantasies that never made sense?"

The wind curled around us, disturbing a grouping of fallen leaves that gathered along the cold chimney at the center of the deck. The surround was made up of stacked river stone, gray with streaks of black running through it. The skin on my legs pebbled from the touch when I sat.

"It's sad," Freya started, stretching toward the stack of cut wood to hand me several pieces, "because I'm a witch with excellent vision and a keen sense of observation."

"Meaning?" I didn't watch her as I arranged the wood, not bothering with a lighter or matches to get the fire going. The incantation for fire was elemental, simple. Something I could no more forget than the sound of my name, since Bane had been the one to teach it to me the night we'd gotten ourselves lost in the forest.

"Meaning that I saw you both when we were kids, and he'd scare away anyone that so much as look at you even a little bit funny." Freya moved to the other side of the chimney, watching me as the incantation caught and the wood ignited.

She wasn't wrong. Since that storm, Bane seemed to make it his business to protect me. It had started in the forest, him seeing me safe, holding my hand, neither of us understanding what that flash of red light meant the tighter our fingers twisted together.

Then, two years later, I ran from Micah Allen and his stupid cousins, through the pecan grove north of the Grant's territory. I wanted to hide, to scream, to forget that I was a girl, to forget that my body and magic stirred and broke inside me, that I could no longer twist hexes just because they were funny. I couldn't give Micah lice with a snap of my fingers because he called me a loathsome mongrel bitch, even though the old coven insults were the worst, because they cut the deepest.

The stupid Allen boys—all gingers with too many freckles and lopsided ears—crowded around me among all the black-bark trees with pecans falling from the limbs like fat, leaking grapes rotted on the vine. Then, there was only the tree at my back and my feet slipping as I scrambled over fallen pecans.

"Maybe I should make those big eyes of yours look damn foolish with eyebrows that cover your forehead," Micah said, wiggling his fingers over my face. "Or maybe you'd like a broken arm to match your twin's."

I didn't want a broken arm like Mai's. It was her and my folks and even my stupid brother Samedi that came to my mind just then—not how Micah and his cousins were stepping closer. She should have never tried skating backward off the dock...and suddenly, for some reason that made no sense to me at all, I thought of Bane Iles and his glowering frown and the stupid way he bullied anyone who spoke poorly to me. It was Bane who was in my thoughts as one fat Allen cousin grabbed my arm and pulled my hands behind my back so I could not hex Micah.

And just as suddenly, and with the same lack of reason or sense, in the fussing and confusion and me kicking and cursing, there Bane stood, in the grove, towering over Micah and all his dumpy cousins.

He was just a kid, like the rest of us, but even at twelve Bane was scary. His temper was something that had gotten him into a lot of trouble with his uncle. And he was big for his age and getting still bigger. He could threaten anyone with a sharp glare of his silver eyes.

"Leave." It was all he said, all he needed to say, and just like that, as Micah and his cousins ran away and Bane stared down at me like I was a bother, I knew I had a protector.

I never knew why.

I never cared why, but at ten and twelve and other formidable ages, I'd acquired a bodyguard—one that seemed to know when I was afraid or worried, or whenever I wouldn't admit that I needed help.

One that I could never quite remember speaking to for more than a minute.

One that my papa said it was best not to be too friendly with.

A boy that watched when he wasn't asked.

Freya laughed at me, snapping her fingers in my face to get me out of the memory that had taken my attention. "And," she continued, "I saw you tonight bickering with the man. There was the same crackle of energy humming in the air that there's always been, Jani." She reached for one of the dried leaves, tearing at the edges. "That sort of chemistry doesn't just disappear, even with time. It might get forgotten. It might get ignored, but it doesn't ever really go away."

*"I don't really care about anything but the way you feel against me."*

I blinked, desperate to shake away his voice and how that last time together before I left still haunted me. It was the one and only time we'd touched each other. What stung worse was he had no memory of it at all. Freya's assertion didn't help. Neither did being in his home, being around him.

"It doesn't matter," I told her, watching the flames rise higher and higher up the chimney. "I'll keep it buried."

"Jani..."

"No, Frey..." The smell of woodsmoke was the only comfort I'd taken from this place. It was the only thing that settled my nerves since being back home. "Buried is where it should all stay."

"But being around him has to be..." She went silent when I glanced at her, hoping the look was warning enough that I didn't want to get into this. Not here. Not now. "Okay. I get it." Freya leaned forward, threading her fingers together as she turned toward me. "It's a shitty situation and being here, doing this job has to be a gut punch." I could only manage a quick nod, one that my friend seemed to accept before she went on. "So, here's what I propose..."

"If this has something to do with you and Landon *Damn* Lucas..."

Her laugh was loud, infectious. "Nah, he moved away years ago. Probably bald with a dad bod by now and not the *hot-dad* bod kind either." She sat up, rubbing her hands on her jeans. "I'm going to go back to town and grab a few things from my place and give Ivy a call." She lifted her hand when I shot my eyebrows up, not sure what the point of contacting the chief of police would be. "I have vacation time due me and I don't want you out there on your own. I'm going with you."

Something warm and light moved inside my chest. Nothing of the kind had set off inside me for years. Not since I'd left this place. Freya watched me. Her eyes unblinking. Her hands flat and still against her thighs, like she waited for me to say something that would allow her to release a breath. It had been a long time since anyone depended on me for more than just a piece of promo art or to find something they'd misplaced. But Freya seemed to depend on me now. She watched and waited, and as she did, I realized I might be waiting too. For what, I wasn't sure.

"Frey, I'd...love it if you came along."

"Really?" She stretched her mouth wide with a smile, then moved her lips further apart when I nodded. "Good. Okay, great." She stood, bouncing a little on her feet. "Okay. Sweet. I'm gonna go."

"I should drive you. You're drunker than me."

"Nah, Bane's got a million people to give me a lift." She pulled out her cell, moving her thumb across the screen. "I come out here a few times a month to keep him updated on stuff Ivy asks about so I know a few of the guys." Freya moved her cell back into her pocket, curling my sweater tighter around her as she clapped her hands together. "Alright. Give me a couple of hours and then I'll be back."

"I'm not going anywhere." Despite the distance I tended to keep from everyone in my life, I didn't stop her when she grabbed me as though she was overcome with excitement and gave me a tight hug. "This will be great...like old times. And don't worry about...you know." She pointed with her thumb over her shoulder, toward Bane's house. "I've got your back. Always, Jani."

"Thanks."

I waved her off, laughing at her smile, how wide it stayed when she jogged back into the house and disappeared into the dark den. Freya hadn't changed much. She'd always been ready for an adventure, and she'd never let me down when I needed her. Of course she'd be there now.

It was my friend and the dozens of stupid stunts we'd pulled as kids that I thought about as I watched the fire, staring at the orange and white play of light as it ate away at the wood. My senses were dulled only slightly by the whiskey, but I still detected the presence of someone's signature as they walked near the deck. Straightening my back, I kept my fingers curled into a fist. There was no one I recognized in that heartbeat or the approaching scent and so I stood, moving my fingers as though I stretched them, readying a hex that would protect me from any threat that came my way.

But as the noise of steps moved closer and the creak of wood hit my ears, the heartbeat quickened and the signature, though faint, and mildly unfamiliar, became clearer.

"Jani?" the man said, holding up his hand, a small surrender I guessed he made when he glanced down at my lifting hand, ready to level a curse at him. "It's me! Malak!"

*Impossible. Utterly impossible.*

He paused long enough for me to tilt my head, my gaze sharp, examining as he took two small steps toward me. The eyes were the same, still round and light, like crystal and aquamarine all at once, but where the boy had worn a round face with dull features and a heart-shaped mouth, the man standing before me was completely changed. The bones of his face were angular, the chubbiness completely vanished, and the sharpness of chin and jaw were so pronounced and exaggerated I could have sworn he'd picked up a keen glamour skill, something that wizards weren't ever particularly good at.

"I swear, Jani," he said, two more steps slipping away, "it really is me. Malak Grant. Bane's cousin."

"That just...doesn't seem right," I admitted, dropping my hands to my side. "The last I saw of Malak, he was tripping over his untied shoe laces in the school gym trying to make it up the rope hanging from the ceiling."

"I did manage it...year four." The smile. That too was the same, though it was also exaggerated and more pronounced. "And by then there was no baby fat or unlaced shoes to keep me down." He took tentative steps closer, bringing his face and features nearer to the firelight, and I relaxed, then released a small exhale when I spotted the only flaw on that beautiful face: a gash that ran from the bottom of his jaw, across his neck to disappear beneath his shirt. He lowered his gaze, following my distracted attention and his smile shifted down.

"I'm sorry," I tried, feeling stupid for staring.

"It's fine. Everyone looks at it." Malak adjusted his collar to cover most of the scar. "Kind of hard not to." He sat next to me on the fire surround, warming his hands as he passed glances between the flames and my face, lingering a bit more on the latter. "*Man.* Janiver Benoit."

Not wanting to pry about the scar, I jumped on his change in attitude. "Why do Grant wizards use my full name?"

"Do we?" he asked, bringing that sweet smile back to cut the tension. "I take it my cousin does it too?" He shrugged at my nod, dismissing the answer. "Maybe because we're both a little awed by you." He was so unlike most higher coven wizards. Malak was always free with his compliments.

"Now I know you're related."

"Why's that?" Malak's smile shifted again, like he expected the small tease before I spoke it.

"Because you shovel as much bullshit as he does."

His laugh was deep, heavy, and sounded like an old curse you were compelled to obey, but it didn't last long before he spoke. He almost made me forget he consorted with the likes of Ethan Rivers, Cari's brother. "Well, that might be true, but I've never once heard Bane shovel shit to flirt with any witch."

"Is that what you're doing?" He moved closer and my only response was to laugh at his boldness. The Malak I'd known back at Crimson Cove Regional would have probably vomited before daring to even look at me. "This is you flirting?"

"How am I at it?"

There was a compliment hanging around somewhere near the tip of my tongue. Malak seemed to sense it was coming. He even moved closer and I forgot about who and where I was. Just for a second, I appreciated being a witch getting the attention of a handsome wizard.

"You, little cousin, are shit at it," Bane said, breaking the spell just as easily as if he'd shot a hex between us as he walked out onto the deck.

Malak lowered his shoulders, but he didn't jerk away from me. That smile kept on his mouth and he even managed a quick wink before he stood to face his cousin. "Oh, I dunno. If my history is anything to go by..."

"Edie Daniels has worked her way through most of the wizards in the Cove and Sarah Proctor is addicted to Elysium. She'll flirt with anyone with means."

"That's below the belt. Sarah is..."

"With that vamp from Ruston, strung out by now." He slipped his gaze to me, grunting when I frowned at him before he looked back at

Malak. Addicts were nothing to tease anyone about. Bane knew that. Elysium had killed many a good witch and wizard in the Cove the past few years. Though he hadn't proven it yet, Sam suspected the kid that killed his wife had been strung out on the drug.

Bane cleared his throat and rubbed the bridge of his nose as though he was already tired of the conversation. "The Shreveport den is ahead of schedule and will be here in an hour. Can you get with Lennon about their quarters? I need to talk to Jani."

"Later, Miss Benoit," Malak said, a tease in his tone that made me smile and his cousin release a noise that was half grunt, half growl.

"Mr. Grant," I said, rolling my eyes when I caught Bane's tight jaws working. "You need to relax."

"You need to...to..." He shook his head and that in-check temper he'd managed to keep under control slipped to the surface. "You're being unprofessional."

"Me?" He didn't move when I stood in front of him. Bane squared his shoulders, glaring at me like a kid pouting for the lecture he knew was coming. I ignored that expression and the temper that flared to the surface, coloring his skin. "I'm not the one fussing at a kid for flirting with one of your *temporary employees*. That's what you called me, right?"

"I didn't mean..."

"What did you mean then?"

It was stupid. The entire argument. It was rash and immature and utterly pointless. There was little sense in either of us being angry or lashing out. And when I realized where we were and what was happening, a rush of embarrassment flooded me.

Bane opened his mouth, seeming ready with another argument, but remained quiet when I held up my hand. He dented his eyebrows, bending them together as I walked to the edge of the deck and stepped down onto the ground that led toward the lake.

"What is it?"

I didn't answer immediately, deciding instead to slip my eyes shut and tilt my head back, letting the hum of energy around us vibrate against my skin. "It reacts to everything, doesn't it?"

"Of course it does." He moved to my side. Even in the darkness I could make out the shape of his body from the warmth his wide frame gave off.

"I'd forgotten about that."

"Your nexus is open now and wide." Bane moved closer, and the scent of bourbon and woodsmoke mingled with that familiar smell of sandalwood that always came from his hair. "The lines will exaggerate everything you feel tonight. Anger, happiness, frustration..." His voice was so deep, I swear I felt it rattle my insides, shatter any control I pretended I had around him. "Desire..."

The breath in my lungs froze and I jerked my gaze to him, knowing the look I gave him wasn't hidden, couldn't be remotely concealed this close to the lines. Whatever irritation Bane felt, no matter what he couldn't remember, Freya had been right, there had always been chemistry between us. It was there now, pulsing and pulling until I turned to face him.

A small breeze picked up against the water and I shuddered, trying to push back the sensation of longing building inside me at Bane's scent. Did the lines push us together or some other mystical force draw us closer despite the expectations laid at both our feet? I had no clue where that inclination came from—didn't much care, if I was being honest. But out here under the bright moon, with the lines humming behind us and Bane standing close enough that I could feel the heat of his body, nearly feel the whisper of his breath, that closeness was like a weight I thought I'd dropped years ago.

*It never left you,* the lines sang, and in my mind, I imagined that tone was a bit smug.

Still, it wasn't wrong. But it was pointless. The truth was useless when reality serves up a generous helping of impossibility.

He blinked at me, then tilted his head as, I guessed, he also sensed the steady buzz of magic pulsing from the lines. Bane closed his eyes, his nostrils flaring as he inhaled and rested a hand on my shoulder as though he needed help just standing upright.

He was so ruggedly beautiful, so impossible to resist that I had to remind myself we weren't alone, his guards would likely notice if I stood there staring at him helplessly for so long. But before I brought my attention away from his sharp features and the subtle, soft hint of stubble along his jaw, Bane grinned, a slow, amused twitch of his mouth, and then he glanced at me as though he found it the height of funny to catch me gawking.

"Your eyes are telling secrets, Jani."

"Hardly." I tried forcing an eye roll I didn't mean. Bane wasn't buying it. He didn't seem overly concerned that his guards were inside and the Shreveport den would soon arrive. He, in fact, somehow stood closer, arms crossed so that his elbow brushed against my bicep.

"It doesn't mean anything, you know."

"What doesn't?" My question came out too quickly, the words too clipped as he inched closer. He liked to torture me, I knew that, but I'd never seen him enjoy doling out that torture so openly.

"The attraction you feel." Bane shot his thumb over his shoulder. "The lines, the raw feel of them—without the Elam they aren't buffered." He twisted his head as though he tried to shake off a sensation that was teasing and good, but very bad for him. "It's in our nature, Jani. The lines unhindered, raw, they just bring it from us." Bane was easily five inches taller than me, and as he crowded closer, he used that height to his advantage with his breath fanning over the top of my head. "They'll only get stronger." It wasn't anything I hadn't already guessed, but that claim coming from him, with that air of seduction in his tone, made me realize, finally, what that might mean. Uninhibited magic influencing every magical creature, no voice of reason to temper our behavior should we get too close. God help me, I'd cave.

"What is it about you, Jani?" He'd said my name like that once, a long time ago. But one look, one real, honest examination of my expression and Bane had guessed. I wanted him, and my name falling from his mouth in that throaty, eager whisper was all it had taken to unravel my hesitation. "You love this, don't you? The raw feel of the lines. It frees you so much, doesn't it?"

My fingers rubbing against my eyelids, another breath against the top of my head and the sweet, warm bourbon scent brought my awareness away from the never-dimming desire to kiss him. He was twisting magic, working me over on purpose. Bane let the lines take him over, just a bit. His control was waning as he moved his fingers through the ends of my hair.

"It would free anyone who...who'd been away for so long," I told him, curling my arms around my waist like I could really protect myself from him.

"They'll get stronger," he said, taking one wavy strand of hair off my shoulder to curl around his finger. "They'll get stronger and you'll want to lose control."

Eyes closed tight, I saw what that loss of control would look like. Something erotic and inappropriate involving that large wizard next to me and lots and lots of fallen red maple leaves sticking to our naked skin.

I blinked, stepped out of his reach to block that imaginary scenario. "That is not going to happen."

"Why not?" he asked, moving in front of me, keeping me from retreating further away from him.

I arched an eyebrow and smiled. "Why do you think, *Mr. Iles?*"

His shoulders fell and the tension crowded around his features again when my small words pushed reality right back into his mind. One low grunt and Bane turned his head, attention back on the sky above us. "You know how to ruin a moment, don't you?"

"Was that a moment?" I teased, trying not to laugh when Bane started working his jaw.

His gaze flashed back at me and some of that irritation lessened the severity of his expression. "Could have been."

Sometimes Bane let a little emotion—real emotion that had nothing to do with teasing or trying to bait me into a reaction—pass in his eyes. I saw it just then. It was sincerity, maybe a little longing, but I couldn't stop and give it much weight. How could I when that would lead to nothing but disappointment?

I cleared my throat, bringing my gaze down to the ground where I kicked a rock with the tip of my boot. "I don't think your fiancée would have appreciated any moments you might have wanted with me."

"Probably not," he said and the humor in his voice was forced, as though he'd noticed the real emotion had snuck in for a moment and he needed to tamp it down quickly. Bane put back on that dominant, in-control mask and moved his head, trying to catch my eye. "But that doesn't mean they won't happen anyway."

"That's a little selfish of you, don't you think?" When he squinted at me as though he were confused, I clarified. "You engaging in moments not reserved for the witch you're supposed to marry."

"Maybe, but you know, Miss Benoit, I'm not married yet." He stepped even closer, bringing my hair back between his fingers. "And when the right moments come, I generally don't care who they're with."

It was a lie, one that I saw clearly through his arrogant demeanor. "That doesn't say much for your pending marriage. Or future happiness." I pulled on his wrist but couldn't find the energy to move his fingers from my hair.

It was then that I saw the hardness of his features for what they truly were: regret. "Who the hell ever said there would be a happy future for me?"

He let me hold his wrist, let me hold the moment between us, forgetting our lives and the situation he'd soon find himself in. In that small pause, we were kids again, in that room, sharing a moment that was ours alone. But Bane was never one to linger on sadness or things that gave anyone a reason to pity him. Pressing his lips together, he dislodged his hold from my hair, pausing long enough to brush his thumb over my cheek before he stepped away from me.

"Which reminds me why I came out here in the first place..." The professional coolness was back and behind it was the hard edges of irritation. "Caridee will join the search and, at the insistence of my uncle and your father, so will your brother."

*Of course they will,* I thought, cursing both men.

"Is that right?"

"You and your sister can keep the guest room for tonight, and when we leave, she can remain with Lennon. We'll split into camps when the other covens and dens arrive." The way Bane cleared his throat, how that small pulse ticked on the side of his jaw, told me enough that he was irritated by the next bit of news. "You, Sam, me, and Cari will be in one camp..."

"You're joking."

"Wish I was," he started, hurrying to explain when I shook my head. "If that..."

I looked up at the sky, catching the moon overhead, not interested in any excuses. "I'm home. I get it. Higher and lower covens. Hierarchies...and our family is bound to yours. I understand the rules." Bane's frown relaxed and he took a step toward me, though he didn't touch me. I didn't give him a chance. "Save the reasoning. I haven't forgotten how things work here, but let's get one thing clear. I don't play well with mean girls. Especially with mean girls who think I'm after their man."

The look he gave me was quick, sharp, as though he wasn't sure if he should be offended or amused. Bane was never one to show his cards, not if he could help it. "Cari will be fine..." I moved my head, releasing an unamused laugh and he amended. "She'll behave or I'll send her back. That sound fair?"

"None of this is fair, but I can handle it."

Before he could ask to elaborate, I waved him off, walking away, looking back only once. I didn't miss the expression on his face, one that had me thinking he wanted me to see the promise in his expression with the low glance of his eyes over my body. That expression, that promise he gave, was a challenge he wanted me to take. But as I climbed back up the steps, I knew the challenge would be unmatched. Just like us, it'd be the game I'd refuse to play with him.

# SEVEN

THERE WAS FIRE IN MY VEINS. IT RAN DEEP, BLISTERING ACROSS MY skin, curling the fine hair of my arms, and I crawled from it. The lines were feet from me, teasing, tempting, a hum of energy that wanted to claim me. I needed only to reach out with my flaming fingers and touch that lick of magic as it waved like a current, burning hotter than the inferno beneath my skin.

*"No! Get away!"*

It wasn't my voice. The tone was frantic, tight. Desperate.

Familiar.

*"Get..."*

But I was so close and the power inside that current, the sweet freedom it offered, was too much. Even the slow drip of raw power emanating from the active line made me drunk. It compelled me closer, had me reaching nearer.

And then...there was blood and a piercing scream. It rattled me to the quick, soaked inside me deeper than the fire, harsher than any scorching mark the lines could make.

*"Jani! Help me! Please, someone...no!"*

The thin blanket tangled around me as I thrashed awake, kicking the small table at my side. "Mai! Where are you?"

The room was dark, with only the dim lights from the overhead oven light giving me any clue that I'd fallen asleep in the connecting den waiting for Freya to return. My head spun and a burning throb rushed through my fingers and along my arms. Holding them ached and I hurried into the kitchen, turning the faucet, half-dizzy, still not sure if that had been a dream or some sort of vision sent to warn me.

Then the familiar sensation began to creep into my stomach. It burned worse than the fire from my vivid dream. Scorched deeper.

"Oh...gods...no."

It couldn't be this. Not again. Not...fucking again.

Before I hit the kitchen floor, overwhelmed by grief and fear, the thunder of running feet came to me then, Mai's arms, soft, sweet and the smell of her skin, the feel of the silk wrap holding her hair up, smoothed against me. She held me so tight, her fingers pulling at my shirt like she wanted to hold onto me just so I would know she had me.

"Jani...it's dark. It's so damn dark. I feel the darkness everywhere. You're in so much pain... Just like when...oh *Circe and Hera*...just like..."

"Mama," I finished for her, gripping my sister's arm.

We were connected. Blood bonded us. Magic and DNA sealed us. What I felt, so did my twin. But if our instincts were linked, so was our magicks. Mai was a healer. I was not. She couldn't spin hexes to maim like I could, but we shared visions, sensations when we dreamed, when there was danger; what it was and how dark it would be. Mai may have not seen all that I'd dreamed, but she felt the darkness of whatever that beast had been.

Helpless, I gripped her tighter, inching closer to her. My twin let me rest my face on her shoulder, giving me a second to breathe, to let her hold me for once, despite the tremble of her arms and the chill pebbling her bare skin. It was a reprieve before I told her what to do. It didn't happen often. Mai wasn't good with panic situations, but she managed just then.

"Jani?" I heard Bane ask, his voice deep, worried. His signature and scent thickened the air around us, and I tightened my eyes, trying not to let it overwhelm me. Bane was anxious, that much I could sense. He had always been my protector, and seeing me like this had to fire off something basic and primal inside him. It triggered that connection we had and heightened the need to touch him.

The old charms and incantations came to me then, flashing behind my closed eyes like glyphs flying in the air so that I caught them, seeing the runes until I knew which one to focus on, which one would center me so that calm would burn away the fear and worry. Mai's touch helped. Her soothing, sweet voice was like a melody as she held me. Bane's scent did as well, though it did nothing to ease that deep, dark desire I had to cling to him. Especially when he knelt beside us, seeming to wait for answers that would either have him charging off to kill whatever thing had me weak and helpless or take Mai's place to protect me from the world.

Neither option would be smart.

"Call Papa," I finally told my sister, pulling away from her when the spell had done its job. "We have to make sure it's not Sam." When she stiffened and gripped my fingers, I knew the possibility hadn't occurred to her. Her job at consoling was done. "Go," I told her, unable to settle enough to stand. "Hurry."

The taste of blood was still in my mouth and, fainter, more bitter, a hint of sweat and the sound...my body shook as that noise echoed inside my head. Bane would be no help. He couldn't take this from me, so I went into myself, gave myself the only comfort I could with my face in my hands and my tears forced tight behind my eyes. I would not cry in front of him.

But still he came to me. Slow. Easy. He was at my side, his large hand on my shoulder, his fingers brushing the damp hair from my forehead. "Tell me," he said, the words like a plea.

"A...death." I shook my head, realizing how wrong that sounded. "No. That's not..." His hand was hot against my skin and I couldn't find it in me to tell him to back up. Just then, I'd take the small comfort he offered. "Murder," I continued, finally looking up at him. "I can still taste their fear and hear the...creature."

Bane's expression shifted from worried to surprised with that one word. "An animal?"

"No. Couldn't have been. Magical. I...felt its signature. I felt its...power."

He nodded, his expression softening, mouth moving into a frown when the tears I tried suppressing escaped my lashes. Bane always took control. He always knew how to command. But I'd never seen tenderness from him. Not like he was then. He moved closer and held my face in his large hands, his gaze working over my features. His expression was rigid, like he didn't know what to do and didn't like that sensation. I couldn't help myself, needed the calm he offered when he pulled me closer and rested my forehead against his.

"Take ease, Janvier...take comfort," he whispered, muttering something I recognized as a spell under his breath. It was meant to calm me. It was meant to dry my tears. But all there was then was Bane, everywhere, in my head, beating back the taste of blood and the vision of that vicious attack. "Jani..." he finally said when my heartbeat returned to normal and the screams I heard inside my head lowered to a soft moan. "Do you know who..."

But there was no answer I needed to give him. Of course I knew. He did too. Everyone in that house did when my Mai's cry echoed through the hallways and she thundered into the kitchen, her face red and her expression horrified.

After all, Mai had loved her too. We'd never been alone out on that roof drinking that wine. Mai had always been with us.

Every single time.

# EIGHT

THE MOON WAS WAXING.

The faint glow glinted over the slow lake and flickers of golden light shined against each rustle of water as it slapped against the bedrock near Bane's back deck. The fireflies were flickering in the black sky, zipping along the bank and between the tall grass, but I could not make out anything beyond their peripheral image as my vision unfocused.

Whiskey had been the balm I used to distract myself this past week. It numbed me. Kept me silent. It kept me from raging and screaming and hexing the lot of the town.

*"You can't be here." My father had thought to actually stop me. He was the town's fixer. He cleaned the messes, and something had made a mess of Freya. "Mon petite, she wouldn't want..."*

*"You don't know what she would want. You never bothered to know anything about her, Papa."*

It was cruel to lash out at him. But my father had only been kind when it served the higher covens. I was his daughter, but I was still lower coven, just like him.

I'd wanted to see her. I'd wanted to see what it had done to her.

There hadn't been much left.

Papa hadn't done much to hide what happened. To Ivy, the mortal chief of police, his deputy would have appeared to be attacked by some sort of wild animal while she walked the main road leading out of town into Grant territory. Bane's driver hadn't waited for her. No one knew why or could ask the wizard since he and his car were missing.

Papa had covered the tire tracks and Bane hadn't mentioned her getting a ride from his driver. Ivy would wonder why she was walking instead of driving toward Grant territory, and Papa had fixed that too. With the help of her family, Freya's Nissan had been brought onto the main road and one of the tires deflated, and the town's surveillance cameras spelled to alter any appearances of Freya's car that night. The rest was made to appear like a horrible accident of nature. Black bears had been known to frequent the area and huge bobcats had been spotted in the marshy lands around Manchac. It would not be much of a stretch. But my father had collected hair and a claw, things that would enable him to work a spell to find what sort of creature had done this.

But it wouldn't matter.

It wouldn't bring her back.

*"Someone summoned it. It had to be a rougarou!"* Selene, Freya's younger sister insisted. Of all the Douglas sisters, Selene had taken her death the hardest. They were close and a cloud had come over the entire family. A dark wave blanketed much of the town, in fact, but the emotion Selene seemed to feel most deeply, like me, was close to blinding rage.

*"I don't know about a rougarou, Sele,"* I'd told her, passing a flask to the *woman on the back porch of her family's home the night of Freya's funeral, "but I can promise you whatever the hell it is, I damn well will find it."*

I don't think she believed me. Selene wasn't like Freya. She didn't have many friends. Didn't blend into the town or covens and have drinks on Fridays at Batty's. She'd gone off to Europe for college and came back changed, quiet, reserved, but still fiercely loyal to her sisters.

*"You do what you have to, Jani," she'd told me. "And I'll do the same."*

It hadn't been lip service I'd given her.

I sat out on that porch watching the Cove's magical congregation milling around the square, making polite conversation with mortals from the police force who likely had no idea they were consorting with witches and weres and a few demons and vamps for that matter. All that time, all that watching, I analyzed and listened. I marked the gaits of people's walks and the way they conducted themselves.

With good reason. Freya may have been taken by a creature. It may have been summoned, but my guess was it wasn't a creature that was always a creature. And, like the good cop she'd proved herself to be, my friend had taken a bit of that bastard with her, gashing their thigh with her pocketknife, something she never went far without. It wasn't found at the scene or in her possessions, but that much of the attack had come to me. The slash against a thick animal's thigh and the lunge of the blade inside it. Since it wasn't left at the scene, it had to be left inside whoever had killed her.

I hoped it hurt like hell.

"You cold?" I heard and glanced over my shoulder to find Bane standing behind me with a mug in his hand. When I glared at the mug, squinting, not speaking, the wizard shook his head. "Tea. Hot." I started to shake my head, but Bane amended. "With bourbon."

"Hand it over."

He did, sitting next to me on the lowest step that stretched near the lake. Bane passed over the mug, nodding at the small tilt of thanks I gave him but, thankfully, didn't speak until I'd gotten one long sip down. When he did, his voice was low, calm. "Your brother would bitch and moan if he knew I gave you that." I glanced at him, not moving my head, and Bane shrugged. "You haven't slept far as I can tell."

"You never sleep."

"There's ten dens and four covens on my property ready to help us search for the Elam." He pulled a flask from his inside coat pocket when I offered him my mug and pushed the silver tip to his mouth. "No one's going to sleep with that much going on."

"We'll...get started tomorrow night." Freya's death had delayed us.

It had put a kink in everything, for everyone. Crimson Cove may have been a small town, but its reach and that of the magical community stretched wide. She may have worked with the mortal police, but she was first a witch from an old, respected family. Her death was felt across the region. "This week has been..."

"Everyone is hurting..." Bane said, surprising me. He kept his attention on the lake, his eyes unblinking as he drank from his flask again. "She was a good witch."

"She was a better friend."

I hadn't meant to speak so openly. Not in front of Bane. Not in front of anyone. Being this close to the lines, feeling their raw power did something to me; it heightened what I already felt and Bane seemed to sense it.

When I dipped my head down, hiding my face with my dark hair, pretending to sip on my tea, he moved close enough to bring his shoulder next to mine. "If you want to cry..."

"No," I said, cupping the mug, my body going stiff when he touched my shoulder. "Bane..."

"She was your friend." He pushed my hair back, his forehead wrinkling as his attention shot over my face. "Emotion doesn't make you weak." I wanted to shake my head, tell him to leave me to my rage and anger. It cradled me. Gave me energy to lead this search and find who did this. But there was only so much control I had whenever he was around. There were buttons I had Bane knew how to push. He had each one connected with one hand against my face and his thumb brushing over my bottom lip. "Jani..."

I knew what he tasted like. The memory was faint, but so clear.

Woodsmoke and whiskey.

Home and heartache.

That was Bane Iles.

He leaned forward, and all around me everything coalesced—my grief, my anger, my desperate damn longing and the moments I never got and always wanted with him.

The hot breath from his full lips tickled over my mouth just as he pressed closer. I could make out that sandalwood smell, hear the low, sweet hum of his throat working before he spoke and then, just like that, I realized this was midnight and magic and the lines around us.

"St...stop..." I said pushing away from him. "Don't...don't do that."

"This was just..."

"I know exactly what this was. Please don't..." I stood, leaving the cooling mug behind as I did. "What I need is for you to understand I'm here to do a job." I took two steps down, away from him as he watched me, his hand back around that flask, elbows on his bent knees. "The job you paid me to do and the one I've set for myself."

"Which is?"

"You're really going to ask me that?"

Bane exhaled, nodding once before he replaced the flask into his coat and stood but didn't approach. "Did it ever occur to you that you aren't the only one determined to find out what happened to her?"

"I know what happened to her. I saw it!"

Bane's expression hardened, his jaws clenching as he looked out over the water. That look only ever crossed his features when he felt lost and powerless, when something was beyond his control. He had the power to dip into my mind and erase the vision. A long incantation and his fingers twisted in my hair would give him freedom to take that pain from me.

But my pain was mine. The losses were what fueled me, and if I was going to find who did this to my friend, I needed that vision— every aching moment of it.

Bane rubbed his mouth, smoothing his fingers through his hands as his focus shifted from the water and the humming energy of the pulsing magic that lay beyond it. "The lines..." he tried, not looking at me.

"They're affecting everyone. I know that." I turned to him, curling my arms to keep myself warm. The air had turned, and the temperatures were dropping, making the night frigid. "You mentioned it. But that has nothing to do with how angry I am or the fact that I don't want you to kiss me."

He watched me, eyes calm but shifting to my arms, then down my body as he moved closer, coming two steps from me. Without my asking, Bane waved his right hand, moving two long fingers as he muttered, "*Éirigh te,*" his gaze piercing, brightening to a sharp silver as the small spell fired and a circle of warmth surrounded me.

The coolness dropped slowly so that I wasn't suddenly overheated. A slow lick of warmth began at my feet and zipped around me like a wave, cradling, hugging until I dropped my hands to my side, struggling between gratitude and irritation at the wizard.

"I can warm myself, you know." Even I knew what a brat I sounded like.

"I know that well, Jani." Another step and he was in front of me, not too close, but near enough that I could make out the sharp features of his face and spot the silver from his spell dimming in his irises. "You...*don't* want me to kiss you?" Just like that day in high school, Bane took the ends of my hair and smoothed them through his fingers, watching each strand as they slipped away from him. "But you kissed me first."

*Circe*...this was dangerous territory. Bane could never know what happened that day, not all of it. In his memory was my parting kiss, the forward witch saying goodbye to him because she wanted to.

"That was a long time ago."

"It was a memorable kiss."

He reached for my hair again, but I stepped back, taking all of my hair into my hands to knot it into a bun at the top of my head. "Like you said. This, all of this, is the lines. You wouldn't be interested if it weren't for..."

"Maybe." His grin returned, the same half-smile that always came over him, but this time Bane looked away, like he tried to fight it and looking at me directly would give away how amused he was. Gods, it was my favorite expression he made. "Or maybe there's always been something there. Maybe I've always been drawn to you for a reason."

"And that reason doesn't matter, does it? Not when we have a job to do and a search to lead. And especially not when you are betrothed to a viciously jealous witch who will be on that search."

He didn't seem to like when I leveled reality at him. He'd called me a mood spoiler the other night. I supposed I was, but then, I'd just lost my best friend. There wasn't anything or anyone that would take the anger from me. Not even a kiss from the boy I let slip through my fingers.

Looking down, Bane moved his fingers into his beard, rubbing it smooth before he nodded once, seeming determined when he glanced back at me. "Let me help you. You know I can. No one knows this land better than me."

He wasn't wrong. Bane had made this land, Grant land, his playground when he was a kid. It was a running joke how often his uncle had to send out wizards and cast spells to find him when he was a kid and wanted to keep to himself. If the creature had killed Freya near Grant territory, then its scent and trail wouldn't be far behind. I could track, but Bane had been schooled in the craft by some of the best clerics in the world. He could find this creature faster than anyone.

"Fine," I finally said, the word like nails in my mouth. "But understand this: whoever killed Freya doesn't get a pass." He watched me, the threatening smile dying the longer he kept his attention on my face. When my mouth tightened and the flash of that scream returned inside my head, I frowned, the anger surfacing again. "They're dead and I get to do it."

Bane opened his mouth, posed to speak, but closed it again, moving his head to the right. "Have you ever..."

"Promise me," I interrupted, waving my hand to kill the warming spell he'd conjured. Depending on him to take care of me wouldn't make watching him with Cari any easier. My defenses needed to be up, beginning now. "Or I go on my own."

Whatever gave Bane pause, he didn't mention. But the look he gave me spoke volumes. Maybe there were memories, ones I hadn't taken from him running through his mind. Maybe he was remembering us before our mothers died, before higher and lower covens meant anything at all to either of us. Maybe he remembered the girl I'd been when I doodled his initials in my notebook and erased each line the second I did, knowing he'd likely taken sneaks at the artwork on my paper. Maybe there was a repeat of my kiss moving through his head and Bane wondered what had changed that girl who poured every inch of herself into the slow, methodical ministrations of her lips and tongue against his because she wanted to make an impression. Whatever he thought in the delayed pause, he watched me, shifted his worry into something that looked a lot like resignation. Then Bane nodded, pressing his lips together like it was the only way to keep from asking why or who or how many. "I...promise you."

"Good," I said, my voice breaking before I cleared it. "Now, hand me my mug and keep your lips to yourself."

# NINE

THERE WAS LIGHT AND DARK IN THE WORLD. THERE WAS LIGHT AND dark in the lines and we were taught from an early age that they were like a raging fire—beautiful, magnetic, something of great, shuttering power, but also deadly, destructive.

I knew about pyros. I knew that the bend of one's will to the siren call of the lines was sometimes more tempting than the heat of a blaze or the destruction one single flame can cause. But until I stood on Bane's empty porch, watching the convergence of were packs, dens, and regional covens flocking around the property, I never knew just how naive I'd been. Even the din of their voices, their laughter, their arguing, did not register above that sweet, melodic hum of the lines. That siren song was strong that night, stronger than I'd ever heard it before.

The song was something out of a fairytale. There was light and melody, love and comfort coursing in the lines. There was truth and beauty and a dozen, a million truths I never knew I needed to know coursing between those hums. It was all that I was, all my folk would ever be, and all of it—all that truth, all the answers—was a few hundred feet away. Batty had unlocked something inside of me, something more volatile than my nex, something that opened me up completely to the raw feel of that magic and the pulse it brought to the forest around us.

I wasn't the only one to sense that great power. For weres, the raw song of lines unhindered by the Elam tempted them with the animalistic need to join, to meld with the earth and embrace their primal selves. For witches and wizards, the pull was not so subtle. My fingers itched to strip myself bare. My skin was tight. My pores, open. I wanted to be naked. I wanted to feel the vibration of the ley lines against my skin and bathe in the moonlight that fell brightest in the hollow of trees at the center of Bane's property. Perhaps especially with the rage and weight of Freya's death heavy in in my mind, I wanted to be free from the hindrance of civilized society.

I wasn't alone.

Lennon kept fidgeting with his sleeves, rolling them up, untucking his shirt and casting eager glances toward the forest and the darkness that hid the lines. And when Mai walked along the riverbank, shedding her light jacket, Lennon's baser inclinations seemed to rise to the surface. His gaze followed my twin, watching her every movement like an animal prowling, and she seemed to eat up the attention, smiling, giving him some ridiculous come-hither glance that had me blinking.

The other guards, the cook, even Cari seemed antsy, not themselves. I didn't care about her brother Ethan chaperoning the search, but found it verging on hysterical that the lines were making Miss Prim and Proper yank out the pins in her hair and run her fingers along Bane's bare arms, near his waist. For his part, he seemed little disinclined to acknowledge her attention.

Bane seemed, in fact, very unaffected by the raw, pulsing heat the lines sent out into the forest. At least, that's what I told myself. That's exactly what I thought until Bane walked away from Cari and joined a group from the Oxford coven down on the grounds below. Each wizard kept their distance from each other but still found it impossible to be still or keep their hands from their collars or the hems of their shirts. The witches, most of them, had tugged off their jackets and sweaters and walked among the dens and covens in nothing but their tank tops and jeans, despite the cold temperatures. It was the witches that caught my attention—

particularly when two of them congregated toward a wolf pack from Jacksonville who seemed a little too eager to entertain them. I was considering the result of the missing amulet and wondering what would happen if there'd be a sudden rash of inter-species breeding and offspring when I sensed a warm, intense stare watching me from the grounds.

Bane always had a way to pull my attention back to him. No one could scream at me with one slow gaze and have it be as clear as if he'd yelled my name into the open darkness. A slow turn of my head and I met his gaze, doing a little staring of my own. His eyes were tight, his bottom lip pressed hard against the top one. God, he was beautiful. Beautiful and compelling and so off limits, I reminded myself, bringing forward the scream of the attack and the recall of what else lay in that forest once we recovered the Elam.

But I had to admit, Batty had woken up more than my nex. He'd reminded me of what I'd given up, of what I'd taken from Bane, and as the magnificent wizard stared up at me with his mouth relaxed and eyes scorching like a flame, I had to remind myself that what I had done had all been for the best. It had all been for the coven, for the Cove, for his own peace of mind.

Not able to stand his gaze for another moment, I turned away, giving him my back as I watched the lake on the other side of the forest. Closer to the water, the lines were less evident, and I walked off the porch, eager to put some distance between myself and that sweet, haunting song. I nodded at Lennon and several of Bane's guards I didn't know as I headed toward the bank.

The lake was calm, it barely moved at all, and a small swarm of fireflies danced above the water. They'd be gone soon, taken by the fall, then the winter, and the lake would grow black and still until spring. But for now I watched the insects zip through night to skid along that water like there was no threat beneath, as though their lives were endless, and nothing loomed on the horizon for any of us.

"It's a little too quiet, don't you think?"

Lennon seemed more relaxed now that Mai had disappeared back into the house, less formal than was his usual manner as he came to my side, joining me in my observation of the fireflies and their show, skimming above the water. "The calm," I told him, not sure why my voice came out slow, small.

The guard's gaze was heavy, but nowhere near the intensity Bane seemed unable to keep from shooting my way every time he decided to gawk at me. Still, Lennon's presence was a comfort I didn't realize I needed until he was standing at my side. "You believe that's what this is?" In my peripheral vision I noticed his quick nod toward the water. "The calm before the storm? Something is headed our way?"

He couldn't be serious. Maybe it was his inexperience with the Cove. Maybe it was because he'd spent so little time here that made him seem so naive. Still, he was a wizard. I assumed he'd have experienced his fair share of upheaval when magic slipped over onto the mortal world.

"We're magical folk living amongst the mortals. A witch from a highly respected family has just been murdered by a magical creature who was likely summoned." A quick glance in his direction, that quick head shake I didn't seem able to stop, and I stepped closer to the bank. "Something is already heading our way."

Lennon considered me a moment longer than I'd expected. Mine was a way of thinking realistically, based solely on the hurdles life had tossed in my way time and time again. It was just the way of things and I was surprised Lennon didn't agree. He was from the UK, and every magical creature knew the suffering mortals had put magical folk through over the centuries. Hell, it's what caused the mass exodus to the new world. So Lennon's overtly positive attitude was a bit curious.

He kept watching me, moving his gaze over my face as though he half expected I'd poke him in the ribs and tell him I was teasing. Instead, I kept my attention forward, watching the lake as the wizard kept to himself. "That seems ominous." His voice was gentle, kind, and bordered a little too near placation for my liking. "It makes the future seem hopeless."

"Not hopeless." Another shrug and I waved my hand, passing off his claim. "Inevitable if we remain in the shadows."

Not seeming to like that response, Lennon stood in front of me, hands deep in his pockets and the most ridiculous, incredulous expression on his face. His green eyes sparkled against the moonlight reflecting off the water. That deep wrinkle between his eyebrows set harder, it seemed, as though Lennon fought to question my seriousness. "You think we should make ourselves known?"

I didn't pause to soften my response. I'd been repeating it for years because it was what I truly believed. "I think it would loosen some of our self-imposed shackles."

"They'd revolt." Lennon's mouth worked like a guppy struggling for water and I thought I'd tell him he'd started to look fish-like, but that shock and worry was far too serious to be teased. "They'd try to overtake us, Miss Benoit. On the whole, there would truly be nothing but disaster."

"Maybe."

"Maybe? You're serious?" He touched my arm, looking very shocked, looking like he was generally concerned for my mental health. "You can't be serious."

"Oh, she is," Bane said, coming up behind us. One glare at Lennon's hand on my arm and the guard stepped back. "It's the same assertions her brother has made for decades. Jani's only repeating what she's heard her whole life."

"Doesn't mean it isn't true," I told him, narrowing my eyes when he laughed. I glared at Bane, but that didn't lessen the smile on his face. I hated being written off as some dutiful sister not capable of thinking for herself. My brother's opinion might not be popular, but I truly believed he was right. I didn't need Bane being condescending to me because he didn't agree.

"No, I suppose it doesn't." He rubbed the back of his neck, nodding as though seeing at least some of my point, but then quickly dropped the argument before it led to something heated. "Right now, though, we have more pressing issues than whether or not we should jump on broomsticks and fly across the moon for the mortals to see."

Bane turned back, nodded toward the clearing beyond the house where several more dens and covens had arrived and were greeting each other. "They're all here?" Two shifters immediately transformed as they came closer to the lines hidden deep in the forest, and I grinned at their enthusiasm.

"All but Birmingham." Bane's expression was relaxed, a little pleased, but then he faced me again and that ease stiffened until his features became tight. "They'll be here in a couple of hours and then we can leave." Bane grunted, his attention on me, not his guard, and in my peripheral I noticed Lennon shuffling his feet before he cleared his throat. "Well then...I'll see that the supplies are arranged."

"My brother here yet?" I asked when the stare Bane gave me went on too long. I'd thought we'd settled things the night before, but he seemed unable to keep his attention from me.

"Five minutes out. He just sent me a text." Moving closer, Bane's shoulder bumped mine when he folded his arm and we both spotted the slow slide of a snake moving off a stump and into the black water. "I've...been thinking about that promise last night."

Jerking my attention to him, my chest automatically went tight. "You're backing out already?" I turned, dropping my hands, fingers shifting as though the instinct to attack was something I couldn't reign in. "It hasn't even been..."

"You don't know what you're..." Bane's eyebrow shot up and instantly he grabbed my wrist, covering my entire fist with his hand. "Were you...going to hex me?"

Swallowing, I tried to pull free, but his hold was tight, unrelenting. "I wasn't going to do anything."

"I...think you were, little witch." Head shaking when I frowned at him, he pulled me against his chest and leaned forward but didn't try to kiss me. "The Janiver I knew was sweet, bit of a smartass, and very smart." He let me step back when I yanked against him, but he still wouldn't release my hand. "She wasn't mean or cruel and she damn well didn't have it in her to kill another living creature." The glint of amusement that had just been on his face dimmed and something dark, something hard replaced it. "Taking a life changes you, Jani, and you don't come back from it. You live with it, but you aren't the same. So tell me, can you look in the eyes of a creature who may not be aware that they've attacked anyone and snuff out their life?"

Head shaking, I glared at Bane, ignoring the warmth that had bubbled inside my chest the second he touched me. "I know what death does to you, Mr. Iles. I'm very familiar. Please don't pretend to imagine you know anything about me anymore. And that thing didn't attack. It murdered my friend. For doing that, I'll look it in the eyes with my hands around its neck and watch it breath its last breath if it means no one has to feel what I do right now."

The tears burned in my eyes, but they did not fall. Bane must have spotted something in them that sparked some well of pity, because his grip loosened and he reached for my face, resting his hand against my cheek. "Gods, Jani, what happened to you?"

Eyes closed tight, I shook my head, ignoring the nagging internal urge to tell him the truth, to explain what had turned me so cold. But I'd taken something from him and kept a secret. He'd never understand or forgive me.

"I left the Cove. I had to survive."

*   *   *

"Here," Mai said, handing me the bag she'd packed while I grabbed several bottles of cold water from the refrigerator. Outside, dozens of weres—wolves, ravens, panthers, and eagles among them—as well as a handful of skilled witches and wizards organized into groups of five, following Bane's command as he pointed out markers among the vast acres of his coven's property.

My twin stood next to me, shoving the pack over my shoulders, and we both watched the activity through the large window in the kitchen.

"That's a lot of people coming here to find something that maybe can't be found." My sister's voice vibrated as she looked up at me. That frown, the stupid, scrunched up dip between her eyes—there was real fear and worry in her expression. "I'd hate to be you."

"It does suck sometimes."

"But you aren't worried?"

The water was cold with the smallest flecks of ice floating around the bottle when I drank from it. I could deflect my response to my sister's comment, but not for long. She knew me too well. She'd see right through me if I tried to deny I wasn't generally concerned about how things could turn out during our search.

"You worry enough for the both of us." I took another swallow when she only continued to glare at me, forgetting for a moment that

Mai wouldn't let me hide my fear for too long. "Besides, this is nothing compared to the search party last year in Ohio. The mortals brought out the National Guard and four different sheriff departments from three counties. All of them going off of my direction."

Mai made a little sound of surprise and touched my arm to pull my attention to her shocked face. "You told them you were psychic?"

"I told them I had a gut feeling. They didn't much care how I knew, just that I did." My sister relaxed with my explanation and leaned against the counter as I mirrored her stance. "Mortals see and believe what they want, you know that. It doesn't matter if the truth is right there in front of their eyes. They'll only see what their brain tells them makes sense."

Mai nodded at the crowd outside that window. "These aren't mortals, Jani."

"Which is good. No need to lie to them."

When I straightened and turned back to stare out again, Mai joined me and we both watched the weres and covens tossing their packs and listening to Bane as he and his shifter friend Wyatt pointed toward the forest.

"Yes, but that means they'll expect more from you." She paused, taking the bottle of water from me. "I'm worried about this. I'm worried that whoever took the Elam is going to target you."

"They won't touch me."

"How do you know?"

Mai didn't fight me for the bottle when I took it. "Bane won't let them."

My twin's smile was wide and hopeful, advertising the intent behind that look. She wanted me back in the Cove, and I guess being around Bane gave her a little too much hope that might happen. I almost hated deflating that pretty bubble of anticipation. "Get over yourself, nosy witch. It's not like that."

"So you say."

I stared at my twin, shaking my head when that wide grin didn't falter in the least. "It's like you forgot that we aren't eighteen anymore."

"I know what I see, and I know what drove you away ten years ago." She didn't, not really, but Mai liked to think of herself as all-knowing when it came to love. More specifically, when it came to me and love. She'd been way off her game for a long damn time.

I wouldn't tell her everything. Mai was my twin. We were connected, but if she knew I was also angling for this trip to be a hunt for the creature who killed Freya, she wouldn't get a second's rest. I had to play off the threat that loomed in that forest.

"He's engaged, Mai, and not interested in anything with me. Besides, this is a job. The money will help with my debt and doing well will help Papa's business save face." She frowned, as though only just remembering that it was her husband who'd ruined things for our father. "Stop with the grimace. You'll get wrinkles."

"Ronan..."

"You were stupid in love with him." She didn't loosen the tight set of her mouth when I nudged her, seeming unwilling to let me tease her a little. I hated Mai letting that guilt get inside of her. "He was a charmer and good looking. We've all done stupid things when our libidos are firing on all cylinders."

Finally, that frown eased, and my sister shook her head. "What have you done because of your cylinders?"

"Stupid, stupid people, sis."

"You aren't the only one." Two shifters approached the door, pulling our attention away from talk of wayward cylinders, and I smiled at the slow grin that came across Wyatt Rimmel's mouth when he nodded to us both.

Ten years back, I'd met Wyatt one afternoon after I had ditched the last fifteen minutes of English Lit. He'd been waiting on Bane, a surprise visit, he'd claimed. *"It's his eighteenth birthday this weekend," he'd told me as I nodded at the comfortable spot he'd taken up on the hood of my patchy, rusted, holes-in-the-bumper '68 Shelby.*

*"That right?" The shifter hadn't moved, so I edged him off the hood and dumped my backpack onto the front seat. "This information should matter to me somehow?"*

*"You're Jani," Wyatt had said, laughing when my face heated and likely went blotchy.*

*I slammed the car door, which rattled the front window and the shifter finally slid off my car. "How do you know?"*

*"Folks talk." Eyes shifting to my tight grip on the door handle, Wyatt relaxed, seeming like he found my little bout of curiosity funny. "Especially smitten folk who try to play like no one touches them."*

*"Who on earth..." But I hadn't needed to ask the question. I knew, of course I did, but couldn't seem to bring myself around to thinking that Bane wanted anything other than to trade long, knowing, unresolved looks with me. "What'd he say?"*

*With another laugh, Wyatt had leaned against my car. "Ah, beautiful, what kind of friend would I be if I let my boy's secrets spill?"*

*"Honest," I offered. "Helpful." My smile couldn't quite match his, but Wyatt seemed to have gotten a kick out of my exuberance.*

*"Shameless. I like it." He moved in closer, too close for my liking and he knew, saw that he made me a little uncomfortable as I stepped back. He didn't follow, but did offer a generous examination of my frame, my face, before the smile he wore turned genuine. "I see now. You're something else."*

*"You've heard different?"*

*"No. I haven't heard anything but good. Maybe," he'd said, sidling a little closer, "just maybe you should take initiative, jump before he can break away?"*

*My go-to defense was always to curl a bit inside myself, and back then Wyatt's confession had stirred up a lot inside of me. Still, I thought that maybe he was messing with me, just to get under my skin. Teenage boys did that. Hell, my brother still does that.*

*When I didn't respond, Wyatt cut me some slack and stepped away, a decent enough distance that relief washed over me. "Listen, Jani, it's only my gut instinct, but I know what I've been told and I know what I see in front of me. You like him, get him."*

*"It's not like that. He's...taken."*

*"Hell, beautiful, no one's taken, not really. Especially not that one." Wyatt nodded over my shoulder and I looked around, eyes blinking fast when I noticed Bane watching us closely as he came down the steps of the school. I kept my gaze on Bane and that curious, mildly irritated expression of his. But Wyatt moved closer, stepping to my side so he could whisper in my ear. "Sometimes, you gotta take what's yours before anyone else can latch on to it."*

*"He's not mine." I had my door open and my butt on the seat before Bane made it into the parking lot.*

*"No? Well, shit, maybe I should change my plans and keep you company this weekend, Miss Jani."*

*Engine running and my hand on the wheel, I'd smiled up at Wyatt and laughed at the glint in his eyes and the way he hadn't looked at my face. "You're a hell of a lot of trouble, aren't you?"*

*"Absolutely."*

*"Then I'd probably be better off ignoring everything you just told me."*

*Wyatt shrugged and glanced to his left as Bane walked closer. "It'll probably keep me from a busted nose if you do."*

*"Well, I'd hate to come between two secret-keeping friends."*

*"You do that, Jani, and I'll owe you one."*

*"I'll remember that."*

And I had, just then as Wyatt strolled into the kitchen followed by a younger, smaller version of himself. The Rimmell genes were excellent and Wyatt still had the same soft features that were exaggerated by the smooth shape of his jaw and the whirl of green in his hazel eyes.

"You here so I can collect?"

Wyatt's laugh was still loud, still carried around the room with very little effort. He remembered. "Never said a thing, did you?"

"Nope."

"Then why'd I still end up with a bloody nose that weekend?"

He leaned against the counter, sizing me up, looking like he wanted to see the differences, the similarities from the kid he had met that one time, years ago.

"Got me," I said, folding my arms as Wyatt kept looking me over. Only this time I didn't mind the examination. This time I could stand the scrutiny a man often gives a woman. They could look all they wanted. At least until I shut them down. "I didn't tell a soul."

"How you been, Jani?" he finally asked, ignoring the shifter next to him when he cleared his throat.

"Good. Only back for this one job." At my side, Mai shuffled her feet, and I finally pulled my gaze from Wyatt's handsome face. "This is my twin sister, Mai." A nod and Wyatt shot her a smile.

"Twins? Wow. That seems a little unfair." My sister and I both frowned at Wyatt's friend when he laughed, his gaze volleying between us. "Two beautiful women, twins at that, in one small town. Not fair at all."

"Look at you with the flattery," Mai said.

"I call 'em like I see them, miss."

Wyatt slapped his friend on the shoulder. "This is my little cousin, Joe Arvel. He's from our pack in Columbia."

Pleasantries were exchanged, handshakes were given, and at Wyatt's explanation, I noticed how similar the two shifters were to each other—same narrow eyes, same elongated noses, and each had high cheekbones that made their eyes nearly vanish when they smiled. But where Wyatt was sandy-haired with a few waves touching the back of his neck, Joe had dark, thick hair cut short and tight.

"So, this is the famous Janiver Benoit?" Joe asked, waving off his cousin when Wyatt elbowed him. My cocked eyebrow had Joe shrugging. "Sorry, but Bane said you were the best at finding lost things."

I bet he did, and just for a second I wondered what else Bane had said to the two cousins.

"She is the best," Mai said.

"Oh, Joe, there you are," we heard as Lennon walked into the kitchen. He offered me a nod, then smiled easy, but still the professional. "Mr. Iles said that you and Wyatt..." Lennon nodded to the pair of them and then moved his gaze back toward me, straightening his spine when that gaze stopped on my sister.

There was a quick pull against the lines that we all seemed to feel. My skin went warm, tingled like I'd run around a carpeted room in fuzzy socks, and Wyatt and Joe stepped back, away from Lennon as though he threw off a pheromone only the shifters could sense. At my side, Mai's voice hummed, but she shook her head, blinking when Lennon cleared his throat. "Miss...that is, Mrs. Phillips. How...how are you feeling?"

"Fine, thank you, Lennon." I'd never seen Mai so timid around a man. I'd certainly never seen her fidget the way she did then with her foot bouncing against the tile floor. She'd never had to be timid before.

My sister was beautiful, with her skin a shade or two lighter than mine, and she had beautiful natural waves in her hair and light eyes that shone against her complexion. Men gravitated toward her without any encouragement on Mai's part.

She never had to cajole or flirt. And she'd never done the awkward, anxious thing when a man she liked paid attention to her. So this, between my sister and Bane's guard, was just plain weird. We all stood there a moment, watching, it seemed, for who would speak again, Lennon or Mai, and when this ridiculous back and forth shyness would play itself out.

Finally, with Joe clearing his throat, Mai stopped staring at Lennon and the guard nodded at her. "I'll just...I'm..." And with that she stepped away from the counter to fuss with the cabinet next to the fridge, out of sight of Lennon's gaze.

"Pardon, Joe, Wyatt...Mr. Iles says your pack will head out first."

"Nice to meet you, Janiver," Joe said, shaking my hand again, and I blinked, pulling my attention away from my sister's odd behavior. Joe's skin was rough with calluses on the inside of his palm, and as he gripped my fingers, a cool, relaxed sensation passed from his skin to mine. It made me wonder if Joe had a little more than shifting magic beneath that tall, wide frame.

Wyatt nodded, gave me a small wink before he left, and I ignored that flirty smile as I took my hand back from Joe. "Please, call me Jani. Everyone does."

"Or Miss Benoit," Bane said, coming into the room. Wyatt slapped him on the back as they met at the doorway, but I waved Joe off, doing my best to remind myself that Bane was the client. If he didn't want anyone being too friendly, that was his prerogative.

Still, I didn't need him speaking for me. "Jani is fine. It was good to meet you as well."

From my peripheral, I could make out Mai's shifting gaze, how she watched Lennon as Joe left and the guard listened as Bane said something to him in private. This skittish, shy twin burgeoned close to sad. "Here." My sister frowned when I handed her a glass bottle from the counter, whiskey with a bite, but she didn't outright refuse it.

"I don't..."

"Please. You're a smitten kitten. Have a drink. You'll be all on your own with Lennon tonight. You're gonna need liquid courage."

"Look who's talking." She handed me the bottle, glancing toward the two wizards as they chatted. Well, Bane chatted and Lennon nodded after every instruction his boss gave him. "Mr. Senior Year Fantasy will be right beside you for thousands of acres. You'll be sleeping under the moonlight three feet from him." *With his fiancée and our brother in tow,* I thought but didn't mention. I still choked on the liquor and my twin laughed. "Uh huh, now who's the smitten kitten?" She laughed when I flipped her off and then kissed my cheek. "Be safe. Be smart," she said, leaving me in the kitchen with that bottle and the Fantasy.

Another swig, this one going down with a burn.

"That's not going to hinder your reach once we get out into the forest and you try to search for the Elam?"

"No," I said, closing my eyes when Bane stood next to me. "It'll heighten it."

"So you say."

I took another sip. "I do." Then another before I nodded at the black runes that were tattooed around his forearms. I couldn't make out their meaning, but knew there were many Celtic and some Druid markings that seemed vaguely familiar. A majority of the patterns looked Viking influenced. They weren't tattoos, really. They were marks of knowledge, lessons taken and given, used to hone his craft.

"Some of us didn't need to train in Norway with thousand-year-old mages to learn our craft." Made a little bolder by the liquor, I stepped into Bane's personal space and ran the tip of my fingernail over the runes wrapped around his forearm. "All these runes, all that pain and blood, I never once had to suffer so much for my craft."

"Maybe," Bane said, taking the bottle from me, "if you had, you wouldn't need the liquor."

"Maybe I like the liquor." My tongue was heavy in my mouth and I wasn't sure why my voice had suddenly lowered or how I could feel the ley lines whispering against my mind.

But Bane wasn't drinking, and he seemed able to control how the lines affected him. He was too versed in blocking raw magic. Still, he didn't seem wholly unaffected, and for whatever reason, he at least didn't object to how closely I stood in front of him. "You strike me as the type of witch who likes things that are bad for her."

The laughter came quickly, the first I'd released in over a week. Just then, I didn't think about the darkness that took me with Freya's death. Something light, almost sweet came into my head and I glanced at that bottle, only just realizing that I hadn't been drinking whiskey at all.

"Berry Burn wine?"

"You didn't know?" He laughed, scrubbing his face. "*Circe*, Jani. I thought you were more careful."

Shrugging, I let the elixir work through me, enjoying the way its potency made everything feel electrified and sweet. Dipping my head back, a sudden reminder of the worst possible thing for me—the wizard standing inches away—seemed so attractive, so sweet, and I licked my lips, my inhibitions lowered as I watched him.

Unbidden, a memory of that solitary day when I'd bitten the forbidden fruit and I forgot myself for just a moment filled my head. "And, baby, you've got no idea how much I like things that are bad for me."

Bane blinked. I blinked and just for a second I savored the silent room, the energy that built between us then. "Did you...did you just call me baby?"

It was if he'd unstoppered a drain and I twirled down into its belly. Berry Burn wine or not, I immediately sobered. Mortification, humiliation, it had to be all over my face, easily read in my expression. But I was not a witch who would admit defeat or mistakes made so quickly. I was a natural survivor. I'd say anything to weasel my way out of a tight spot. Or utter humiliation.

"No." There was a touch of humor in my response—forced and clearly fabricated—but it didn't stop me from making that sound or stepping back when Bane held my wrist.

"You did." He pinned me in the corner of the counter with that wide body nearly engulfing me in shadow and heat. "Damn." Bane came so close, mouth too near my neck as though he was just managing to control himself and not devour me right then and there. "Why do I like that?"

*I knew why and just then, I hated that he didn't. Because you claimed me! Ten years ago, I wanted to scream. Because I am yours, because you belong to me.*

Some part of him had to know the truth, despite the block I had put on his memories. Somewhere, behind all that power, the knowledge, the lists of lines of duty and expectations, lay the hidden memory of that one blissful afternoon with me in that empty classroom. The day our nexuses melded. The day we claimed each other.

The way Bane looked at me, the deep focus of his gaze on my mouth, shifting across my fingers brought us closer and closer to the edge of something that could mean nothing but misery. For him, at least. And I couldn't stop it. I didn't want to stop it.

All around us seemed to settle, every sound, every scent, just like it had that day, just like it had the first time we kissed. The only sound I could clearly hear was the steady, rhythmic pulse of his heart and mine —two separate bodies moving toward each other, closer, nearer until Bane's stubble grazed on my cheek and he held my head still, insistent between his fingers.

I had only to tilt my head back a little. Move my chin, wet my bottom lip and he'd take my mouth. It was all there on his face. Expressions that told a thousand stories, made a million promises, and I wanted them all inside me with him, where he was meant to be.

Just one small movement and it would be done.

Bane tilted my chin, held my face between both hands now and I heard him come closer, waiting, making my mind up that I would only take a taste...

A taste that wasn't mine.

A touch that belonged to someone else.

Eyes shut tight to clear away Caridee's perfect skin, her perfect hair —the flawless Rivers coven regalia that Bane deserved. The one taught over and over to us as expectation. Certainties that had never been changed. The way the Cove existed so that there was no upset, no chance of shaming all of the Cove by letting the mortals know what we are and how we lived.

Expectation.

Certainty.

Things that had been constants for everyone in the Cove. Each coven depended on the other. Each den, every pack, all connected.

The way of things.

The things I'd left behind.

The things Ronan had tried to topple.

The things I was there to recapture for my family.

And, louder than any of that came the scream...Freya's scream.

She was gone. My friend was gone and I had to find who killed her.

Before I realized I'd uttered a sound, the word came out, my hands pushing against that wide chest and "Parley!" echoing around the kitchen.

Bane steadied my hands when I tried to push at him again, holding me by the shoulders so I wouldn't leave. Eyes wrinkling as he squinted at me, the expectation was evident. He wanted clarification. He wanted me to explain why I'd used the most antiquated, passé respite possible in our world.

*Parley?* Had I really said that?

"What...did you just?"

But the black flag had been lifted and measures were maintained even in such...personal matters. Bane was heir to the most powerful coven in the Cove. Even he had to mind the rules we all lived by.

"I did." Damn. An inhale to push back the tension crowding between my eyes and I glanced up at him, grateful that I hadn't spelled him to back away. "Parley. Back off. Don't...don't touch me. Talk only."

"Why in the hell would you..."

"I have reasons." I waved my hand so he'd step back. "Please, I already told you...I have a job to do and a creature to find. I can't have you being a distraction."

"*I'm* the distraction?" He moved his gaze over my body.

"Didn't you say we're on a time crunch here?"

He nodded, reluctantly agreeing. "Fair enough." He stepped back, pulling on the neck of that bottle fisted between my fingers. "We have to get this search going." He set the bottle on the counter next to the sink. I nodded, started to walk away, but Bane tugged on my arm, his fingers touching right on my skin. Shuddering in my limbs, in his, and his eyes grew wide. He twisted his head to the side like he needed to shake the sensation away, then jerked his gaze up at my face. "What... what the hell was that?"

"I...I don't know."

He stared at me a long time, then at his fingers still gripping my arm before he dropped it.

"The search?" I said when Bane had stayed too quiet. "I'll see you out there in ten minutes." Before I left into the hallway, Bane called my name. Stopping would be stupid. Not stopping, though, might tell him I couldn't control myself alone with him. He'd already gotten enough of my fear in the past few days. I wouldn't hand him anymore.

Eyes, chin twisted toward him, I didn't dare stare right at his face. I can admit that I was a coward when it came to him. But Bane didn't seem to care that I wouldn't look directly at him. He clicked back into control mode. "We finish this...all of this, as quickly as possible."

"That's fine with me." A little more relaxed now that he was back on task, I turned around. "I've got...a life waiting for me in New York."

"That's not why I want to hurry."

"Why then?"

Two long strides put him back in front of me and I immediately cursed myself for stopping. Bane's mouth was tight, eyes narrowed as though he needed to concentrate on anything other than the rip of energy that bubbled between us. The lines feed off anger, passion, lust. All of those things, with a few other emotions, permeated the room. It made the lines pulse square into us.

"The sooner the job is over, the sooner we can discuss what the hell that was and what you've been running from for ten damn years."

He didn't wait for me to answer. He didn't want to see me huddle against the counter or try like hell not lean across the granite just to get my skin to cool. It didn't matter that Bane was curious, that he wanted answers. I was there to do a job. I was there to save my family's name. None of that would include a conversation with Bane Iles about what had happened to us when we were kids. I'd be long gone before then. Again.

# TEN

MIDNIGHT WAS BEHIND US ALONG WITH TWENTY MILES OF WOODS, and the forest whispered like it knew something we didn't.

"Another half hour and then we rest. We'll reach the spring by then."

The spring. That was what Bane thought had kept me quiet the entire hike into his coven's property. The deeper we got into the woods, the greater my senses aligned with traces of the amulet left behind. Familiar. Ancient. Part of my brain recognized that faint hint of magic not coming from the ley lines. The Elam had been gone for weeks now and since my arrival in Crimson Cove, the faint whispers had grown louder, hindered only by the constant memory of Freya's screams dulling them in my mind. The spring was some three miles ahead and as we neared it, the Elam felt closer.

We walked single file with several feet separating Bane, in front of me, Cari who was virtually on my heels, two guards I didn't know, along with Joe, Wyatt, and his sullen-looking cousin, Hamill, leading us through the thick woods and my brother taking up the rear. Clover Springs rested near a small settlement of Bane's folk, fourth or fifth cousins by my estimation, that Bane hardly knew.

"They are quiet, only two or three families large, and we never see them at the yearly coven gatherings. They always send their regrets and my cousins never have anything but grief to spit about them."

"Isn't that the case with everyone they don't know? Blood or not?" I ignored the snort Cari released at my small dig and walked forward.

"True enough," Bane answered, shooting a glare to his fiancée. She stepped back, pausing near a clearing to dig water from one of the guard's packs as we moved on. Bane continued, "But this sort," he nodded at the faint rush of water up ahead, "they are odd to say the least."

"Maybe they just like keeping to themselves." Bane grinned as though he'd half-expected my reaction. And when he kept smiling I stopped walking. "What?"

"You, Jani." The laughter held just a second longer and then Bane sighed, giving up the idea about keeping things to himself. "Never once have I heard you say something hostile about anyone. Well, except Cari for being rude to you, and Ronan, but even his mother talks shit about him." That grin moved a little but didn't disappear when he glanced back at me. "How is it you've lived for ten years in the city, with mortals, no less, and you still don't speak ill of folk?"

I shrugged. "What good is ill speak? Isn't there enough wrong in this world? Why add to it?" The smile left his lips and they went soft, easy. Not quite a grin, nowhere near to a frown. And then came that long, aching look of his again. There'd never be a time when that look was usual to me. "Come on, Bane. We're getting close."

"Jani Benoit," he started, ignoring my little demand as I passed him. Bane didn't move, but I heard his words as he watched me walking away. "Jani Benoit and that sweet, sweet tongue."

"What?" I stopped, scared that he might try to pick up where things had come too close to losing control in the kitchen. Surely he couldn't remember what had really happened ten years ago. My block had worked. I knew it. But that didn't keep the worry from my mind or ease the burn of anxiety in my gut.

"You think I've forgotten the last I saw you?" The familiar teasing glint came back into his eyes and some of my worry lessened to see him lighten up.

When I remained silent, shooting a glance to the group behind us, my brother and Cari among them, who had stopped in the clearing to rest, Bane's gaze followed mine. Then he stood, facing the woods, his back to the group, face forward, but his attention was on me. He didn't seem to hold a shred of hesitation when he spoke. "I meant the day in Matthews' class when you came at me like you wanted to climb inside." My eyes widened and he laughed. "Didn't think you had it in you, Jani, but one minute I'm standing there watching Matthews talking to you about some mortal career advice, and the next thing I know you're all around me with your mouth on mine." Bane was large, primal, and it took only his approach and that smooth, slick look in his eyes to have me retreat, looking for some purchase that would keep us from touching. How was it he was remembering even this much?

I walked further up the trail, moving away from the wizard and the crowd, and deposited my pack against a pine tree among a small cluster to distract myself. But Bane seemed intent on following, intent on not keeping to any agreements we made about sticking to the job at hand. What was it? Why did he seem capable of maintaining any professionalism with everyone but me?

Pulling out my water bottle, I downed what remained, doing my best to ignore the man when he squatted next to where I'd sat against a thick pine tree. Suddenly, I didn't feel anything but his signature and that low, earthly whisper of the lines singing to me.

"Funny how I didn't mind you clearly subduing me with a spell, but damn if I didn't care." He looked at me like he'd never seen my equal. "For the life of me, I don't know what it is about you." His gaze lifted along with his fingers, skimming along my forehead. "Anytime you're around me I go a little stupid." He narrowed his eyes, dropping his hand as though something had just occurred to him. "You twisting a hex on me?"

My small laugh took the glare from his expression. "After all this time? Really?"

"Hmm." There was the slow, cautious rake of his gaze down my body, the hesitation of that look over my chest, to the small curve of flesh barely visible beneath my thin shirt and heavy scarf. Still, Bane looked as though it was his right to take whatever he wanted. And exactly like he wanted every square inch of what he saw.

"You know, Mr. Iles, when a man looks at me the way you are now, I generally ask that he buy me dinner first, at least say please."

Bane licked his lips, the bottom of his mouth twitching between a smile and the fight to hold it back. "I'm not a *man*, Miss Benoit." He moved closer, close enough to kiss me, fast enough to make it a threat. "And I damn well don't say please."

Behind him Wyatt cleared his throat and I offered the were a relieved smile, but Bane didn't let me pass when I stood, grabbing my pack. He treated me to another of those long, dark looks, this one promising how eager he was *not* to say please.

* * *

"It's higher coven blood that maintains the balance," Cari told Bane, who seemed to not be listening to her. He nodded intermittently as we moved through the trail, his attention on the woods and the movement through them as his fiancée droned on. "It's why we are left unaffected by the lines, don't you agree, my love?"

Next to me, Sam threw me a look, complete with an eye roll at the asinine witch's droning voice. For his part, Bane didn't seem inclined to agree.

"No, Cari, I don't agree." He nodded toward another path leading to the left and we followed.

"There? You're sure?" For all her flaws, Cari wasn't useless. She held him back, her hand against his chest before any of us followed him toward another trail. "Something...just around that bend."

He paused, shooting me a look, and Sam and I both moved to flank him. Wyatt led the weres, each crouching, not transforming, but on alert as Bane's guards pulled Cari back and we readied ourselves for whatever lay hidden in the brush.

Sam nodded to the far right, twisting his hand to bring forth a hex, and I followed with my left, drawing on the lines to pull in the smallest sliver of raw magic to strengthen the hex just as Bane drew in a long inhale, squaring his shoulders. He was a brute, letting the lines fill him, the visible runes on his arms glowing as he lifted his hands over his shoulders.

*"Ionsaí,"* Bane said, and a burst of light shot from his hands, circling the brush and the saplings around it. Sam and I moved, flanking the wizard as he charged forward and met the biggest bobcat I'd ever seen, scared and crouching in the center of the now open woods.

I thought of Freya, my sweet friend and what that creature had done to her. My heart could not stand it. My rage would not be tamed.

The animal pounced. Its loud scream cracking like a whip across the forest, it lunged at Wyatt, catching the were across the arm before the animal went still, as though suspended in amber, frozen by the charm I threw at its chest. With a thump, it hit the ground, sagging, unmovable.

"You've...killed it..." Sam said, grabbing my still-charged and tingling hands. He covered them, face tight as the raw magic coursed through me, pulling at me like an electric current. "Is it...Jani, is this the one..."

"No...no," I told my brother, tightening my eyes when Bane knelt at my side, looking over the fallen animal. "This isn't a magical creature."

One look at his face told me my brother was right. I'd let the lines bleed too much magic into my hex. An innocent animal was dead by my hands because I'd let it rule me and hadn't controlled myself.

"You see, Bane?" Cari said, approaching the dead bobcat, her gaze shooting to me and my shaking hands still covered in my brother's grip. "This wouldn't have happened to a higher coven witch."

I stood, ready to charge at her, but Sam held me back just as Bane took Cari's arm and led her toward the trail.

An hour later, Cari slept, aided by whatever potion it was I'd smelled her brewing—lavender and valerian root from the scent of it— in a tent on the opposite side of the encampment with her own fire and two guards watching over her. Wyatt sported a make-shift bandage I'd fashioned from one of my scarves, staying the bleeding from his wound. He, Sam, and Joe moved around the woods with Bane's remaining guards to scout for any lingering predators or the creature that had killed Freya. I was left with Bane and Hamill, trying to focus on centering myself and controlling my magic. I couldn't let the lines overtake me again.

Lost in my failure, my thoughts, Cari's words hung in my mind, teasing, taunting, each one a bitter rake against my self-confidence.

*"This wouldn't have happened to a higher coven witch."*

Was she right? Was there some innate power gifted to the higher covens I'd never understand? Is that why Carter and my father had been so insistent about keeping me away from Bane?

A chill worked up my spine at the thought and I lowered my forehead against my arms, thinking how close I'd come to destroying everything. What if that had been a magical creature I killed?

The covens came from every region within a thousand miles. Some from even further away. As we'd ventured through the forest, bypassing small encampments made up of tidy cottages and solitary cabins barely noticeable if you weren't really looking for them, the realization had hit that Bane's coven and the influence it held stretched throughout most of the Gulf Coast region. Possibly, all states south of the Mason-Dixon line.

There had always been this unspoken knowledge about the Grants: of the fifty or so covens in Crimson Cove, theirs was the oldest. They held the deciding vote when the board could not reach a unanimous decision. They sorted out the most delicate squabbles among the lower covens. They oversaw but didn't judge—supposedly. They counseled, not controlled, and if the vast acreage and reach of the neighboring covens was anything to go by, the Grants were wealthier, more powerful, more important than I had ever understood.

This stuck in my mind as we settled for the night near a small pecan grove. The trees had begun to lose their drying leaves and most of the nuts had been gathered or eaten by the squirrels who jumped from limb to limb above us.

"Feel anything yet?"

That was the third time Hamill Donaldson had asked me that question within an hour. He was a tall, lanky wolf shifter from Birmingham, a third or fourth cousin, I'd gathered, to Wyatt. He, like Joe, had been added to the group when a warring pack from Memphis decided they didn't want Wyatt's kin near their daughters. Not surprising. Those wolves were a cagey sort.

Hamill had the look of a man not well suited for company, someone who wasn't altogether unpleasant looking, but he frowned just enough to seem unapproachable. Where Wyatt was friendly, maybe a tad too flirty, Hamill was distant and kept glancing at me as though I didn't warrant much more than a passing thought.

"No," I told him yet again, settling closer toward the fire on my side of the encampment. There were several pallets of sleeping bags and small, flat pillows made up beyond the tree line. Bane had kept Cari away from me, thank the gods, especially since she'd taken great pleasure in my failure. Her insults hadn't ended when I killed the animal. But at least Bane knew my nerves had been tested.

Hamill stood across the fire, looking as though he expected me to elaborate why I couldn't feel the Elam yet, and when I only sipped from the thermos of warm Yorkshire tea, spiked with whiskey that burned just a bit, the shifter made a small noise that I supposed might have been a threat.

"Is there a problem?"

He didn't answer and rocked on his heels, looking as though he might strip and shift into his wolf right then and there. But I wasn't some simpering coward completely neutralized by a decade in the big city. I knew who I was, what I was capable of doing.

His low warning growl deepened as my gaze swept over his face, to the tight snarl of his top lip and the twitch that moved his cheek just below his eye. In the breath I took, there was a hint of his pheromones, thick and earthy, but I knew they had not been released to entice me. Any witch with half a brain knew that shifters, and even some wizards, let arguments and certainly violence wake some primal beast within. Just then it seemed that Hamill wanted to fight or fuck, and only one of those options were open for me, as far as he was concerned. There was definitely no "let me have you" vibe coming from the shifter.

He stretched his neck, that growl muting his words when he spoke. "Hadn't you best do your job?"

Another sip of tea and my gaze stayed right on his face. The warning was still there, and I got the feeling that whatever it was that had made the shifter irrationally angry had little to do with me. At least, I hoped that was the case. Still, I wouldn't sit around waiting for him to strike.

"Back off."

But my anger only induced a deeper growl from the shifter, and as he began to transform—the crackle of bone twisting and the smooth, fine sheen of fur emerging from his skin—my thermos hit the ground and I absorbed a touch of the lines in the distance. It took little effort, barely a call to the lines at all, for the funnel of strength, of blind, raw magic to come right at me.

Big damn mistake.

I was too near them. There was no buffer, and my anger, my fear bubbled up and shot out of me, made my body a conductor, feeding on emotion as I lifted my arms, fingers pointed right at Hamill's morphing chest. A blinding, swift flash of light, a swirl of heat, and the shifter yelped, a wolfish squeal of pain, and then I heard the familiar rumble of a curse behind me and someone or something clamped down against my arms, taking me to the cold ground with a thud.

Moments passed like melting ice. I couldn't say how long it was. But suddenly, there were a lot of voices—Wyatt's, Joe's, Sam's, ones I didn't know, and then Bane, soothing, consoling just as he held me to the ground.

"Is he dead?" Bane asked.

Bile thickened in the back of my throat.

It wasn't me asking the question, and the fear that had me rushing to grab hold of the lines morphed into something ancient and ugly. Worry, remorse—two things that tended to control my stupider decisions—flooded me like a wave I could not swim away from.

"Wyatt, check him," he said, my cheek against the dirt with his chest planted on my back.

I shuddered, and the air came back into my lungs, then out again with a ragged cough. "Off," I ordered Bane and he shot up, releasing my body, but his attention remained focused on my face.

"Jani..."

"Did I kill him?" I asked, rolling onto my back, my hands scrubbing over my face. No need in delaying. If I'd let the lines consume me again and the full force of my power came out of my fingertips, then there was no way Hamill could have survived.

Bane knelt beside me as rocks and twigs from the ground bit into my back and he covered my body with his shadow, guarding me from the small crowd that hovered near Hamill's downed body. He looked over his shoulder, seeming seeking an answer.

"Good." Bane only spoke, only exhaled when Wyatt nodded at him, a wordless acknowledgement that I hadn't killed the wolf. "He's fine," he confirmed as I sat up. My brother moved to the left, stepping as sentry, on guard as though Wyatt and Joe would want some retribution for my attack. Bane seemed to be of the same mind and didn't move, keeping his back to me and his elbows out as if he anticipated a reaction as they carried Hamill off.

Finally, the worried conversations, the theories on how to treat a half-transformed, fully unconscious shifter died beneath the crunch of dried leaves and the faint sound of the river running past the grove returned.

Sam turned, tossing the large limb in his hand to the ground as Bane helped me to sit up. "*Sè,*" he said, scrubbing his face, "you cannot..."

"I know...I know this, Samedi." I lowered my head, rubbing my neck as I tried to block out the worry I felt pulsing from both my brother and Bane.

"Hawthorn," Sam said. "Will that help you?" When I didn't answer, he touched the back of my head. "Near the ridge behind the camp I spotted some new blooms. I'll fetch a few and brew it. *Wi?*"

I nodded but didn't answer, keeping my head down until my brother's steps and signature grew fainter.

"You going to be okay?" Bane asked, moving his hand to my back.

"I was protecting myself." I told him, my focus still on my boots and the mound of clay dirt at my feet. There was an imagined look of disappointed I didn't want to see from him.

"Which is why they didn't demand any recompense from you."

"I didn't expect..." I jerked my head up, worry and surprise making my pulse increase.

Bane watched the fire blaze bright. "Untethered lines, unsecured lines, Jani, will kill you, take you over if you let them."

"I know that."

"Do you?" He spun around, expression twisted and angry. "We've been walking for hours, trying to get you as close to the Elam's signature as possible. After the animal...why in Hera's name would you tap into the damn lines?"

"It was...instinctual... Besides, you can handle it. I thought I could too."

"*You* are not *me*." He stared off toward Wyatt and his group, head shaking.

"Because Cari's right? Because I'm lower coven?"

For the first time, Bane expression when he looked at me was cold. A small twitch curled the skin beneath his right eye as he turned, moving toward me like he would attack, but stopped short when I got to my feet. "You...would think that...of *me?*"

Unthinking, I stepped closer than I intended. I didn't notice, until Bane's jaw worked and he ground his teeth together, that being close to me might be too much for him to stomach. Something shifted in the air. A spark of light that pulsed and flickered but would not ignite. It didn't come from the lines or from any magic either of us conjured. Bane watched me, his expression open, wounded, and I was powerless to do anything but stare at him, trying to organize the words and make them make any sense at all.

*No,* I thought. *Bane had never been like any of his fold.* He might have their name and their money, their power and influence, but he'd never much cared about hierarchies or social standards.

"I don't think you believe that," I finally told him, swallowing when he nodded, holding my breath when he stretched his hand to rub his fingers against mine. This time I shook for a reason that had nothing to do with the lines. Clearing my throat, I inhaled, reminding myself where we were and who slept just a few feet away. Her draught must have been powerful. How had the commotion of my attack on Hamill not woken her? "I didn't realize it would affect me like that, but I...can handle myself."

"Jani, you've been away a long time."

"Are...you...thinking of sacking me, Bane?" He stepped back, but I held my ground in front of him. "No one can find it but me. You know this."

"The lines are too volatile."

He wasn't wrong. I was still a little high from the wild hex that flew from my fingers. Moving away from him, I let the sound and scents of the forest move through me. It *was* volatile—all this sensation, all this energy. Couple that with the heat coming off the shifters and what the raw lines were doing to all of us and you had the makings of an impossible mission. Of all of us, Bane was the only one not cracking at the seams. He remained cool, guarded, and in control. But he would. He'd trained for years to hone his abilities and alleviate any weaknesses.

"You can spell me," I told him, spinning around when the idea came to me.

"No."

"Bane, come on. I can take it."

"I don't think that's a good idea."

"Will it hinder my awareness? Will it block the Elam's signature from me?"

"No. Not as such."

"Then do it."

"Jani, it requires more than you're likely willing to give."

"What do you mean?"

Bane ran his fingers through his hair, grunting as though the thoughts spinning in his head were too much. "If I spell you to mute the lines then you'll be vulnerable."

"Okay."

"It means that I'll have to watch over you. It means that you'll have to willingly submit to my protection."

"Submit?"

"Your magic, your energy, you have to let me hold it, corral it if the lines begin to overwhelm you again." He stepped forward. "I'll be able to see inside your thoughts, your emotions." He licked his lips, looking like he wanted to smile. "It means I'll always be connected to you. I'll always be able to hear you if you want. Even after I release the block."

That was a hurdle I hadn't expected. Let Bane inside my head? Give him access to my thoughts?

"Will...will you know my memories?"

He frowned, but didn't pause, like there was a question he had, but didn't linger on it. "No. Your memories don't have anything to do with your magical signature. But Jani, you'll be vulnerable...to me. Everything will be there for me to sense."

"I can't have lines overwhelm me, Bane." I reached out for him instinctually. Holding his large hands, feeling his warm skin under my fingers, it's what I wanted. But in that motion, I realized that maybe whoever took the Elam knew exactly what they were doing, so much better than we expected. Maybe they understood something about Bane, about me that no one else did—that eventually, the lines would pull us back together. And they were using that to their advantage.

Rumors had flooded the town about what happened that day in Matthews' class and there had been lots of speculations on what I'd done, why it was that Bane Iles had stumbled after me as I took off. But except for me, my father, and Mr. Grant, no one knew what really had happened.

And just then I realized that the Elam, the amulet, had been securely in place back then. It had allowed us the control to keep the lines from overrunning us all. All of us, yes, but me and Bane especially. Without that control, what would me coming back to the Cove do?

The lines exploited like this would destroy us all. Not just me and Bane, but all of us. I wasn't strong enough by myself to keep from lashing out without the Elam's help. I could be used to bring us all down. I couldn't let that happen.

"I can't let them take control like that again. I need to temper them. I can't risk it, not again."

Several minutes passed without him looking away, without him uttering a sound or doing anything but pinching his eyebrows together as though he needed to figure out my angle. There were arguments, objections working in his mind. I could see the result of them in his expression until finally Bane dipped his head, barely an agreement, more an acquiescence. "Alright. I'll do it, but Jani, don't say I didn't warn you."

"You think I should worry about you knowing how I feel?" He didn't say anything. So I tried the only thing I could think to do—teasing. "Mr. Iles, you think a lot of yourself don't you?" Just then I realized I loved his grin. It made him look so unencumbered by the life he'd been handed. "That kiss was ten years ago."

Bane nodded, nudging his foot against the rocks at his feet and his attention on that small task. "It was a damn fine kiss."

"It was." I stepped closer, my feet shuffling the rocks, my presence bringing his gaze back at me. "But I never said it was the best."

# ELEVEN

DARKNESS CREATES ITS OWN KIND OF MAGIC.

There are spells working in the twitching calls of insects and the low, close cry of the owls warming the night with their songs. This night was different. It seemed darker, denser somehow, and as I sat in the clearing, shivering from the campfire's absence with Bane on his haunches in front of me, I thought the magic had nothing to do with the whispers of nature around us and the low, quieted call of the lines.

"You can change your mind." His voice was low, maybe a hint uncertain, but Bane's comment came off as bland, point of fact.

I doubted his concern was from any inability he thought he might have at working the spell. Maybe he was worried what he'd see inside my head. Maybe he didn't want the burden of taming my magic. Whatever his worry, the wizard pushed it down, shifted closer as though he didn't expect me to heed the warning he gave.

Eyes closed tight, I fought off the shiver that threatened to move across my skin as Bane's scent got closer. "Just do it already. I'm damn cold."

"You won't be for long."

There was a lot of threat, a good deal more challenge in that statement, but Bane couldn't frazzle me. Not when the risk of losing control was just a mile away, near the camp, near the spring and group of sleeping shifters giving us space to perform the spell. This was too important to read much into. Besides, the one-sided connection to Bane was something that settled inside me ten years ago. I had gotten good at pushing it aside when I needed to.

"I'll need to touch you." The flash of my lids opening almost pulled the small frown from Bane's expression, but he let my reaction pass. "Just your wrist. I'll need to feel your skin."

He'd touched me before, a handful of times, incidental, but still it had set something off in Bane that had me worried. What would this spell do? Would it somehow loosen the block on his memories?

"Jani?"

"It's fine. Just get it over with."

And he did. His warm, wide fingers curling around my wrist, his scent, the heat from his large form all crowding around me and then... that touch tightened.

"I won't hurt you," he promised just as that grip clamped on my wrist, pulling until Bane held my left arm off my lap and my open palm close to his mouth.

The words that passed Bane's lips were ancient, like the sound the sea would make if its crashing had voice or reason. The sound of his voice in that language was something that warmed my stomach, edged around my nexus as if just the words, the lyric and melody in their cadence, could somehow cradle it, keep it safe.

I didn't recall just when it was that I'd shut my eyes again, or why the sensation of floating came to me. There was only a liquid warm bliss of being held as though I was precious, as though the heat of his breath against my palm meant more than a spell, more than protection from the insistent pull of the lines. The way Bane touched me was possessive, assured, and though I was certain I was reading too much into it, I still enjoyed the sensation it gave me.

"Bane." The whispered word slipped from me like a plea that held no fear, and the moment I spoke his name, I understood where my embarrassment and regret came from. That grip, at least, grew tighter.

"Stay quiet." For once, I listened. "The spell will take me around your blocks, all the damn walls you've constructed to keep everyone away." I opened my mouth, thought of dozens of excuses that would challenge Bane's assumption, but he'd know. Somehow he was beginning to know the truth of me already. "Don't bother," he told me with the smallest laugh in his words. "I see them plain, Jani. They're there for anyone you don't share blood with. You trust no one but your kin. Not even your coven." A few more whispered words and those excuses became weak. "That's sad, Jani, but I understand the point."

Bane didn't need to be in my head. The thought of him there, aware of things I didn't want anyone to know, made my chest tighten. Instead, I pushed forward the thought of the beach and the small house that met the white sand of Biloxi. There was a cobbled stone walkway from the front porch and the green, tidy grass that met an azalea and crape myrtle-lined white picket fence and dipped down to the sandy beach below. It was my dream. I wanted to call it *L'Abri Reach* and rent out two of the four rooms on the second floor.

"The beach?" Bane asked, distracted by the image. My only reply was a small hum, happy, content. "It's...nice, Jani."

It was. It was my fantasy—living on that beach, away from the Cove, away from the covens and the city and the sleight of hand I had to use living in New York just to do my job well.

Writers were a strange group, wanting a certain look, a unique vibe for their covers, their promotions. For the most part, I could create something that satisfied, but lately, the pull of the Cove, the worry over my family, had me losing focus, relying too much on my abilities just to pull off the design jobs for my clients.

"How do you do it?" Bane asked, and I didn't hesitate answering, something that should have warned me how easily it had been for him to tame my magic.

"Dream...dreamwalking."

"Without their permission?"

"Yes."

The tension from his body flooded into my skin and when I moaned, uncomfortable, Bane pulled it back. "How do you manage that?"

"Take...take something from them. Their napkins from business lunches, the sketches they send me to show me what they want." I took a breath. "It has to be something they've touched or created. I get that easily and slip right into their imagination."

"And it works."

A quick nod and I spoke dispassionately, as though the words were pulled from my mouth with little effort. "Last month I cleared enough money to pay off my credit cards."

"Whatever it takes, right?"

He sounded disappointed, preoccupied, and then there came the whisper of something from behind the tallest wall, the one with the highest safeguard. The one that shielded who I'd claimed that day in Matthews' classroom. Even if I allowed that wall to crumble with Bane's influence, he'd never know it was him. He might sense familiarity, maybe even recognize my age, my train of thought from that time, but he couldn't latch on to those memories—the where, the who. Still, even the smallest hint of recognition could weaken the block I'd placed on him years ago.

He couldn't have that one.

Bane inched around that wall—I could sense the old spell brushing against it as the other walls protecting my subconscious came down and I quickly learned that this little push and pull wasn't one-sided. Bane forced the spell toward that mammoth wall and I pushed back literally and metaphorically, blocking the intrusion in my mind and shifting my arm, fighting him as he held my wrist.

"Easy, Jani. Be still." He did not pursue that one as aggressively as before, but that push remained, like a curious horse eager to bust away from the gate keeping him corralled. "What are you hiding..." he whispered, a thought voiced unchecked.

"The spell, Bane. Finish it."

He hesitated only for a moment, touching my forehead with the tip of his fingers, resting them there as the chant he uttered rushed up, pulsing at first, like a heartbeat, and then as he spoke louder, faster, those words bent and melded together until the chant became a beacon, a thriving element that fused and spoke into the darkness. Inside my mind there were flashes of thoughts made real, vivid, the emotions that drove my magic, markers that would set me off, and then, with the whip of heat searing inside me, through me, Bane stopped speaking, held tighter and tighter to me until all was still and silent and the only thing I heard was my speeding pulse and the sounds of the forest around me.

Gods, how I wanted him. He leaned so close to me that his breath dampened my bottom lip. "Something is there," he told me, shifted my body so that my cheek was in one of his hands and the other held the back of my neck. "I used to daydream, as a kid, especially that senior year. Pushing against that wall, I remembered that daydream...nails... your nails on my neck, over my chest, your teeth...skimming." He frowned, head shaking.

I remembered it too. How could I forget?

For a moment, the temptation became too much and I let the memory slip, just a hint that he would not be able to decipher from the daydream he thought he had. It would be vivid. It would feel real, because it was. Because I wanted him to remember before it was too late. Before he belonged completely to this place and his people.

To her.

Closing my eyes, I let loose a slip of sensation—taste and smell, the hint of perfume I'd borrowed from Mai that day and the graze of my tongue against his neck. His reaction was immediate and Bane shuddered, eyes clenched tight, lost, it seemed, in the recall of what he didn't know was fact or fiction.

*My fingertips against his hard nipples and my lips and tongue wetting down the center of his throat. Heat...some sort of spell cast between our bodies, a hum that mirrored the heartbeat of the earth, the faint but constant hum of the ley lines pulsing through the Cove. That's what had zipped around the room, the sensation foreign to anyone mortal. Bane had tilted me back, his large, strong hands holding my head as he'd smoothed his mouth and nose down my neck, in the valley of my breasts, and my hips had moved, grinding against him, making our centers touch and then I'd felt him, long and hard and gloriously hot through my thin shorts.*

*We had let ourselves go too far. There'd been too much touching, too many months of pent up attraction, that we could not see the light flickering through our limbs or hear the slow thump of each other's hearts beating beneath our skin. Bane's low, hurried groan of pleasure, my eager, needy moans had grown louder, stronger until that great whip of electricity between us moved hard, easy through our touching bodies.*

And then, the break of my exhale fashioned a thicker, strong wall in front of the only one barrier left. He couldn't see it, but the memory of that day, the emotions it had stirred inside me, the moment Bane felt what I felt, the recall so similar, I supposed, to him that he jerked away from me, stunned, looking more frustrated than he had a moment before. But Bane—cool, calm, never flustered Bane Iles—brought back in the control that was never far from his reach as he watched my face, his gaze working over my features, as though he was trying to catch a flicker of movement, some small tell that would clue him in on who had conjured the emotions from me.

There was a small distance between us then, him guarded, me on watch, making sure he could not get more from my thoughts than I'd already given. When I only returned the stare he gave me, Bane moved away, standing, eyes still focused, consumed, confident.

"Your secrets are your own," he finally said, a little of his confidence dimmed, but his resolve stronger than ever.

*Good, I thought. He'll need it.*

"They are." I nodded, following his stance, moving in front of him.

One step forward and Bane stared down at me. "Then why do I get the feeling that what's behind that wall isn't just for you?"

Beyond us, I sensed the weight of the lines trying to breech across the safeguard Bane had placed inside me. He sensed it too, even nodded toward it when I looked at him, expecting confirmation. But he wanted an answer, didn't seem to care that his spell had worked on me.

"Don't go poking, Bane. Not all secrets need telling."

Bane was only a foot away from me, his mind likely lingering around the confusion of that day, ten years ago, and the heat he thought he'd imagined. But it had been real. Hell, it was still so damn real, and even with him tempering the lines from me, Bane seemed to know it too.

"A warning," he started, looking as though he wasn't sure if he wanted me or wanted to be angry with me. "I may not be able to have complete awareness of your thoughts, but I can tell what direction they're heading toward."

"Meaning?"

"Meaning if I piss you off, I'm gonna know." I shook my head, not caring if Bane knew how often he pissed me off. "Meaning that if I do something you like," he moved his gaze down my body, then back up, "Well, I'll know just how much you like what I do."

"And if someone else does something I like?" He grunted, but remained silent. "I mean, if say, one of the primal, alpha shifters does something I really, *really* liked..."

"I'll damn well know." The clip of his voice was a warning I took to heart.

"I see."

There was little time left now for us to squabble or argue over what I kept from him so when I turned away, needing the distance, and he grabbed my arm, stopping me, the shock was quick and, despite knowing him as I did, unexpected. "That daydream..." He pressed his lips together. "Seemed pretty damn real."

My gaze kept steady on my wrist in his grip, as though on their own, my eyes decided looking at Bane wouldn't be smart. "Why are you touching me again?" Finally able to control myself, I looked up. "The spell is over."

"Is it?"

There was something new, something strange to how Bane pulled me in. The lines weren't calling me, insisting that I take him, claim him once again. They were, in fact, nothing more than a quiet whisper I could barely make out, begging now instead of insisting. The sensation had no bite, not as it did before Bane's spell, but there was still heat between us, that constant energy that no block could keep from us. We were drawn to each other even without the lines' interference.

"Bane..." He inched nearer and I held my breath as that pull—our pull—drew us closer. "What am I thinking now?"

He growled, rushing toward my mouth, warming it with just a brush of his lips. "The same damn thing I am." He gripped my face between his fingers and kissed me hard, scorching against my mouth like he wanted to claim it. God, how I wish he would, and just that thought made that low, deep groan in Bane's throat transform into a growl of pleasure.

The air around us dropped, the temperatures cooling the wind, bringing brittle leaves and small twigs from the trees around us. Nothing slipped into my thoughts as we came closer, as I forgot that I wasn't supposed to touch Bane, that he belonged to someone else, that he was meant for something else in which I played no part. But just for that moment, I wanted to take him. I wanted his touch and taste all over me.

At the thought, Bane broke away, his hot, hurried breath fanning down my nose as he rested his forehead against mine. "This spell was an insanely bad idea."

"Why?" Fingers fisted in his collar, he moved when I pulled him toward me, too eager, too anxious to keep from touching him.

"Gods, Jani, because now I know you've been thinking the same thing I have since the second I walked into your apartment in the city."

But I knew, I knew that it had all started for us far longer than a few days before.

"Bane..." *Tell him no,* I thought. *Remind him who he is, who you are.* But even thinking it was enough to settle him.

"I don't think I much care." He stopped me, answering my unspoken question about what would be or what should be. "Circe help me. I don't fucking care about any of it."

Like a flame igniting, like the rush of decision that is never given much thought, a choice that is more instinct than logic, we moved away from ourselves, from the people we were always supposed to be. There was no duty, no honor, no distinctions to be maintained, no expectations that needed to be protected. We'd come this close before, the near making of something new, something forbidden, but this time I gave no thought to what would happen if I let Bane forget that I was not for him.

Just one flashing moment where we pulled against each other, where his touch was like liquid fire on my skin, where my mouth against his throat made that huge man shudder at the feel of it.

"I don't care either."

It was all it took. Providence, destiny, the twist of some life-altering event set in motion by the lines, by the gods, by whatever it was that bent our wills, directed our paths down the roads we took. My declaration, my small lie that I truly didn't care, was enough to pick apart the moment that might keep us from it. It was enough to ricochet into something that could never be unmade.

That's when the screaming started.

In the quiet din of darkness, with Bane holding me, devouring my mouth, insisting my body bend this way and that, a scream rent through the moment and tore it to pieces, followed by another, and another.

"Bane!" Joe called out from seemingly so far away, sounding desperate, appalled. "Bane where are you? Get the hell over here!"

We ran together toward that frantic voice and the smell of blood that thickened in the air the closer we came to the campground.

# TWELVE

DEATH WAS COMING TOO CLOSE TO ME AS OF LATE.

Cancer took my mother before I said goodbye. That death came in the form of a pristine body, laid out with roses and gardenia petals in her hair. She'd looked lovely, peaceful, like some ethereal fay resting in white lace and vintage silk.

The mortals from the mission where she volunteered couldn't believe she'd been sixty. They'd kept their focus on me and my sister, as if looking at us closely enough would reveal some great secret to the age-defying genetics beyond the ageless melanin my mother had passed down.

But even Mom's still, cold body, as beautiful as it was, came in the form of custom and preparation. It ended in a marble mausoleum, engraved by my father's hand, while the mortals slept through the night.

And Freya... *Circe*. There had been no beauty in her death. There had been no spell fixing her body into anything resembling the witch she'd been in life. Nothing could. It ached to remember her that way.

Death, like the one at my feet, was bloody and vicious and looked damn painful.

I could not pull my attention from the body. There was a great clot

of tension in my stomach, one that had been given life the second
Bane and I stopped running after a screaming, fearful Joe.

The moment we saw Wyatt's neck twisted beyond its limits. And
the blood, lots of it, pouring from the cut near his neck and rib. That
smell—metallic and bitter—filled the night around us, peppering the
darkness with a stench that was unmistakable, unforgettable.

The weres around us bellowed, cried with their primal voices
begging vengeance. Around us, the other group converged, smaller,
true, but on alert. The Biloxi contingent—a group of witches who
instantly split around the area mentioning wards and signatures—and
Ethan Rivers, Cari's brother, and Bane's cousin Malak both came to
our sides, their normally smirking grins vacant for once.

At my side, Bane knelt next to his murdered friend, fingers
covering his mouth, eyes hard and squinted. There was a heaviness
around him, that deep, angry venom the lines loved to stoke pulsing
from him, shifting a heated, white energy between his fingers. Him
lashing out would not do. Not if we wanted to keep the scene of the
crime untainted.

When Bane's hand closed into a tighter fist, I squatted next to him,
not caring that it was probably improper to touch him. Not caring that
the others might talk about me offering my boss comfort.

Then, a rustle from behind us, and the rich smell of expensive
perfume announced Cari ambling from her potion-influenced sleep as
she stopped short, gasping at Wyatt's body.

"Gods," she cried, angling around Bane, her arm snaking over his
shoulder. "Sweetheart." There was nothing more she needed to say. It
was enough to remind me of my place. Cari leveled a look at me, one
not tinted with sorrow and pity over the were's death. One, in fact,
that told me plainly I needed to back away from what was hers.

I did, because it was proper.

I did, because I knew Bane well enough to know there would be no
words to still his anger. Nothing anyone said would ease this ache, and
I made no attempts to soften this blow with words that he'd never
remember. But he let Cari console him and he did not push her away.
He didn't retreat from her or make her feel useless. Bane, in fact,
seemed to take the comfort she offered and let it soothe him.

That hurt more than it should have and I felt the sting of it deeper than I wanted to admit. Something, it seemed, Bane noticed. He stiffened away from her touch and moved his head toward me, not looking at my face or glancing in my eyes, but enough to let me know he understood my misplaced offense.

"I don't understand what happened." That customary Iles calm had slipped for only a moment—a little gaffe when Bane let the worry, the fear that this attack had been meant for him, outweigh the mourning I knew he craved. But it was a dangerous moment. Only when it passed did he square his shoulders.

"We heard him yell. It was Wyatt's watch." Joe's voice cracked at his cousin's name, as though saying it delivered pain he couldn't quite bear. "It was seconds. Seconds and we ran to him here." The shifter's breath released in a sputter of noise that sounded like a wheeze. Something that could not be controlled. Anguish hidden within the patent ache this death had caused. "He was just...he was laying here."

"Where was she?"

Bane and I both stood from our crouch over Wyatt's body as Hamill Donaldson's question had the crowd around us looking my way. "What?" I stammered, incredulous.

"Convenient that you weren't near the camp."

"She was with me," Bane said, ignoring the glare Cari gave him at the admission.

The accusations in the silence that followed were still deafening.

"She takes off, no one sees you, Bane, and then Wyatt gets dead." Hamill didn't back down from the glare Bane gave him. Instead, the angry shifter kept his attention focused on me, the thin line of his top lip making him look even more hostile than he had earlier that night when he nagged me about doing my job. How the others had managed to shift him back from his were form, I had no clue, but the angry, bitter man stood in front of me now.

"I said," Bane started, walking away from his examination of his friend's body to step close enough to Hamill so that he could look down at him, "she was with me. I never let her out of my sight once."

"And why is that?" The question was honest, if not invasive, and when the wizard asking it stepped forward, I understood where the curiosity came from.

"Something I'd damn well like to know myself," Cari said, glaring at me, but I didn't bother answering her.

Things were tense enough without engaging the jealous fiancée.

"Funny," Hamill continued, "how you have an answer for everyone where this witch is concerned."

"Funny?" I said, tilting my head. "He hired me. Most employers want to know what their workers are up to. It's how they know whether or not to pay them."

"And what job is he paying you for exactly, Miss Benoit?" Ethan asked, folding his arms, a question his sister seemed to approve of.

Bane shot them both a glare of warning, but it didn't take the bite from their expressions.

"Not to kill people." I told Hamill, who still held his expression tight and his eyes like there was an accusation on his tongue reserved for me. "And certainly not to fuck him," I said to Cari and Ethan, their twin smirks unconscious, I was certain, just as sure as I was my comment had made Sam's frown dip hard. My brother looked on the verge of wanting to thrash Cari and Ethan for what they were implying. It didn't matter. I wasn't a real consideration to anyone. And my attempt at a blunt joke likely wasn't funny to them. Crude, possibly, and I couldn't argue with that.

There was a haughty snobbery about the way the Rivers carried themselves. Their clothes were too clean, too above rim to be convenient for a long hike and search through the forest. The black leather boots were made for looking good, not walking; the long trench coats had begun fraying at the hem from the hours they had been brushed against the ground.

The ridiculous penchant for appearances over practicality, the perpetually lowered gaze down their long noses, none of it was new to me. I'd seen their sort my entire life in the Cove. I'd seen more of that entitled, rich-bitch swagger working catering events in Manhattan when one of my friends needed an extra pair of hands serving New York's richest. Money is the same no matter where you are. It might come in different clothes, speak with different accents, but the attitude is the same; it's the unbendable belief that just being born into their lives, their station, engenders some sort of declaration—the fierce determination that the world is theirs to take and anyone not in that same station didn't warrant a second thought.

"Please, Jani...Cari, there's no need for this cool attitude." Malak stood next to her. It had disappointed me when Sam told me that Bane's little cousin had become thick as thieves in anything remotely decadent with Ethan Rivers. But at least Malak was subtler than Ethan. He was kind, sweet still. He wasn't like Ethan, who wore smiles that weren't friendly and spoke with the glimmer of kindness without sentiment he'd never mean.

"And Hamill, really," Malak said, waving between Wyatt's body on the ground and me. "What kind of idiot would blame Jani for this? What possible motive could she have?"

"She had opportunity." But even as Hamill spoke, his voice held little conviction. The small amount of pride he had deflated as he scanned Bane's face. "She's not one of us, Bane. You know that. Who's to say she wasn't hired. That...father of hers..."

"Excuse me?" I said, charging forward, but Bane caught me before I could lift my hand and pull a bit of the line into my limbs.

"Not going to work now, remember?" he said against my ear.

"At all?" I asked, suddenly worried that the block would render me helpless.

"No. You can still fight." Bane released me when the conversations around us sounded a bit too much like judgment. He was better at ignoring them than I was. "You just can't seriously injure anyone."

Something heavy, something that could not be easily lifted from me had crashed onto my chest. "I won't have any power."

"You have power, Jani. More than you know." Bane's voice was softer, lower, though I could still make out his sadness, that foreign emotion I knew he tried to keep off his expressions. There also was a peak of pride, a little swirl of confidence in me that slipped to the surface. Bane could not block me from the lines without letting me feel what he felt as well, and as he stared down at me, defying the murmurs surrounding us, I realized that block may have uncovered more than it held back.

"This is fucking adorable, really." Ethan's whine broke the spell, and Bane stepped back, keeping enough space between us that Ethan and Malak could corner him, usher him away from the crowd and, it seemed more importantly, away from me.

"I don't damn well think it is," Cari said, moving between us, her back facing me as she jabbed a finger into Bane's chest. "What do you mean you blocked her? You went into her mind?" When the wizard only stared down at her, the small witch's face contorted, her mouth bunching up into a snarl. "Have you lost your damn..."

"Careful," he told her, grabbing her pointing finger before it landed again. "I did what needed to be done in order to focus her." He slipped his gaze up at me, not hiding his small grin before he looked back down at his fiancée. "We need her to find the Elam. I was only doing her a favor."

"And what other favors will you do for her, I wonder?" Cari asked, knocking her shoulder against Bane before she walked away, muttering a low, dark phrase under her breath that he must have taken for a hex. Bane waved his hand, deflecting something over his shoulder—a whip of energy I took for a hex coming from Cari. Then it rebounded with a flick of Bane's finger and shot back a spark straight at the witch's ass. She released a yelp of pain, glaring at him again, then marched back toward her tent.

"I don't care what Bane says." Hamill walked behind me through the throng still looking for evidence, clues around Wyatt's body. "I don't damn well trust you."

"Yeah?" I asked him, not caring that I'd hurt him just a few hours before.

"By the *sodding* gods!" Joe cried out, his voice ragged. "My cousin has been murdered right under our noses and all you do is bicker and point petty fingers and stir up trouble? What is wrong with all of you?" His voice broke, and he fell to his knees next to Wyatt's body.

Bane knelt down next to Joe, spoke to him in quiet tones, words that mentioned revenge and love, but words that were meant to bring Joe alone comfort. I could see, though, by his clenched fists, and I could feel that it was all he could do, kneeling next to his friend, surrounded by violence and blood, that it was all he could do to keep from lashing out himself, in his grief and his anger. I wanted to go to him, but now was not the time. He needed space and to keep from being a target that he would feel obligated to defend. And Joe was right—Wyatt deserved better from us, from all of us. Even in death the were was handsome. Pale, ashen already, but still rugged and handsome as he'd been years ago when I first met him. *Circe,* had it only been a few days since he'd teased me about the past?

The body was solid, growing stiller by the minute as the weres moved around the area and Ethan and Malak dispersed, looking like they at least attempted to help search for anything that might give away what creature had done this.

His shirt was in tatters, his jeans and boots shredded as though someone had taken a weed whacker to them. Even the sleeves on his thick jacket were ripped and his tan skin and hairy arms were visible. Then I spotted the wrap I'd used to bandage Wyatt's injury from the bobcat attack earlier in the day. The knot was still intact. The center was still bloodied, but the ends had been torn in several places, as though whatever had attacked had done so in a fit.

It was similar to the state Freya's clothes had been left in, particularly the sleeves of her sweater.

*My* sweater.

"Gods above..." I whispered, covering my mouth when Bane shot a look my way. He moved his eyebrows up and narrowed his eyes at me as though he expected me to disclose what had made me upset, but I couldn't say. Wouldn't. Not here in front of everyone. Not while Wyatt lay right there.

So I held back. But as I did, my mind was racing. I couldn't help it. The one day I had met Wyatt he was witty and fun, and he obviously cared about Bane, but in his death it became clear that there were threats and danger abroad of which we had no clue. And something else was dawning on me, something that came unbidden but seemed important. It had been my experience that unwarranted anger came from somewhere. Hamill Donaldson was a shifter I'd only just met. He wasn't even local. Logically, there should be no real reason for him to hate me. But for some reason, he'd mentioned my father.

I glanced over at where Hamill had been pacing, a cigarette in his hand. He stood apart from the crowd, eyes down, but his gaze did slip up once or twice to glare at me. What had my family ever been to him? Maybe Papa or Ronan had screwed up a job for his pack. Maybe they hadn't done everything they were supposed to cover up the trace of magic. Whatever it was had angered Hamill, and that rage was now being directed right at me, despite the chaos in the camp, despite the murder of a fellow shifter.

Could that anger and my giving away items that smelled of me have gotten both Freya and Wyatt killed? If that were true, why would anyone target me? Who was I compared to anyone else in the Cove, least of all Bane?

Bane had blocked me from the lines, but he hadn't completely tempered my magic. I could still draw the lines toward me, though I suspected Bane would have to release the block for me to control its power. But I could still rely on my innate abilities—the power to focus, feel the remnants of magic left over from the Elam. It had been brought through the forest and as Bane debated with his cousin and Ethan, and Hamill guarded himself from my attention or the draw of the crowd, I let that small trace of remnant power slip into my senses.

And suddenly, I sensed it. The Elam.

It was close, closer than it had been in days and the moment I realized what I was feeling, the second I stepped away from the bustling crowd, Bane knew it too. He stood up from where others were now also comforting the still grieving Joe, and followed me as I walked into the darkness, feeling, listening for the Elam.

But this time when he followed me, he wasn't alone. Hamill didn't trust me for reasons that likely had more to do with my family than me. My brother didn't trust Hamill to keep a civil tongue in his mouth, if his glares were anything to go by. Ethan seemed quite eager to remind me of my place and Bane of his responsibility. It was the makings of an argument of epic damn proportions.

I followed the remnant of the Elam.

Bane followed me.

Hamill followed me. Sam followed Hamill.

Ethan complained, bitched at losing Bane's attention, but still followed the rest of us.

"Jani? You feel it?" Bane watched me standing in a small clearing, far enough away from the scene that the voices around Wyatt's body were nothing more than a low hum.

"You can feel it?" Eyes closed, I stretched my neck, let the hint of magic that perfumed the air fill my senses. "Can you see it?"

"No. Not like you can." He stepped closer, ignoring everything around us but the energy the Elam pulsed behind its trip within the trees. "It's a damn whisper, as if your brain is muffling the song it's singing. I can only feel what you do and you're seeing it now, aren't you? You're hearing it?"

"A little. Yes."

"A little? That's muted? What the hell is the full force of it like?"

My eyes were still closed and the scent of the Elam, the heat of it still a distance away, yet so close, mixed with the warmth pulsing from Bane's still hyped-up body and almost perversely, that sweet, honeysuckle scent coming off his skin.

"Full force it is like life itself. It's a great piercing scream, louder than a crowd, penetrating through the thunder of a hurricane."

"And you hear it all?" Bane asked, his voice sounding astonished and very close.

"No," I said, blinking, smiling despite the circumstance, despite Wyatt's loss. "It's an aftershock. What was laid waste as the Elam travelled through the forest. It's lesser but still damn powerful."

When Bane only stared down at me with an impossible, amazed expression on his face, I took his hand, eager to let him feel more of the signature that crowded closer toward me the harder I concentrated.

"It's like air,' I told him, looping my fingers through his. "It's just like the lightest, fiercest air burning your lungs, but you can't help the sensation. You crave it." He squeezed back when I fell silent and the action brought my attention to him.

"You know what that's like? Feeling something that you know is horrid for you but you..."

"Still want it inside you."

"Yeah. Well." Bane didn't stop me when I pulled my hand away. "That's my gift. I feel what others can't. Anything lost has energy. Hell, anything in life has it. Every single element on this planet, anything with mass, creates energy. It's the energy I can hear. It's the energy that calls to me." I wrapped my arms around my waist, Bane's gaze glowing hot against my neck. I continued, walking up the small trail set in front of us. "I just have to focus on the object. It's the small details that no one pays attention to. That's what I can sense."

"Then that's what we'll follow. You just keep feeling for that energy, see where it takes us and I'll get things sorted out here with...well, Wyatt."

"Sorry, Bane, but that's not gonna work," Joe said, coming toward us, followed by two weres I'd spotted at Bane's before we left but hadn't seen much of on the trail. Bane, too, frowned at them, pulling Joe aside.

"What is it?"

"We'll send a sonar charm to town to alert the Board of Covens. They'll need to send Jani's father and wizards to collect the body. We can't have the mortals discovering an unmarked grave. Besides, I couldn't let him..."

"Easy," Bane stopped Joe when his voice cracked, squeezing his shoulder. "Send the charm. It will take some time for them to make the trail up. Until then, we'll keep the search to the a few yards in this area. I don't want to break camp just yet anyway."

"Thank you," Joe told him, nodding to me before he moved back toward Wyatt's body.

From my peripheral, I spotted Malak and Ethan leaning against a tree, sharing what looked like a bit of jerky, and my brother, who seemed to scope the ground for plants, something he always did when he spent any time in the forest. Mainly, his attention was on Hamill as the man pulled out a pack of smokes and rested against a boulder.

I ignored them all, except for the wizard at my side and the growing sensation of the Elam as its song grew louder.

"There's something you should know," I told Bane, pretending to focus on the Elam as I shut my eyes and tilted my head back. My stomach knotted tight as dread and worry inched inside of me like a tapeworm.

"This is going to be bad...I can feel how bad this is going to be."

I nodded, not bothering to confirm anything for him, and turned, folding my arms before I dipped my head, watching the ground. "Freya was wearing my sweater when she was attacked."

"Yes, I remember," he said, stepping in front of me, his voice soft, a little confused. "And?"

"It was ripped to pieces and my father took it from the scene." Bane nodded, moving his head into a tilt that reminded me of a confused puppy. "And Wyatt...earlier, he got hurt. With the bobcat..."

Bane's expression dropped, his mouth opening as though whatever he thought might choke him. "By Hera...your bandage..." He looked over my head, glancing at Hamill, then to where Sam and the others had taken their rest before he moved me out of earshot. "You believe its searching for you. Is that right?"

"It makes sense, doesn't it?" I turned, making sure no one heard me before I continued with my theory. "If you've told anyone you're hiring me, if anyone at all knows and thinks I can find the Elam, the common assumption would be that stopping me should be a priority."

"And the creature is hunting your scent." He caught my gaze, holding it as he kept whatever he thought to himself. Then, just as suddenly as he'd gone quiet, Bane grabbed my arm. "We've got to get you out of the forest. You and Sam, Cari as well."

"Why?"

"You and your brother have similar scents and the creature might take Cari for you..."

I shook my head, ignoring the look Bane gave me. He was gearing up for an argument and probably knew what I'd say before I spoke. I did it anyway. "We're not related..."

"Doesn't matter," he said, waving a hand when I opened my mouth to argue. "They smell pheromones and can only discern male from female. It may not be able to tell the difference."

"I'm still not leaving," I told him, moving nearer to the call of the Elam.

"Jani, be reasonable..."

"And you know that Cari won't leave either." I sat on top of the largest boulder near a clearing where I could feel the signature the strongest. "And Sam won't leave without me."

"If you stay here..."

"You will protect me," I said, covering the small flinch that twisted my mouth before I stopped it. It was too honest an assumption, but it was the truth. Bane had always protected me. Why should now be any different? I closed my eyes, inhaling, holding a breath when he knelt next to me.

"You're so convinced I can do that?"

The smile came without a fight, but I didn't open my eyes. There was no need. Bane's breath was closer, moving the hair from my shoulder when he leaned down to hold my arm. It was a small comfort, perhaps the smallest gesture of appreciation that I'd take from him.

When he squeezed my fingers, I finally opened my eyes to look at him. "Of course I'm convinced, Bane Iles," I told him, feeling drunk on the Elam's power and the look in that beautiful wizard's eyes. "It's what you do."

\* \* \*

Two hours later, my father arrived with workers from the Board of Covens and two higher coven investigators who took control of the inquiry the second they came into the area.

"Max Wilson," one nodded as way of introduction to Bane, barely looking my way when he greeted us. "This is Lyle Simms. Tell us what you know."

"We have a lead," Bane told them. His voice bordered on finality that would typically work on anyone. But the investigators were used to powerful wizards using their force and names to get their way. "And we need to get on the way before the trail runs cold for Miss Benoit."

I ignored the stare my father shot my way and how his expression seemed to harden the longer he watched Bane standing next to me. It didn't lessen until Cari joined Ethan and Malak near the small grouping of trees behind us.

The investigator called Wilson glanced at Simms but didn't hesitate for long to answer Bane. "Sorry, Mr. Iles, but as the most senior coven leader here..."

"I'm not a coven leader yet, Wilson."

"This is your investigation. It's your case. Your blood took down the Elam. The Board chose you to provide the means to find it." The investigator glanced at me, but his gaze didn't linger. "Protocol dictates that you stay until we've completed the investigation."

There was indecision, a little hesitation in Bane's stance. He popped his neck, twisting away from the wizards, turning away as he came to my side. It was the second time his indecision seemed to crumble just by his standing near me.

"I can't let you go on your own." His profile was sharp, a stark silhouette edged against the moon as Bane looked out over the forest. "You're vulnerable."

"I can take care of myself."

Bane glanced at me and debated what he would do as the guards took the opportunity to question Cari, Ethan, and Malak as Sam worked with our father to clean the field and tend to the body. When Wilson and Simms got nothing but bored attitude from the Rivers pair and little else from Malak, they moved on to talk to Hamill, making sure to stand downwind of his lit cigarette.

"If anything happens to me before I can unleash the block..." Bane almost whispered.

"What's going to happen to you?" The idea was ridiculous and there was the smallest hint of frantic worry that made my lungs feel tight at the thought. "I know how magic works. That isn't a higher coven secret." Smiling helped. Him returning that smile eased some of the needless fear. "You die, your hexes and spells die, too."

"I have no intention of dying, Jani." The shadow of his famous smirk flitted across his face, as though the suggestion was insulting. How could the likes of Bane Iles die? Even he doubted that was possible. Still, he knew he wasn't immortal. Yes, we supernaturals take a long time to get old. Still longer to die off, but that doesn't mean we aren't susceptible to disease, to decline, to decay. That doesn't mean there isn't ever danger. Bane seemed to know that well enough and the longer he watched me, the more that realization took away the smirk from his face. "But...if I'm not there..."

"You think there's a traitor," I realized. He glanced at me again, as though it took effort not to smile or control his shock. It wasn't something I'd given much thought to, actually, but it did make sense. Bane was smart, calculating. He didn't think like the others. He didn't tackle anything without first analyzing the possible outcomes. I knew this because I knew him. No matter the time we spent apart, I still knew the wizard he was.

But I had managed to surprise him, if that slow-working, impressed grin meant anything at all. Then came out his devious secret. His body language changed, limbs and fingers heating with excitement—the swell of heat from his body, the drip of truth pulsing between his subconscious and mine.

"You know there's one." My voice was low, hissing. "You handpicked everyone, didn't you? To draw out the asshole who did this."

Bane waited and that headshake, that impressed, amazed look on his face was torture. Beautiful, but still torturous. "Either I'm losing my touch or you're a lot cleverer than I gave you credit for."

There was no need for flattery. I wasn't the kind of witch that thrived on any of that. And when he kept smiling, and that small wedge of pleasure swept up my stomach, I decided that only Bane could make me someone who wanted to be complimented. "You got any prime suspects?" He nodded once, but kept silent. "Who?"

Bane cocked his eyebrow, but said nothing. "Okay, fine," I said, tilting my head to make him look at me. "Anyone I should be wary of?" He rolled his eyes as though I was simple and stupid. "Ah, I forget. Everyone, right? Trust no one?"

"Me," he said, reaching for my arm, but he dropped it when Cari called his name. We both looked up at her, and that simpering, put-upon glare, but Bane waved her off, asking her with one hand gesture to give him a second's pause. Then he moved me away from the crowd, from my father and brother, from his grumbling fiancée and the investigators. "You trust no one but me." He rubbed the back of his neck, watching me. "There was no way for me to guarantee a spell working before, since we were so close to the lines. The further into the forest we go, the less intense they become. A spell to draw out the traitor might work now, but I can't do that and run an investigation at the same time."

But I could. Bane didn't have to say what he meant. He wanted me to trust him because he was trusting me.

And I did trust him. It was the melding, had to be. It was our two nexuses reaching out to the other, reminding us that there had been a moment when they'd touched completely. He had my trust because everything in me demanded that it be given to him freely.

The block had worked but had not hampered the call of the magic swimming in the wind or the low, still song of the Elam ahead of us in the ether. My eyes fell shut when a small bustle of wind brushed through the limbs of the trees around us to sweep the ground. The subtle smell of mint and honeysuckle hovered in the air, reminding me of the spicy brilliance of the life around us, pulling me closer toward it, wanting me to follow.

"Bane, it's calling." Reaching for him, the tension in my chest eased even as my pulse quickened to feel his fingers entwined through mine still. "If I don't leave soon…"

"I know it." He squeezed my fingers and the pressure in his knuckles shook his entire hand. "Damn it, I know." He looked behind us, to Hamill and the small words he exchanged with the guards, then Bane's focus was back on me. "Hamill…"

"You're serious? He hates me. He attacked me. I almost…"

"No, you didn't. As to his hatred of you, I get the feeling he'd rather parade you and your family around the Cove as traitors and hacks than try to do you any real harm."

"You willing to bet my life?"

"No fucking way."

"Then Hamill is a no." I nodded toward Ethan, Cari, and Malak. "And them?"

"You'll want to hex Cari and Ethan inside fifteen minutes."

"Too late. My fingers are already twitching."

Bane's neck was corded with muscle, and the thick veins stood out when he twisted his shoulders and his neck to work away the tension there. "I don't like this, but Malak will be there. He's my blood. He knows how I feel…" Bane looked away, staring at his cousin as though he needed an excuse to cover whatever it was he almost let slip. "And

Sam. We'll have them all go. Between Malak and Sam you'll be protected, and Ethan will watch Cari."

"I...suppose there's no choice, is there? You have that mess to deal with and I have to follow the Elam."

"Hamill will follow as well," he finally said, as though sensing my need to get nearer to the Elam. "He doesn't trust you, but he doesn't like your father more, and I want to avoid a problem while he's here cleaning things up."

"I think you're being optimistic about who will cause drama."

Bane frowned, the muscles in his neck tightening. "There's a liar among us, and I'm counting on you and your brother to sort out who that is."

I shrugged, an idea coming to me. "I think I can manage something."

Bane stared at me as though he tried hard to discern my thoughts but couldn't quite get a read on what dominated them. "You want to twist a spell?"

It was amazing how well we'd both adjusted to his block, to that quick back and forth of knowing what the other needed.

"I want to find out who I can trust." Stepping away was easy, ignoring him behind me, standing close, that voice and sweet breath right at my neck, wasn't as simple.

"Do you need me to..."

"No." Another step ahead and that time he knew what I was thinking. *Stand back. Give me a little breathing room. Stop looking at me like that.* The only thing I said was, "I got it."

He watched me step toward the clearing again, the crowd behind me, the hint of the Elam ahead in the distance. And just one small chant, old, comfortable, easy, and a spell spun from my mouth, collected into the night, and twisted outward. Those words, the magic they invoked, would carry around me, around Bane. It was a Judas spell, and it would mark a traitor, show them for the lies they told and the truths they held close to the chest.

"Any lie?" Bane didn't ask, likely knew the answer before he asked for it. He was in my thoughts, privy to the tug of every emotion I felt. He'd have recognized the Judas spell when I spoke it.

*Won't be that easy. A glance over my shoulder and I knew Bane understood me. They'll have protected themselves from any detection.*

"Good," he said. "It'll make the truth clearer and louder when it comes." The soft crunch of leaves signaled that he had moved closer, but I was focused as the weight of the spell continued to fall. Bane stopped near me, but not too close.

Commander and soldier. Client and employee. Yin and yang. I wasn't sure what role fit us anymore, but Bane played his part well. Net cast and now we'd hunt.

"Don't let them fill your head with pointless shit."

"Too late." But my joke didn't seem to ease him. "There's a lot of pointless shit in there already."

"Cari and Ethan, they'll aim to tell you your place, make you see them as superior somehow. Don't let them do that. You're better than them."

I stared at him, frowning. "They're your coven."

"You're better than them to me too, Jani."

No way I'd touch that one. Not with that frown making the muscles in his face tight. There was no use in saying goodbye. There was no longer any point for belaboring warnings or clarifications on what I needed to do. He had his job; I had mine. The Elam called me, wanted me. I didn't need anyone to get in my way, not Hamill, not Cari or Ethan. They'd follow or they'd fall behind.

"Jani?" Bane said, holding my wrist. "I'll find you as soon as I can. Keep your guard up, don't trust them. The spell will work." I nodded and took two steps before he called after me, bringing my gaze right to his. "There isn't a thing about you that's pointless. Don't you damn well forget that."

# THIRTEEN

When I didn't think about my surroundings, things became clearer. There were no distractions around me in the night, only the clear sense that ahead I'd find the Elam, that it called and beckoned, like it knew I was close.

The sense of it, the way it drew me in, was like something I was meant to do. It was very much like a path I had no choice but to take. But there was a hurdle, three in fact, keeping me from that path. I wanted to hex all of them to clear my way.

"You know," Ethan began, "for someone who'd been running from this place for ten years, you certainly came back in a hurry."

"I didn't run."

"That's not the way I remember it." Ethan sounded smug, but in my brief experience with him, that was pretty typical.

"The way you remember it?" There was no need for me to stop walking, no reason to slow my pace. He'd follow. He'd have to if he wanted to annoy me. "You mean the way you heard it. You were a kid back then, barely thirteen years old. You have no idea..." I quieted when Ethan's smile went lethal. "Bait all you want, little wizard. I won't bite."

"Oh, you will." Ethan looked merely bored, not worried, not scared that he was deep into Grant territory with little protection from the elements or whoever it was that had killed Wyatt. Only an idiot like him would walk around the forest like he was on a stroll and not a mission. "All witches take the bait. It's in your nature."

He wanted to play, to lead me straight into a debate that would only annoy me and make my spelling fingers eager to wiggle a hex over his fat mouth. "I'm not here to entertain you. I'm here to finish this job and keep the lines from flooding the Cove."

Ethan took a quick turn on the edge of the trail and only caught himself from a fall by jumping in front of me. "And saving your father's business in the process?"

*No, ass, and discovering who's responsible for my friend's death. Both of them.*

Still, curiosity is a hell of a thing. It can make you question motivations, tempt you to forget your purpose. Ethan likely knew that, and anyone who'd heard even the vaguest thing about my return knew it had everything to do with my father's business and the mess Ronan had made. Ethan was a dunderheaded jackass, meddlesome, and catty, but he did likely know more about what had led my father's business into the ground than I did. "Know something you'd like to share?"

"Ronan is pathetic." That he admitted freely, but Ethan wasn't coy about the sideways look he gave me or the condescending smile that held no humor. "He's a useless piece of garbage."

"And that makes my name dirt now, too?" The trail twisted this way and that, keeping us single file as it narrowed, with Cari, Malak, and Sam at the rear and Hamill ahead in front, but I moved onward, not bothering to see what reaction the annoying wizard offered. "If we are judging each other by names and connections then I'd have a sharper cut to judge Bane by, wouldn't I? With the two of you soon to be in his family."

"Say what you want, Jani." Ethan sped up, moved just a half a step ahead of me, but kept speaking. "We know the game you're playing. We know your father would do anything to protect his business."

That wasn't true. My father was ruthless, but only when it came to protecting our secrets from the mortals. This talk of him setting up the burglary of the Elam and interjecting me into the fold to rescue it, was ridiculous. It had been when Caridee mentioned it as well. Lundi Benoit was ruthlessly loyal to the Cove, but that didn't make him a criminal.

That was what Ethan needed to hear. It played loose to lifting off my tongue when Ethan's jab had cut too close to the vest. But then his taunting, as well as my desire to defend my family's honor dissipated when the brambles snapped about ten yards ahead.

"I don't think..."

What Ethan didn't think died immediately as my quick hex took his voice. Cari, who had been thumbing nosily through her cell phone, and Hamill, who seemed to pick up on the sounds behind us as well, joined us, followed by Sam and Malak, who mimicked me as I narrowed my eyes through the thicket of trees.

Ethan tried speaking, grunting and jabbing his finger near his throat, but I waved him off, tugging on his jacket and beckoning the rest to follow me into the dense crop of limbs around the next bend.

"How dare you..." Cari started, but closed her mouth tight when I waved my fingers in her direction and the small flickers of white light from the silencing hex I threatened sparked to life. Her glare was sharp, but the witch had to know I was good for the threat I made. She need only to look at her brother to see that plain enough.

Two hunters, or maybe three, came down the path, sounding like a herd of cows, with little stealth at all. They were untrained, stomping in a way that was certain to leave tracks, making all sorts of noise, but they carried mortal weapons, big guns that would be difficult to disarm if we surprised them.

"You sure they went this way? This way exactly?"

"I can smell the damn shifter, can't I?"

We kept still and silent as the pursuers neared the small outcrop of limbs that gave us cover. But Ethan, looking terrified as well as highly pissed off to have lost his voice, squatted nervously behind us, making attempts to see through the small opening in the limbs.

Pointless, all of it. The tracking, the hiding. This put me off my mission and kept the Elam's signature distant. The time for hiding had passed, and though Ethan was useless for anything other than annoying me, the others might be of some help. Even Cari could sense danger before it came at us.

Bane's future brother-in-law gripped one of the limbs, cracking it before I could stop him and the trackers ahead stopped where they stood.

I reached out then, pushing my senses into the darkness, catching the signatures of what now proved to be two men, one shifter, and one...something else I couldn't quite name.

We needed to find their identities, and I was the finder of all lost things. Seeing their shapes—one small, wiry man with bushy black hair, and a stockier, clumsy guy with too much paunch around his middle—it was easy enough for my gift to tap onto them. But their purpose was clouded behind something that had never interfered with my power before: a seclusion charm. It was a thick, heavy thing that covered the men like a cloak, tacky, and it smelled of sulfur. Simply sensing it had me covering my mouth to prevent my gag reflex from loosening.

"Enough." My mutter wouldn't be heard by the men outside of our hiding spot but it did catch Hamill's attention and kept Ethan from moving too much.

I had never been happier that Papa always insisted I wear a guise charm around my neck than I was now. The charm was smooth, a tiny stone cut from the quarry some hundred miles away, in no one's territory. The leather band I wound it on brushed my hair from the ends as I pulled it from my neck and twined the strap through my fingers as the stone rested in the center of my palm—bright, glowing white and pulsing with ley line energy.

My father had gifted it to me when I turned thirteen and the rite of passage dictated I venture out of our lands and make treks into the forest around the Cove that would test my mettle. This charm hadn't left my neck since then, but it damn well would keep us undetected.

"*Diegol.*" The charm came in low and slight, and at least the others had respect enough to pretend they didn't hear me as I cast it. Magic was personal, intimate. It was bad form to eavesdrop on someone else's spelling.

A quick flush of light expanded around us, a ripple of movement, like light bending as we watched the arch of shadow and light move around us, setting the spell so that no one could hear or see us.

"Who are they?" My companions had no answers or if they did, they weren't talking. "Fine then, you don't know."

Ethan protested when I stepped away from our hiding place, tapping my arm as though I'd forgotten to unbind his voice. I hadn't and gave great thought to keeping him silent, even went so far as to bypass the trackers who sniffed the air and squinted around us as we passed them undetected. We could shout in their faces, rustle their clothing and they'd be none the wiser. No one could craft like my father, and that guise charm was the strongest of its make I'd ever seen.

Another jab on my arm and I jerked around, knuckles popping when Ethan got a bit too aggressive with his silent insistence. "Touch me again and I'll keep you quiet even longer."

"Be still and let him loose." Cari's voice was clipped, sharper than I'd ever heard it, but the look she gave me—that frustrated, stern manner reminded me of the mission, of the role I was meant to play. There was little time to dole out punishment, no matter how richly it was deserved. Ethan Rivers was an ass, but that wasn't my concern.

A snap of my fingers and Ethan coughed, clearing his throat as though he'd swallowed down a thick swig of whiskey.

"Don't you ever..."

"Threaten me," I told the wizard, smiling because I guessed it would annoy him more than a glare, "and I won't unbind it next time."

"Leave her, Ethan." Cari kept her palm against Ethan's chest, pushing him back. "Help Hamill clear the trail ahead." My brother and Malak came to my side, doing their best, I reckoned, to back me up, though it would do no good. Cari and Ethan didn't need anyone's loyalty. Regardless of what happened in this forest, they were higher coven. They'd keep the advantages that status gave them when this mission was complete.

For his part, the shifter seemed as irritated with our little drama as he had my purported slacking while doing my job. He, at least, didn't argue as Ethan walked with him down the trail, securing the way for a return to the Elam search.

But the faint hum of the Elam's magic had quieted in the distraction caused by the trackers. The signature was growing faint, something that pulsed under my skin in the cool dampness that collected over me as the hint of magic faded.

"Has it gone?" Malak asked when I kept to the corners of the woods, not moving, not doing anything but trying to recapture the Elam's power. "Jani?"

He sat on the ground, fussing a bit with his pack and setting up a makeshift camp. He didn't bother to ask if this was where I wanted to stay for the night or if I was ready to give up the search.

"You can make camp if you want. I'm not done searching. I can manage on my own."

Malak let me go ahead by a few steps, keeping to himself as his stare weighed against my back before he cleared his throat. "Not on your own. Bane wouldn't like it." He didn't bother to look up at me when I diverted my attention away from the woods and back to his half-smile and newborn fire.

"That's not your choice or his to make."

"I think you'll find it is, Miss Benoit," Cari chimed in, fussing with the fire Ethan had started before she threw a piece of kindling onto the growing flame. "He's your client. And it's him who gave us our instructions."

"Which I'm sure you're all too eager to follow."

Ethan considered me for a moment, his eyes casting shadows that I hadn't ever seen from him before. "Think what you will of me and my ilk, Jani, but Bane is set to be our leader. I may not like his," he moved his gaze down my body, then back up, ignoring the glare his sister gave him and the way she rummaged through her pack, "proclivities, but he'll lead us one day. Even if I don't respect the wizard, I'll still honor the title he'll soon hold."

"And the investment that title will make in the Cove," Cari said, slumping down next to Ethan. The pair exchanged a look that was both amused and somehow disrespectful. Hamill, it seemed, had caught it as well. He made some odd sound in the back of his throat, working that constant disapproval from his throat with a hard glare at both the wizards.

Cari, though, shook her head at her brother's laughter, and when Ethan could garner no rise from me or Cari, he abandoned his stake in the game and walked further from the fire.

"He has a job to do too, you know."

Giving up the fight of continuing to search for the Elam, my curiosity led me to the flames, across the fire from the smug witch who seemed too eager to tell me my place. I kept my gaze on the fire, letting its warmth and comfort bring me out of the irritation my companions kept stoking in me.

"Ethan, I mean," Cari continued, moving closer, ducking her head to watch for Ethan's attention. "He's the last son of the Rivers coven. I'm his only sister. It's his place to set me into a family that will be a boon for strengthening the lines. You know that the oldest families have the strongest magic."

"That's a theory that hasn't been tested in centuries."

"Maybe, but it's never failed." From her jacket pocket she pulled a flask of something that smelled sharp and bitter when she opened it, but she didn't bother to offer me any. "Rivers, Grants, even some of the lesser covens with the oldest lines are typically the strongest. The hardest to contest."

Cari's throat worked as she swallowed, and my gaze caught on the movement of her slender neck and the large diamond on her left hand as she held the flask. Her smirk was smug, condescending, and if I was petty, I might be offended. I was not. But did she really think I was so basic? Did she really believe I knew nothing at all?

"What's with the history lesson? You think I don't know any of this? You think I've forgotten everything we were taught as kids?"

"I think something keeps you present in *my* fiancé's head." She pointed at me with that flask, still not bothering to offer me a drink. "Hera knows why. There's nothing remarkable about you, and I don't much care why he can't seem to get you out of his head." Some stupid, hopeful expression must have pulled and twisted my features because Cari's frown deepened, hardened so that there was no humor on her face. "Don't get hopeful."

"You think I am?"

Cari wrapped her arms around her knees, letting the flask dangle from her fingers as she stared into the fire, ignoring my question. "Bane has honor. He knows what's at stake." She looked at me squarely, her features set, unmoving. "He'll never forget what he must become and with whom."

"Life is not an Austen novel, Cari." The higher covens tended to forget that not everyone was obsessed with strengthening their bloodlines. "Marriages don't get arranged. Not in this century."

"You're a fool if you think that. You're a fool if you don't think that blood and power and allies aren't essential in securing our world. In protecting it."

She wasn't wrong. The Cove had existed unhindered, undiscovered for centuries. That only happens when caution is taken, when tradition is upheld.

Right then, in that moment, with the fire's heat moving over my skin, settling me and the heavy stare of that smug damn witch across from me, there came a sense of loss. It was something I'd cradled over the years like an old wound that would never heal. Most nights, the pain of it, the ache it gave me could be pushed aside, stuffed down beneath all the emotion, all the tender sting that my life in the Cove had been.

Most days, I could forget it existed at all.

This was not one of those days.

Nothing Cari said was wrong. It wasn't like I hadn't heard it before. You live in the Cove long enough, on the wrong side of it anyway, and a few certainties become abundantly clear. The higher covens never married the lower ones. Mortals had little clue that magic thrived and lived and breathed around them every day, and on the off chance that one caught wind of the truth, they were glamoured, their memories altered until what they thought was the truth could be passed off as some fantastic daydream.

"You're a cunning witch, Jani Benoit." Cari's confession surprised me. So did her next compliment. "You're not unattractive. I'll give you that much." I could be flawless. My hair and skin and body could be something out of the lushest, most erotic fantasy in the world, and still no higher coven witch would admit it. Not out loud anyway. What I looked like didn't matter. Where I came from did. Still, that didn't stop Cari from leaning forward, from looking me over as though she needed to confirm her compliment. "It's no wonder why you've kept his eye."

"I don't have anything of Bane's." She considered me a moment longer than was comfortable before I waved my hand, bringing her attention away from my face. "Why are we even discussing this? Am I that much of a threat to your family's precious plans for Bane's life?"

Cari's expression softened, not for long and not drastically, but the emotion was there. "You have no idea what it was like for him, do you?" It was the first time since I'd known her that I thought she might have some genuine feelings for Bane.

"What are you talking about?"

"You bewitch him. Always have," she said, soft as a whisper behind a swig on her flask. "By the gods, it's time you stop."

She moved away from the fire, disappearing to the tent Ethan had constructed during our conversation, and I watched her, catching the look my brother sent me and the warning in it. He heard her. He knew what warning was meant for me and wanted me to heed it even if I didn't take Cari Rivers seriously.

"Ridiculous," I muttered to the fire, scrubbing my hands over my face, half wishing the crazy witch would have left her flask.

"She's not wrong," Malak said, sitting next to me as Sam and Hamill moved to the edge of the encampment, on their guard. Bane's cousin looked thin and tired, but still handsome, and I wondered if the mission and long trek through the forest was weighing on him.

"You think?" I asked him, leaning back against a small pine tree with my arms curled across my chest.

"I know," Malak said, stretching out his legs. "You forget, I was there, in the same house as him all that time." Malak was five years younger than us, but had always followed after Bane with something akin to severe hero-worship. If my leaving had impacted the wizard at all, Malak would be the one to notice.

"Even before that day you left. Bane doesn't remember much, and for a while we'd half convinced him that you'd twisted some sort of powerful spell on him." Malak glanced at me then, as though looking for a little confirmation. When I gave none, he returned his attention to the fire and his small revelations. "That would have made sense. Hell, I even suggested a love potion, a hex to keep you front and center on his mind. But a week after you left and he was still distracted."

A small noise of surprise lifted past my lips, but Malak continued. "A month and he'd hounded your family about where you were. Two years later and you became a constant sticking point—the girl he drove away without ever understanding how he'd done it. And trust me, Jani, it was a skill he truly wanted to remember." He leaned back against a small, smooth boulder, propping his elbow on it. "You forget who we're talking about. You forget his reach. What witches want from him."

"I haven't forgotten a damn thing."

"Fine then. But let me remind you that he's been hounded, tempted by many a witch. What he'd done to drive you away would have been useful to him, I'm sure."

That Bane would try, would want to be rid of me struck me as insulting, though I knew that made no sense. Malak seemed to be digging for answers, skirting too near the truth. But I didn't give him a thing—I didn't avoid his stare, didn't try in the least to seem apologetic.

"What are you saying?"

"That Cari was right. You were remembered." The wizard shook his head and ran his fingers through his thick hair. "Bane is the eldest among us cousins. And he's the strongest. Our uncle could only choose him. But it took five years to convince Bane to the marriage with Cari. Five long damn years that shortened the preparation needed to make certain the arrangements were settled, that both covens would gain significant assets from this arrangement. The bloodlines crossing, strengthening will ensure the Cove protection from any threat, magical or mortal. The two oldest covens melding magic. Can't you imagine the power of those future generations? Their strength is unfathomable." When I didn't respond, Malak slid next to me and I caught the shift in his expression, the lowering of his gaze as it settled on my mouth. "It doesn't mean that you can be without him completely."

"What?"

His breath was thick, smelling a bit like whiskey. "It happens often. High coven wizards with lesser coven witches. There's no marriage, of course, certainly no children that could be claimed as part of the bloodlines, but it still happens. Wizards, even powerful wizards have... certain wants."

I was too stunned by his words to react when Malak pulled a strand of my hair around his finger. Then sense returned and I moved it out of his reach to my other shoulder as my outrage smoldered. "You're suggesting I play whore for Bane? That I stay here in the Cove and wait on the sidelines as he builds a life with another witch because my coven isn't half as old as his?"

"It's not meant as an insult." Malak frowned, seeming surprised at my anger. "It's simply fact."

"But it *is* an insult." I stood, my fists balling tight as he watched me. "It's damn insulting to expect that I'd want or need to be someone's whore, even Bane's."

"Lower your voice. Your charm can't be that strong. The trackers will..."

"Damn the trackers, you loathsome bastard."

"Jani, calm yourself." Ethan had returned from securing Cari's tent. He made a motion, likely trying to reach for me, but my glare and the bubble of energy that pushed past Bane's block and seared in my fingertips had the wizard raising his hand, backing away from me. "This isn't Malak's fault, you know. He's only...speaking the truth." He cleared his throat, tossing out a low "Some of it," which earned him a glare from Malak.

That small exchange between them—quiet, secret, made the irritation bubbling in my stomach churn harder. "Tell me." I took a step, not backing down when Ethan frowned. "What is it?"

Malak ran his fingers through his hair, looking more worried about where I'd direct my twitchy fingers than concerned about what revealing his little secret might do. "The Elam. When it's replaced back on the lines and things are settled once more..."

For an insulting wizard who was friendly with the likes of Ethan Rivers, Malak certainly didn't seem eager to share what he knew. He hesitated too long, milking the moment, and that stoked my anger. Still, he inched back when I stepped forward. "Go on."

"Our uncle, Carter Grant," he finally said, shifting his gaze between me and Ethan. "He's dying. We cannot be without a patriarch. The treatments, the healing charms he's taken for years, they prevent him from fathering children. Otherwise, he'd take a bride himself. Bane has no choice. Not if he wants to secure the bloodlines. Once this..." He waved his hand at me, around the forest. "Once the Elam is recovered, Bane and Cari will marry." Malak took advantage of my stunned silence to continue. "I wasn't trying to insult you really, though, honestly. This...is just the way it's always been."

At his confession, I lowered my hands and stuffed them into my pockets. At our side, Ethan lifted his chin, his humor returning and that condescending attitude resurfacing as my anger quelled. "Come now, you know what a beneficial position you are in. Catching Bane's eye will be useful to you, especially to your father. Finding the Elam, fixing the lines, will restore his name. Everything else is simply lagniappe, correct?"

Then a great swell of anger and frustration rose up heavy in my chest and I couldn't help it. I didn't fight the feel of the faint lines seeping through the block that Bane had placed on me. I didn't spell Ethan to take that genuine confusion from his face. I didn't hex Malak to keep the smirk from his face. Instead, I let that liquid feel of tension, anger, and frustration flow straight through me.

Behind me, Sam and Hamill approached, and I couldn't be certain if they wanted to subdue me or warn the wizards of the bite my magic held. The two wizards lifted their hands, attempting an offensive block as I charged toward them, fingers twitching with energy. But this time, the pull of the lines did not overwhelm me. The anger and frustration did not seep out in a blast of magic meant to topple and cower anyone. This time, the hex spelled firm, but did not maim. Ethan caught the bulk of my blast, falling backward over the tree he stood in front of near the campfire, while Malak failed to block the remnant of that quick spell, falling face forward into the ground.

Sam knelt down to check the downed wizards as Hamill followed behind me, silent. I grabbed my pack and set out further into the forest. "I don't need a chaperone," I yelled at him over my shoulder.

"Maybe not," he said, trailing at my back. His voice came out muted, then grew louder as he turned back toward me. "But you might need a referee."

My anger and my frustration were too thick and too heavy for me to give much thought as to what Hamill meant, but then I heard Bane's voice and the low rumbling of what was surely admonishment leveled out at Ethan and Malak. My steps slowed only marginally.

"What did you menaces do to piss her off now?"

# FOURTEEN

MEMORY IS AN ILLUSION. TIME, SPACE FROM THE TRUTH TENDS TO draw you in circles of contentment where the memory, no matter the reality of it, becomes this imitation version of yourself, of what held such great happiness for you.

Even when the memories weren't nearly as beautiful as you recalled them to be, the mind, the heart, begs to differ.

It was a glossy memory that brought me into another dream, this one of my own making, part fantasy, part manufactured recollection. It was there, in my own head as I lay sleeping: Bane's reach, the slow, sweet movement of his fingers along my skin, his mouth pressed against my neck. It was like a spell, the weaving together of thought and sensation, misremembered or not, to make me drunk, eager to be lost in that day, the memory of us together in that classroom.

*He was beautiful then—the light from the horizon flooding into the half-opened window, the sticky humidity in the breeze doing little to abate the heat around us. I'd only wanted that touch, that taste to never end.*

*I'd wanted an endless day.*

*But that day, in Mr. Matthews' English Lit class, sitting next to a boy who could likely impregnate the Cove female population with one look, I didn't get my wish.*

*He had never been friendly with anyone. He had, in fact, kept absolutely everyone at a distance: students, teachers, even the handful of wizards and witches that attended that last year with us. Only I seemed even remotely curious enough to exchange a glance or two and, of course, the glances which seemed to always come my way typically happened when I caught the attention of anyone not Bane.*

*Especially the "anyone" boy types.*

*The clock above Matthews' desk had read 1:45. Fifteen minutes and I'd be free from all the hiding, all the whispered living that kept our lives running and our existence, our magic concealed from the mortals in the Cove.*

*Fifteen minutes and I'd lose my chance with him.*

*Forever.*

*The courage I'd worked up had started just a month before that last day. I'd dropped my pencil in the middle of our Persuasion essay exam, and Bane reached down and grabbed it for me. I was going to say thanks, maybe just offer him a smile, but I'd reached for my pencil and Bane covered my hand with his and rubbed the pad of his thumb over my knuckles.*

*And I forgot to breathe.*

*There'd been something in that look, something more significant than his fingers rooting me to the earth that day. There was no need for confessions of admiration, or practiced monologue about how I affected him or how much he loved my smile. There was something sweeter, stronger in the strength of his fingers gripping my hand and the heavy-lidded gaze of his sharp crystal eyes catching me in their stare.*

*Maybe it was the end of things that had forced me into action. Maybe he knew that day would be the last we'd have excuse enough for seeing each other.*

*Things got a little hazy then, but I do remember Matthews telling me to, "Enjoy New York, Jani, and please reconsider college. I've never heard anyone so young explain symbolism like you do." Then Bane staying behind, seeming to wait, and Mr. Matthews pointing out as he was leaving that it seemed like perhaps I'd forgotten something on my desk. But...I hadn't. Had I? But looking back there was indeed a folded piece of paper sitting right there on my desk.*

*It hadn't occurred to me that Bane wanted me to stay behind. But as I opened the folded paper and read the scribble of "Don't go," I realized maybe there was more to small knuckle rub and the months of silent conversations than I could have imagined.*

*I looked over at Bane, who had moved to lean up against the door. "Why?" I asked him, waving the paper between my fingers.*

*He'd opened his mouth but didn't seem able to speak. I'd spooked him with one word and hadn't understood how. Bane had asked me not to leave the room but didn't seem all that interested in doing more than stare at me.*

*Another step closer and the scent of him hit me hard. He'd smelled like honeysuckle and forest.*

*"Why?" I'd asked again, not expecting an answer, even shutting my eyes, giving him an out if he wanted to take it. He could have walked away right then and never looked back. But his scent got stronger as he moved closer, and the tip of his thumb smoothed down my jaw.*

*"Because," he'd finally said as I blinked up at him, "I need you with me. Alone."*

*Alone stretched into an entire afternoon and I'd found myself lost under Bane's control, skimming my touch over his skin, wanting it to always be that way.*

"Bane," I moaned, not understanding at first that where I lay, my mind and emotions were visible, open to him. I was no longer eighteen. He was now out of my reach. But that didn't stop my subconscious from calling out to him. It made the touch that came to me impossible to disregard. "Please."

But the hand on my neck moved up, covered my mouth, its grasp too hard to be a dream, and the shock of being touched, roused awake so quickly, had my eyes jerking open and me gripping helplessly for the lines.

Bane shook his head, his forehead wrinkled with worry as I struggled against him until my sleep-addled brain realized that it really was him. He held a finger up to his lips in a shushing motion and it was then that I heard the sound of lumbering, noisy feet close by—too close.

*My guise charm?* I thought, counting on his spell to keep our silent communication open.

*You were sleeping. It wore itself out.*

I looked around, panicked. We were alone by the dying fire.

*Be still. There's something moving...the creature.*

My heart pounded as Bane waved his hand, throwing a

concealment charm over both of us long enough to make for the tree line.

*My brother...and the others?*

Cari's tent was still erected, but the door flap was open and there was no sign of anyone near the camp.

*I don't know. But their signatures are still here.*

My skin was flush and clammy despite the cool temperatures, and when I pulled Bane's hand off my mouth, that cool sensation only intensified. The way he watched me, how careful he was not to say or think anything that would give himself away, was a little intimidating. I could not pretend to maintain control like he could. Bane was the real power in the woods and I was like a pathetic apprentice waiting for instruction.

Bane worked his own charm from his neck, holding it tight between his large fingers, but I could not make out what spell he twisted to invoke it. Magic is personal and intensely private, and most wizards and witches keep their spells to themselves. Seeing Bane hold something as mundane, as simple as a charm without any real fear of exposure to me was incredibly intimate. With the charm twisted and the muzzle of magic once again concealing us, Bane looked down at me, a half-smile reminding me that he could still read my emotions, hear my thoughts.

"It *is* private," he said, pulling me close when the brush beyond the firelight began to move. We snuggled together, my back against Bane's chest, his large hand extended, ready with a hex as I curled my hand into a fist, centering my own spell to attack.

"Magic, charms," he said against the shell of my ear, his voice reminding me of whiskey and gravel. "They don't work if we keep ourselves from its power. The lines want us." The side of Cari's tent moved and we went still, moving into position, keeping the conversation going to distract whatever would attack and make it believe we were unaware of the approaching danger.

"They want us to crave them," he continued, his gaze shooting to me, then to the tent when Bane came to my side, "but they need us as much as we need them. Light and dark, Jani. We feed off of each other. It's symbiotic. It's a relationship. Of course it's private."

"You...you don't hide it." I answered, swallowing the thick salvia in my throat when the large shadow of a creature moved across Cari's tent.

"Didn't you twist your charm in front of Ethan and Malak and, Gods, Hamill too?"

"Invoking the charm is nothing. Besides, they weren't paying attention to me."

"But you were," he said, nodding toward the tent, taking careful steps. The creature could not see us because of Bane's spell, but it would be able to hear how our voice traveled. It was a tactic I hoped would work as a distraction. "Just now when I invoked it, you listened."

Bane pressed his lips together. He didn't need to explain further. I caught his meaning. Common decency dictated that I look away when a wizard works a charm. It's just good manners, but hell, I was lower coven. He shouldn't have expected me to behave. By the quick smile Bane gave me, I remembered he could hear my thoughts.

"I'm sorry," I said, shrugging.

"No you're not, Jani."

And I wasn't. Why would I be?

The ripping scream that sounded inside that tent shredded apart our distraction and when Cari's voice went flat and silent, Bane forgot about anything else but charging forward, right for the tent. I flanked him, letting the hex bubble between my fingers, holding the curse back when my brother moved from the back of the tent.

"Inside!" I shouted, nodding toward where Bane had disappeared into the tent, to the din of cracking roars and his own curses that rent apart the night.

"Jani, watch your back," Sam said, heading for the tent, his hands extended, braced for a hex of his own. "It may not be alone."

But my brother would not see the inside of the tent or get the chance to attack. He was two feet from the opening with one hand over his head, a great swirl of white light circling from his fingertips when a massive black were shot through the thick canvas of Cari's tent.

"Move! Down!" I heard, but couldn't make out who'd made the command and then, with the charge of several wizards and weres I didn't know crowding into our camp and my brother and Bane charging toward the creature, I was stuck frozen. My gaze locked on the long, sharp claw extended up and its thick flanks flexing as it pounced straight for me.

Thick air circled me as the creature moved, the swish of fur, the flick of saliva and my senses filled with the smell of his earthy scent and the bite of his claw tips as they landed against my neck. I rolled and he followed, but only half a second before my hex flew from my fingers and the dim charge from the subdued lines grazed him as I shouted, "*Toirmisc!*"

"Gods! No...Jani," Sam screamed, running for me just as the creature growled, twisting around to see the crowd charging, ready to corner him as I lay on my back with another hex moving into the center of my palm.

Hatred bubbled inside me. Freya's screams, her laughter dimmed by the animal all coalesced in my mind as I watched it. I'd hurt Hamill with less of a hex. If I had been closer to the lines, if Bane had not subdued me, I could find justice for my friend. But then the creature watched me, his black, dark eyes blinking, staring as though there was something akin to sorrow, to grief lying hidden somewhere deep behind all that primal hunger.

The fury dimmed in me and I could not move, not until the creature shook its head, seeming eager to give up its pursuit of me, and growled, disappearing into the dark woods, forgetting me and the small injury he'd managed to the back of my neck.

It burned and twinged, but it was no greater pain than I'd given myself half a dozen times in some drunken stupor trying to make it into my apartment.

"Jani...where...are you hurt?" my brother said, dropping to my side, throwing back my thick hair to look at my neck. "It's...not so deep." He exhaled, tightening his hold on my shoulder, and I held his wrist but did not mention how badly his fingers shook against me.

"I'll do, Samedi. Do not worry yourself."

But he didn't release me or try to pretend like he had any intention of doing so when the weres ran past us, shooting into the forest after the creature. Hamill trailed Bane, who marched across the camp and knelt in front of me, his expression blank, his complexion pale.

"What is it?" I asked, my stomach dropping when the wizard rubbed the bridge of his nose.

"Cari...is injured," he said, looking toward the tent. Several of the Biloxi witches were moving in and out of it, carrying bags and blankets. "It attacked her."

I sat up, brushing Sam's hand away from my neck. "How...how bad is she?" I said, feeling sick. She was a rotten witch who probably wouldn't worry one fig over me, but there wasn't anyone I'd want to see attacked by that massive creature.

"It got her arm, but it's not too severe." He finally looked back me, tilting his head toward my neck. "And you?" I waved my hand dismissing his question and Bane let it go. There was something else worrying him. The tight set of his expression and hard flex in the muscles around his neck told me that much. When I reached for him, resting my hand on his arm, Bane looked down at it for a long time, like he wasn't sure he wanted it there but wasn't quite sure he had the strength to tell me not to touch him.

"Malak...and Ethan are missing," he finally said, standing.

I came to my feet, dusting off my jeans as Sam stood next to me. "No one's seen..."

"Not a soul. And I can't sense their signatures. They've just...disappeared."

The look Bane gave me was long and worrisome. Identifying no signature for higher coven wizards could only mean one thing. There was no longer a signature there to detect.

"Bane..." I tried, thinking of something that wasn't a ridiculous excuse.

"What else could it be?" He tilted his head back, staring up at the stars like there was an answer he hoped to find there. "This is...my fault." Shaking his head when my brother began to argue, Bane held up his hand to silence him. "You are a good friend, Sam Benoit, but we know it's true. I called the covens. I called the packs. I put everyone in danger to find the Elam and we're nowhere closer to finding it."

"We can..."

"No," Bane said, his voice sharp. "No, Jani, no more planning. No more excuses." Moving his top teeth over his bottom lip he looked between me and Sam, likely not seeing us at all, likely working something in his mind that no one would be able to sway him from. "No," he said again, giving his head the slightest nod. "We do this differently now."

"What...do you need?" I asked him, ready to argue if he thought of sending me back.

"You, Jani," he admitted, ignoring the low grunt Hamill made behind him and the way my brother shook his head. "You can still sense the Elam, can't you? The signature is still strong for you?"

"It's faint, but if we move soon, I can find it. I know I can."

"Not alone," Sam said, but he didn't manage to get Bane's notice. The wizard kept his attention on me, his stare even, focused like he wanted to read me to understand how much I believed what I said.

"Good," he answered, nodding again. "Sam, I want you and the others to take Cari back to town. See that she's looked after. I'll send Joe and the weres to look for Malak and Ethan, but right now, we've got to find the Elam. We're running out of time." He looked up, eyes narrowed as he spotted the moon. "The full moon approaches."

"I can help..." my brother tried, pointing to the tent. "She doesn't need..."

"I'm asking you," Bane said, holding Sam's shoulder. "I'm asking you to protect my...to watch over my...betrothed." He lowered his head, tilting it toward me, but keeping his gaze off my face. "For...for the good of the Cove, Samedi."

It hurt more than I'd let him know. I cleared my mind, bringing in thoughts of Freya and that creature, of the smell of its fur and the fear that filled my blood when it pounced at me. Anything at all to keep the ache I felt at Bane calling Cari his betrothed. It was simple and stupid. It was ridiculous to feel this jealousy about something I'd known for days. But it lay there, in my chest, festering and growing, threatening to overtake me the more attention I gave it.

I stepped back, moving to the fire, stoking it as Hamill squatted across from me, puffing away on his cigarette. Behind me my brother and Bane discussed moving Cari with the witches and how security would be handled. In the end, we would be three. Me, Bane, and Hamill, carefully warded and concealed until we came to the Elam.

An hour later, Cari was wrapped and adjusted onto a makeshift stretcher Sam and one of the Biloxi witches had fashioned out of thick limbs and the unscathed bits of canvas from her tent. She leveled one final warning glare my way, which I ignored, and my brother stopped, loaded down with a pack of his belongings and that higher coven witch's.

"Safe journey," I told my brother, kissing each of his cheeks.

He held me back when I made to step away, grabbing my hand tight. "Safe journey and mindful thoughts," he told me, shooting a look to Bane over my shoulder. "We all have our place, *sè*, no matter how unfair it is."

"I think I've learned that lesson by now, Samedi."

"*Wi*," he said, squinting when Bane called to me, extinguishing the campfire with a cool charm. "But I don't think you're the one who needs to learn it now."

Sam walked away from the camp, following the witches, and I hoisted my pack over my shoulders, nodding to Bane when I approached. He frowned, pointing to the loosened strap near the waist and stopped to adjust it.

His scent surrounded me like a fog, and I had to remind myself of Sam's words and what would happen as soon as we discovered Elam.

"We're all carrying more now," he said, vaguely, as he moved the strap around my waist, stepping closer. When he couldn't seem to get it to line up, the wizard dropped to his knee in front of me. "Well now, this is nice..." His smile was a dangerous thing. Smug and delicious.

Gods help me, my gaze ached for him, wanting to draw in everything I could about him. See all the things I'd missed over the years, remember each detail to keep inside my head when this job was done and it was time again for me to walk away.

At that thought, Bane stretched his shoulders tight and stood, dropping his hands from my pack. "You're just going to run again?" he said, his voice astonished, angry.

"I didn't run, I escaped."

He stood in front of me, hands held in tight fists at his side, and that expression was stern, confident. "What are you hiding from me?"

Just then, I could have told him. I wanted to tell him. I'd have risked his anger, the betrayal he'd feel just to have him know it was me, the lower coven witch whose father dealt with the dirty work in the Cove, that had made a claim on him. And I had let him claim me, back in that classroom ten years ago. But now was not the time. In fact, it never would be the time.

"I have to know." His fists tightened further, but I managed not to react, other than to step away from him.

"It won't matter soon enough. We find the Elam and you'll be married."

He frowned, as though he didn't like the reminder, but didn't comment. Bane was stoic again, and I told him all he deserved to hear.

"I left the Cove because I had to."

"Because of me?" Why did he have to seem so damn eager for the truth? What was the point? Why the hell did he enjoy torturing us both so surely?

"Because it was the only way for me to survive."

Bane didn't answer, and that restraint he held onto so tightly didn't waver in the least as he stepped closer, ignoring my small protest when he touched my face. "Yes, but you forgot the people left behind to survive you."

# FIFTEEN

FOUR HOURS LATER, WE RETIRED, EXHAUSTED, MY NECK THROBBING from the pain and I collapsed next to an oak with low-hanging limbs.

Then the thunder woke me, but that wasn't the scariest sound I heard all night.

That came later.

What was more chilling was that the Elam had completely vanished from me. The forest grew with the first light we'd seen in nearly an entire day, the night ended, and as the sun rose and the presence of Bane's energy left the camp, Hamill's angry, indifferent vibe replaced it.

Then, the thunder. It sounded like the slap of sheet metal, rattled by the shudder of strong fists. It wasn't the sound of weather or the natural vibration wind and rain make together in a storm. This thunder was transfixed, buzzed like the hum of the ley lines, and when a third and fourth clap sounded again, I knew it was a spell.

"They're tracking you down," Hamill said, slipping from the hollow of the still shadowy woods as he smoked.

Above us the swirl of gray and blue crowded in the clouds, pinching out the sunlight to turn the sky black. "Dark wishes." It was something my father called dark magic made with ill intent. "It's a special kind of rotten wizard that will trap one of their own in a spell like this." A quick nod at the biggest, darkest cloud, and the whites of Hamill's eyes stuck out among the shadows and smoke he hid in. "My father says this type of spell work is the worst, the thickest of bad magic. It requires pain and blood to work."

"Like the magic used to spell Bane and grab the Elam?"

Hamill's question made me jerk my attention back to him. There was a hint of something in his voice, some odd amusement in his question that made me wonder if he had other motives for asking it. "Exactly like that." That was not merely curiosity.

"But why would they want you? Why not try to take out Bane?"

It should have been obvious. He should have known, but as the shifter took a drag from his cigarette and let the smoke billow over his head to circle up into the dark trees, I thought, maybe, his was a game that needed playing. For a bit.

"Because I'm the one the Elam is calling. I'm the only one that can find it."

When Hamill only stared at me, I focused on the sky and the blistering wind that danced above us. "They don't want me to find it. They think using this spell will somehow show them where I am. The best way to keep the Elam out of our hands is to keep it from being discovered."

"You didn't steal it."

I shot a glance at Hamill, frowning. "Of course I didn't. How could I?"

"And you didn't touch Wyatt." I didn't bother answering. Hamill stepped completely out of the shadows, like the slow reveal of a wound being unwrapped, and when my gaze landed on his face, the colored complexion of his skin, I immediately stood. "What?" he asked, moving his head to catch my attention when I refused to look at him.

I'd almost forgotten about the Judas spell. Yet there it was, right on Hamill's face—a sharp, jagged line smooth against his cheek, running the length of his neck. He wouldn't know it was there, but I could see it plain as day. We'd been cast in near total darkness for so long, hidden beneath the heavy growth of the forest that the faint discoloration would have been almost impossible to make out. But now, there was light. Now there was truth.

It terrified me.

"What's that look?"

There was nothing to fear, other than the shifter. The forest gave me an advantage. Hamill was a were in his primal self. He knew the woods, but this was the Cove. This was the miles upon miles of terrain my siblings and I had trained to hunt in, to gather and protect along with the other lower covens. It was our calling to know and defend Grant territory. Hamill might be a natural tracker, but I was an earth witch standing on familiar ground. He would not catch me.

"Where's Bane?" I'd need to access what small reserves of subtlety I had.

"Hunting shelter. Some of his folk have cabins deep in the woods. When he saw the storm rising, he went out to find the nearest one. Said he'd be back within the hour."

Hamill watched me as I sidestepped around the camp, my own eyes locked and focused on even the slightest movements he made. "Don't get any ideas," he said, glowering at me as though I were rotten. "Bane will have the final say in what to do with you."

"What?"

"You and your family." Hamill's jaw moved as he gritted his teeth. "If I could, I'd rip you all to pieces."

A swift, dismissive nod and I bolted, zipping away from the camp while Hamill watched open mouthed, unsuspecting and likely confused about my reaction. My father taught me to run and that's exactly what I did. But I'd acted first, analyzed second, realizing embarrassingly late that I had never seen Hamill in full light. Perhaps that was not the mark of the Judas spell after all.

As I ran from the shifter and that brewing storm, I realized that making my way on my own was for the best. Bane couldn't help me, not with the Elam. Hamill certainly couldn't, and so I continued, running through the forest because I needed to. The air, the earth, the rough landscape below my feet—was all a part of the Cove, a part of what made me who I was. All that sensation, all that earthy necessity that combined inside me, in the natural state of who I was. A Crimson Cove witch searching for a lost object.

Then the lightening came, cracking against the darkened sky, illuminating all around me. The low, sprawling hills. The wide stretch of wood and brambles, the slinking, curious eyes of a wild boar that investigated me as I slipped through the woods.

And just when I started to doubt my flight, to suspect it had been hopeless, stupid, to run again, to flee the danger before I could really recognize it as such, the penetrating shock of the Elam flooded me. Its power crashed into me like the lightning bolts above.

"There." My entire body shook as the rain poured from the sky, drumming against my body and the landscape around me. "Just there," I repeated to no one.

It was like a fever, high and searing, and my fingers, my joints, ached to touch it. But the unnatural storm, this infernal spell, interfered, deflected that reach, that power from my senses, forcing me to lean against a large, wet tree and funnel all my focus, all my ability into the signature that called to me beyond the trail merely to keep it from dropping away again.

Eyes tightened, the darkness clouded around my senses until there was nothing but the barely visible smooth curve of the Elam's tortoise face and the turquoise sheen glinting even in the feeble sunlight behind the storm. In my mind, I held the Elam in my hands, its power blistering, burning and so intoxicating, so freeing and bright. It was like pure electricity, some live wire of power that I wanted inside me, flowing through me. Sharper focus, I concentrated on the feel of the amulet that encased the Elam. There was a hunger inside it; I sensed that clearly. It ached and pulsed, a living, breathing element that craved the ley lines. Yin to yang and it wanted that searing power. It wanted to tether it, tame it, and just then, with that strong, blazing energy soaking my subconscious, understanding came to me.

The Elam was mystical, a cord of energy and magic that craved calm and control. It wished for the symbiotic connection to something that was utterly out of control. The ley lines, the Elam, they were two sides of the same coin—one that flipped and rattled, until it finally broke, the other that molded and bent, stilled and coiled and healed.

Gods, how similar that seemed. How ironic it was to me that I would be drawn to something so unlike myself. The very thing I wanted was the one thing that would hold me back completely. Bane was the Elam seeking control, calm. I was the lines craving freedom, reach, the grasp of nothing that would hinder me.

Above me, that mock storm brewed, the sky darkening so that I could barely see anything but shapes and small movements directly in front of me and despite my focus, my grip on the Elam loosened. I was so close, I sensed the wave of its signature as the rain and winds whipped around me, as limbs and leaves fell and scattered, yet my subconscious hold on the Elam became tenuous, weak, and when a loud, heavy crack of lightning sounded above me and the tree I leaned against shuddered with the splinter of breaking wood, that grip left me completely.

I ran.

I'd become the hunted, pursued by a manufactured scavenger. Every length I ran, the lightening followed, cracking, breaking loose the ground, freeing dirt and clay and bits of bark around my feet. Heart pounding, breath an uneven, labored mess, my feet moved just seconds ahead of the streaks of lighting hitting the ground behind me.

Whoever sent the storm wanted me running. But this spell was artless. The markers of stealth and cunning were missing in the forced light of the enchantment. There was little natural appeal to it, and the danger rived up too greatly. Licks of light and heat coiled together, broke across the ground, scaring me, but the damage behind was weak, ineffectual. Each ripped-asunder hole and tear in the earth quickly healed itself as soon as the attack ended. Every whip of light that came close to my limbs, that singed my hair, touched with only the small buzz of a faulty outlet.

For a second I got distracted, watching the sky with a smile on my face, still loving the beauty in the darkness, even in the false storm, just as I'd always loved stars overhead at night, but then another strike blasted and the smile left my face. Something was wrong. Somehow the threat did not seem as angry, as desperate as I originally believed. And then, because I was no longer frantic or frightened, because my thought was so mundane, the spell almost seemed to realize its own ineffectualness, and responded by amping up a level.

"Shit!" My curse barely registered past the wet deluge above head and when the two trees behind me cracked, crashing inches from my head, I stumbled, crawling with grass stuck between my fingers and under my nails as another strike set about and yet another oak slammed close to me. "Holy shit!" Throwing up my hands too late, I knew that the block would not save me, nor would the quick flash of energy shooting from my fingertips as another tree began to fall right on top of me. I held my breath expecting pain, the sound of bone and skin breaking, but instead, all went still.

"Jani?" My name came out in a groan, one I recognized as injury, at the least, excruciating agony at the worst.

"Bane?" The rain still fell and the crack in the distance told me the unsophisticated spell work was dying but not dead. "Oh God, Bane, what did you do?"

"*Shit.* What I always damn well do." He felt around in the darkness, stretching toward the thick branch lying across his left leg, nearly freeing himself just as I reached him. "Minding your ass, I suppose." A small grunt when the branch would not move any further, and Bane fell back, resting an arm over his forehead. "Or trying to, any damn way."

"Stupid, heedless jolthead." When I finally managed to crawl over the limbs and leaves, Bane was still trying to kick off the heavy branch with his free leg. "I never asked you to play bodyguard."

"You didn't have to," he yelled, grunting again, hitting his fists against the wet ground. "I just..."

It was the first time I'd ever heard him sound so open and raw. Bane was not the type of wizard to loosen his guard or be blindly truthful. Especially about his motives. Hearing the difference in his tone completely stilled me.

"It was just something I had to do."

My hands came to his chest just as I moved next to him, not realizing how much his words impacted me. "Why?"

"I don't..." Bane's breath came out slow, as though even thinking of a response was wasted effort he didn't want to bother with. "Fuck's sake, Jani, it's just something I needed to do."

"And look where it's got you." I waved at his leg, fighting back my fear, my anger, and the damn tears that had unexpectedly burned my eyes, making me angrier, making me feel weak and stupid. "You've probably broken it."

"It's not broken." When I glared at him, Bane shook his head. "I've had broken bones before. This isn't one."

A long grunt from my pressed lips and my gaze went around the woods, over the downed trees, and toward the trail covered now with fallen limbs and small saplings. "We should call someone."

"No service out here," he said, trying to sit up. Bane swatted at my hand on his elbow before he nodded toward the branch and together we spelled the massive wood from his leg. "Besides, the real storm is coming, and I'd be a sight more comfortable in that hunting cabin just over the ridge than sitting on my ass with you looking like you want to stun me with a quick hex."

That was a thought, though I'd never tell him I likely couldn't think of a hex strong enough to take him down. Bane was damn powerful.

"I don't want to hex you."

"No?" he asked, leaning on me when I reached for his hand.

"Not yet." He settled against my shoulder and a quick whip of pleasure ran up my spine as I caught the scent of his skin. "But I reserve the right to change my mind."

# SIXTEEN

THE CABIN WASN'T MUCH MORE THAN A SEVEN-HUNDRED-SQUARE-
foot room with a small kitchenette, a threadbare, wool rug in front of a
slight stacked-stone hearth, and absolutely no furniture to speak of.
The floor was scraped pine, very old with loads of blotted stains where
something wet, possibly bloody had spilled and had never been
completely cleaned.

The entire place smelled of wet fur, mildew, and that unique
stuffiness that most places take on when no one has kept the air
circulating or moved around the place. It was damn cold as well.

Bane had enormous feet that thinned at the ankles and sparse hairs
just along his big toe. His ankles were boney and slight and the one in
my lap was twisted and swollen with a nasty gash rupturing the flesh. It
was a bloody, filthy mess, and he would not hold still long enough for
me to mend it.

"Don't move your leg."

"I'm not." Just as Bane said that, he jerked his ankle to the side,
making my fingers slip up his leg, missing the large gash that exposed
the bone.

Dear God, but this wizard was an infant. "You are, in fact."

"I can heal it myself." That promise came with a clipped, irritated growl that I'd heard Bane use anytime he wanted to scare away whoever was presently annoying him. At the moment, that was me. Me and my feeble, subpar spell work that couldn't heal his busted ankle.

"You can't heal it." The jerk of his head and the slowly narrowing eyelids were almost comical, edging toward the pathetic side, but he would not keep me from my fussing. "Not with the pain distracting you. You'll mess up the spell."

Bane made several low, pointless sounds that I took as irritation when I pulled his foot closer on my lap but the noises from his throat did not distract me from the feel of his skin or how I picked up the sense that his stare went on too long, that he watched me too closely.

He didn't seem able to do anything other than watch and silently complain. It was a gift I'd rarely seen—someone who needs your help yet refuses to ask for it, someone mightily powerful but incapable of healing themselves.

Still, the watching, the grumbling, continued and it was that attention and the worry that I'd somehow damage him worse that had my fingers shaking as I tried mending the broken skin with a spell Mai could fashion while asleep.

But my invocations for healing spells were abysmal and that particular craft took skill and patience I had yet to acquire, so when my inflection went wrong and Bane's skin splintered further, I winced, reacting to his loud grumble of "Fuck!"

"Sorry," I said, covering the gash with the meager bandages from the kit Mai had stuffed into my bag. "So sorry."

"Incompetent, stubborn... *Shit.*" He made a grab for his foot, twisting it from my lap before I could stop him. "How is it Mai does such good healing charms and you are..." But Bane ended his question when my eyes flashed and my glare silenced him.

"Because there isn't a nurturing bone in my body." Not thinking about the injury much, I pulled on his toe, jerking that foot right back into my lap. "And because my patient is an uncooperative baby."

The awkward tension leveled thick and weighty around us. We were both soaking wet and tired. Both annoyed by the disaster that the search had been and the ridiculous amount of pressure that continued to build between us. Maybe the silence that quickly descended in that small cabin had little to do with the storm and being attacked or my inability to drum up even the smallest amount of a bedside manner. Maybe it was Bane's lack of effort at being an accommodating patient. I tried very hard not to think it had anything to do with events that had happened so long ago, which still seemed to shape the present: the kiss and the melding and everything I kept hidden from him.

He grunted when I called him a baby, jaw moving as though he'd decided to chew on his insults rather than spit them out at me. Still, my patience, my discomfort and the wreck just being near him did to me as I attempted to heal him again, would not keep my temper from surfacing. "Big, powerful wizard covered in scary runes and you can't even sit still for me to help you."

Bane seemed to give up the fight and leaned back on his elbows, watching my fingers as I attempted the charm again, then at my face when I managed the right invocation. "Who says you're not nurturing?"

I waved a hand over his leg. "Hello?"

His slow smile smothered some of my anger and I shook my head as he laughed. "Who the hell cares anyway?" He nodded at his ankle as though it were nothing. "It's a scratch."

"It's not a scratch, and if we don't heal it, it'll get infected."

Bane pressed his hand over my fingers when I started fussing with the bandage. "I've had worse injuries. It's fine." After a few moments of holding my breath, completely stimulated when he touched the top of my hand, I exhaled, ignoring the small, barely felt zip of energy from his fingertips. If Bane had noticed it at all, he didn't say and let me get on with cleaning the wound and freeing it from the dirt and grime left there from our awkward hike over the ridge.

It was slow work that took my concentration, and it helped me to ignore how closely he regarded me, how I could sense the feel of his stare on my features, eating up every expression I made. "So why did you take off?"

I pushed my eyebrows together at his question—he just wasn't going to give up, was he? But instead of giving him a straight answer, I tilted my head as if I wasn't sure what he meant. "Did I?"

Bane laughed, sounding like something deep and warm. It reminded me of pecan groves and honeysuckle and all the things in the Cove meant for someone else. "You're always taking off, Jani." He leaned back further, adjusting on his side. "The Runaway Witch. That's what Sam and I called you, remember?"

"No," I told him, not liking how the memories collected, like a patchwork doll hurriedly sewn together again without regard for scale or structure. "I don't remember."

"Well I do." Bane pulled two bottles of water from my bag, tossing me one. "You ran from Eldridge Romney in term seven. We were thirteen. He tried kissing you at Joanie Wilkins' first girl/boy party."

"Because you glared at him every time he stepped my way." That night I remembered. But then it's hard to forget when a small boy like Eldridge with big doe eyes the color of a magnolia leaf nearly fainted anytime Bane let that stoic, mean glare land his way. "I didn't want the poor boy to be bloodied."

Something quick and distant flashed behind Bane's eyes, as though the recall of that night didn't quite fit with what he remembered, but then he adjusted his body, sitting up and glancing at me as though he'd remembered something else. "You ran from the coven games that Midsummer when my uncle hosted the solstice. We didn't find you for five hours."

What a retched memory to mention. I'd hated those games and the stupid primal alpha way the men carried on when the solstice arrived. The Grants had hosted, true enough, and all the covens worked themselves into a tizzy over the preparations. There'd been bonfires stacked and set all over the groves, smartly organized with gold and yellow candles, flowers and leaves. Flower wreaths were corded together and given to every girl of the Cove old enough to marry. Even my mother, for all her modern-loving proclamations about logic and bucking the traditions, still laced our pillowcases with herbs and charms to summon prophetic dreams. Crimson Cove on Midsummer was a ridiculous play on sense and reason, and that year had been no different.

"I ran because Mai told me I'd have to float my flower wreath down the river. I didn't know whose bank it would land on and didn't want to be stuck with some strange wizard for the rest of the day."

"Why not?" Bane leaned forward, elbows on his knees, looking too amused by the memory.

"I was fifteen, Bane. I had no intention of letting some wizard I didn't know claim me as a bride."

His frown was forced, as was that small eye roll, but I let it pass, ignoring him when he knocked his bum foot against my hand. "It was just a game. Besides, they'd have only asked for a kiss."

"Which they wouldn't have gotten, hence me leaving."

"Maybe that kiss would have come from me." That I doubted. Bane had spent most of the day hidden away in the tree house near the edge of the grove, taking everything in, looking bored and out of place. I'd remembered that was where he stayed because I'd wanted to follow him just to be rid of all the overcharged Midsummer energy.

"You weren't playing."

"No," he said, taking a slow swig from his water bottle, "but I'd have won you. Trust that."

The little cheater would have done his best to move my wreath toward his bank. Maybe I'd known that even back then. Maybe that's why I'd left. I couldn't be sure. Those memories, of course, were painted with a gloss I had little hope of ever sharpening. That Bane admitted he'd have cheated to get me that day should have made me feel awkward, perhaps a little shy. But the sensation moving through me just then as he lowered the bottle of water from his mouth, leaving a small droplet on that fat bottom lip, was hot and heated and things that should have made me embarrassed.

I wasn't. In fact, with the way he kept watching me, his gaze too focused on my messy tidying of the bandages and rubbish from the cleaning, heightened the edge of tension that we'd managed to push back while we argued over his busted ankle.

Still, no matter what that look did to me, I could no more go to him, touch him, take what I wanted now than I'd been able to back then. Back any time. Save that one day in the classroom.

"You always did that," I said dismissively. He frowned and I shrugged off his confusion. "Chased anyone away who got a little too close. Sabotaged when things weren't going the way you wanted. You were like this giant shadowing me, and I was the only one unable to see you. Big damn warning to anyone I might want to get close to." The wadded bandages and rubbish fit neatly back into the bag and I took to rearranging all the accoutrements my twin had provided, just to keep from looking at Bane. "Maybe that's why I always ran. I knew you wouldn't be far behind." I glanced up at him, not liking it when muscles around his mouth tightened. "Maybe just once I wanted to do something without that shadow, just to see if I could."

It was several seconds before Bane spoke. When he did there was a softness in his voice that came out as mildly annoyed. "You did a hell of a job running that last time."

"What was here for me, Bane?" A small twist of his bottom lip and my heart sputtered twice. "My twin had her own life, my brother and folks, they all had living to do on their own. Hell, Mai was the only person I was close to thanks to that scary shadow of yours." He opened his mouth to speak but I waved him off. "I wanted to see outside of the Cove. I wanted to see what else was out there. There wasn't..." I swallowed, holding my breath for a second before I finished, "anything keeping me here."

What I would have given then to know his thoughts. He could still sense mine; I knew he could. His spell had guaranteed he would, but I had minded what I thought, how intimately I remembered and misremembered things as they had been. Since that test in the forest the night he worked the spell, I'd determined not to let my thoughts seep too freely. He might know my mood, but I worked hard to keep him from my feelings.

Still, his was easy enough to tell. There was the jaw clenching again —the tale tell mark of Bane trying like hell to not blurt out whatever irrational thing was in his head. But if my confession had annoyed him, he wouldn't let me know it. "And tonight? With Hamill?"

"I caught a vibe from him." My flippant shrug did nothing to make that worried frown soften and so I continued, moving my knees up to hold myself together as he watched me. "I thought maybe the Judas spell had shown on his skin."

"Did it?"

"Not sure. I've never seen him in full light. Does he have a scar?" Bane shook his head, shoulders lowering as he relaxed. "Well, he's definitely hiding something, but I don't think he's responsible for the Elam."

Outside the cabin, an honest storm raged on. It was a bitter, windy fight with water drenching and thudding on the tiny cabin roof. Only the dim light of a kerosene lamp and the fire illuminated the small room, and I was grateful I could not make out more of Bane's features. They were too striking, too honest when I looked closely enough.

Bane's cynical snort told me he didn't buy that either. "He doesn't have enough magic to subdue me or to take it."

He hadn't told me much about the attack. There'd been no full disclosures that might have helped me piece together who the guilty party could be. But that was Bane. That was the nature of a powerful wizard from the Cove. Utter bullshit, but that was how they'd lived for generations. Still, this theft and Bane's attack went beyond his wounded pride. He'd have to loosen it and answer me.

"You don't remember anything about the attack?"

"Some jackass got the upper hand. That's all that matters." He turned his head, profile against the flickering firelight, and I looked away, still not comfortable seeing him this close, this apart from the world. "It set in my bones that they pulled that off and my memory went a little fuzzy then."

"It's odd," I offered, fiddling with my damp shirt sleeve to avoid looking at him again. "Whoever took the Elam obviously can't control it, otherwise it wouldn't call to me."

"Can you feel it now?"

I closed my eyes, focusing on the sensory detail around me—the way the fire popped and crackled against the whoosh of wind blowing inside the chimney; the warmth of Bane's large foot in my lap; the texture of his coarse leg hair under my fingertips; and outside, the smell of rain, bitter and thick, the taste of honeysuckle and ozone on the wind. But no Elam, no quiet purr of its signature humming to me. There wasn't even the faintest hint of the ley lines against the storm.

"Storm is messing with the lines." I frowned, focusing on the silence.

"No, it's not."

When I looked up, Bane was watching me. His throat worked, voice low, guarded, and I swear I thought I saw a spark of red-light pulsing from his fingertips. "I'm blocking it from you."

"Why?"

"To help you concentrate, listen for the Elam." He stretched out his hand and didn't seem to notice the small flicker of reddish light glowing from his palm. "Come here. I'll help you focus."

My memory was frayed, but I did remember that spark. There was no way I'd invite it back. It had taken a wickedly strong memory charm to keep Bane's mind clear of the last time that flicker had appeared. I was in no rush to work that kind of spell again.

Instead, I pulled my legs close, looping my arms to mimic having a chill. "No. That's alright. I can't hear it."

"I know. I'll help you." When I didn't look at him, Bane nudged my foot. "What's the problem?" He looked down at his hand when I glanced at it. "What..."

"It's probably the storm. I told you. It interferes with the lines."

There was something in the stare he gave me that felt like an accusation. And then he truly noticed the small spark of light working over his fingertips, sparking out toward me as he reached in my direction. It caught him off guard. Curiously, he stretched his long fingers, moved them in succession like a piano player working through scales, and each fragment of movement ushered up that same red spark—a tingling streak of energy that seemed damn familiar. He moved faster, fingers becoming a line of movement until that spark crackled, shot out and zapped me right as he waved his fingers at my hand.

"Ow."

Scrambling back, my hand on the floor, I managed to get far enough away from him to catch a breath. But the cabin was tiny and the air so thick that my head swam from the heat and the recoil from my thoughts and the magical energy pulsing around the room.

There came a swift flash of memory, a slice of images that I'd tried to forget but could not completely erase from my mind—that light pulsing, circling. Our small, childish fingers touching and connecting, our twelve-year-old limbs brushing together and then jerking apart as that light tried to consume us. And oh, the classroom and Bane's hands all over me, touching, feeling, gripping and that constant red light clouding around the room, inside our heads, surrounding us, joining us together.

This meant finality. It meant completion and Bane did not remember. The flashes came to me disjointed, but still they came, and the one I clearly remembered—our melding in that classroom—was the one that hung in my mind. It was the one that made the most sense.

"Jani..." he started, following me, coming to his knees despite his bad ankle, crawling so close that I had nowhere to go. "You've been keeping something from me. I see it. Even in the damn dark I can see it. It's everywhere." Bane moved his warm fingers to my bottom lip and let his thumb glide across my cheekbone. "You refuse to meet my eyes. You avoid me when I stare too long."

"You always stare too long."

"I can't help that."

He was massive, a sweltering cloud that collected energy, that absorbed emotion so that it became consuming—a vacuous funnel that craved the things it did not need but took what it wanted. That was Bane. He took control, but for the life of me I could not see past letting him take what had always been his.

"Tell me my daydream was invented. That dream of being in the classroom with you." There was a challenge in his voice that reminded me of us as children, huddled and scared, taunting and fearless. But I wouldn't answer, couldn't tell him something that would hurry along his anger. It would be heavy enough when it came.

"Jani," he said, coming so close that I could smell the sweat from his skin and hear the tiny rasp that caught in his throat.

"You'll hate me." It was as close to an explanation as I could offer.

Bane pressed his hand against my cheek, the touch warm and soft but with that small red current still working behind his skin, still flirting with me to cry out that he was mine. "Never, little witch."

Give and take. He wanted, needed, but didn't understand why. He didn't remember, and at that moment, I could not bring myself to remind him. It would hurt too much. But the warmth in his hand, the sweet, honeysuckle scent from his skin weaving like a spell of its own making, intoxicating me, lulling me closer and closer until only Bane—the sound, feel, and smell of him—took up all the space in my head. There was only this man. There was only this moment.

Both belonged to me.

Our mouths came close together, our breaths heated and dampened our faces, our lips—bringing us to the blistering, bated breath before the race begins. A small incline, the minutest stretch of my neck and that mouth, that tongue would belong to me. It was different from the night he spelled me. There was no primeval encouragement from the lines egging us on, inching us closer and closer toward our most basic urges. This was more, and somehow with Bane's face so close to mine, with his fingers tugging on the back of my hair, I knew that one kiss would unhinge me. It would change everything and there would be no stopping us.

"I...this..." My words got stuck somewhere around the back of my throat, clung tight against the hot breath that fanned out when Bane rested his forehead against mine, when he moved his mouth to kiss between my eyebrows.

"This isn't normal, Jani. This..." He paused, shuddering when that pulsing red light shot across his skin, hovering near his fingertips. "Someone spelled us."

Blinking, nodding, it was all I could manage. Bane was too strong, the heat in the room too full, the air too thick. Yes, someone had been spelled—him. Someone had done the spelling—me. But really I was a coward, scared of what he'd think, say, damn well do if he found out I'd taken his memories from before. Even if it was for the best, I'd still lied to him—the lie of omission. I'd blocked him and kept for myself something I had no business hiding away.

But Bane seemed content to ignore the past. He seemed mesmerized by the moment, fascinated by the play of reddish light on our skin and that whip of succulent heat that warmed us every time he moved his fingers across my collarbone. "I think I know what this is,

Jani, but it makes no sense. Nothing between us, then or now, ever made sense to me." And it wouldn't, not to him, not with the understanding I'd taken from him when I blocked his memories. He kept flirting closer to the truth, skating the surface of what that light meant and where he'd seen it before. I couldn't let him find out, not like that. Not just then.

"Bane," I said, pulling him closer, loving the low, deep throttle of his voice vibrating when my nails slid up his neck. "You watched over me. Protected me."

"Did I scare you then?"

"Always," I said, feeling brave, reckless. I exhaled, staring in his eyes like I wasn't a coward. "But I loved you for it."

One swift nod, as though he'd made up some silent decision on his own and Bane picked me up, pulling me closer, his arm around my waist and that busted ankle injury forgotten in his smooth haste to kiss me.

His look was feral and possessive, and even though some loud, *loud* voice in my head told me to stop him, reminded me that it was my job to stop him, I was powerless against the rush of his mouth against my neck and the greedy hold of his massive hand cupping my hip.

"This isn't...this won't lead anywhere..." There was little fight in my protest, my words meant to stop him, only contradicted by how I stretched my neck, giving him greater access to my skin.

"It already has. It started a long time ago."

"It didn't..."

"Yes, Jani," he said, shutting me up with that wide mouth, with the slip of his tongue along my bottom lip. "Every look back then to right now, I was saying the same thing. Every single one."

My body was electrified, stunted by Bane's confession, crippled by the light heat collecting around us. If I asked and was disappointed, I'd lose nothing. I had claimed him long ago and had lived with the empty feeling of that for years. If he claimed me now, not remembering a thing and discovered later how badly I'd betrayed him, could I stand the notion that I was his and he no longer wanted me?

Risk and rules. My life existed around both and just for a moment with Bane watching me, with him waiting for permission he didn't seem familiar with ever having to wait for, I wanted to take something for myself. Just once. "Do I have to ask?"

"No," he said, his bottom lip twitching as he watched me, "just look a little deeper."

And I did as Bane held my face in his hand. I looked beyond the veneer he wanted the world to see. I saw past the expectations, the certainty of what his life was meant to be. There was no alpha wizard, training to lead his coven to the future. There was no looming, angry mage keeping everyone away in some bland effort to protect himself from the world around him.

Right then, there was only Bane. That open, real nexus that had touched mine ten years before. The protector who guarded me from threats that weren't real and the ones that were.

Propriety required that I back away. Tradition, adherence to the way of things in the Cove, told me I had no business touching him. But I was damn tired of doing things I should do instead of things I wanted to.

"Bane..." There was a pause in the name, a small reluctance I wasn't sure I'd ignore, and when he moved my head, tilting my face to look down at me fully, I thought for a second he expected me to reject him.

There was only enough time for two blinks as he watched me, his scrutiny all encompassing, making me tremble, before Bane shook his head, then gripped my face to kiss me. It began simply, tenderly, then his deep breaths grew labored the longer his kissed me. The desperate, greedy noises he made set off something ancient and wild in the pit of my stomach.

His fingers went near my scalp to grip my hair, preventing me from moving away from him—as if I would. He dipped his tongue hard and certain, his teeth sucking in my bottom lip. He pulled away, resting his forehead on mine, exhaling hard, only for a moment before he took to staring at me again, giving me that same genuine expression, the same piercing concentration that could have been anger but was most likely desperation.

Swallowing, Bane exhaled. "Tell me you want me. Not because I'm asking you, but because you mean it." His voice was soft, but I could hear the quiet frenzy in it. "Tell me the truth." Bane pulled me closer, placing his hands on either side of my face, making my heart drum in wild, hard beats. "Tell me, Jani. Tell me now." He wasn't begging, though the tone of his voice, the low gruffness of the timbre and the narrowed slant of his eyes told me how badly he needed to know.

We take life as it comes. The challenges set in front of us become hurdles we must jump. And when you are a lower coven witch in a town obsessed with breeding, when the people you love most in the world are part of that obsession, you take what little you can, when you can.

Bane was all I wanted. He wasn't for me. He wasn't mine, not in the way that our world determined. But just then, I forgot. Just then, I let myself keep forgetting.

"Never wanted anything more."

His hair was thick, curled with a wave, and it slid between my fingers as I yanked him close, an insistent jerk that would bring his mouth to mine. The response was immediate, heady. My loud whine echoed around the room when Bane gripped me, his touch penetrating.

Counter and counterpoint we came at each other—me clinging to him, him insisting, gripping as we kissed, as we moved together against the walls of that tiny cabin, onto the rough wool rug on the floor. My clothes gave way in his desperate, eager movements, his mouth touching each inch of exposed skin he uncovered. Bane was just able to stay upright, then stretched as he held me tighter, twisting our bodies so that he hovered over me. I smiled, watching him tear away his shirt, dislodge his body from fabric in a frenzy of movements, until he was naked above me—so beautiful, so male with wide shoulders that looked like marble, a chest and stomach fit and fierce from the labor of effort. Runes covered his upper body, zigzagged between the small patch of hair on his chest. He smelled wild, like the forest, and my fingers ached to touch every beautiful inch of naked skin. Bane stared down, his lips rolled between his teeth, his nostrils flaring as his gaze moved over my skin.

I ran my fingernails along the deep indentions of his torso, across the considerable sinew of his chest, down to the lean ridges of his stomach, admiring the form of him, the etched precision of his body.

He let me, seeming to enjoy my touch, his eyes rolling up, his hands guiding my wrists over his chest, his hips, within the soft hair trailing down his stomach.

All around me was sound and sensation. It was there, drumming in my ears, Bane's heart beating. I was aware of his desperation, his eagerness and the knowledge had me swallowing knotted clutches from my throat, had me pulling him to me, loving the slick feel of our skin touching. Bane smoothed his fingers along my ribs, flirted against my stomach, descending, as he kissed me, a controlling, pressing touch.

"So damn warm," he growled against my ear. I shivered at the vibration of the sound, skimming my fingers along his naked back, smiling at the small work of red light that collected in the friction of our touching. His movements quickened—mouth on my flesh, on my breasts, cupping, licking along my stomach, and I sucked in a harsh breath when his fingers jarred me into a moan. "I love you making that sound."

I was speechless, anxious, my thoughts becoming inconsistent and unorganized. Bane's mouth, his teeth and tongue, met every inch of my skin, trailed over my body to draw me into a fury of hard pants and a desperate request for completion. It was the same drugging sensation I sensed that day in the English Lit classroom, stronger than the kiss that night in the forest when simple touches and insistent kisses had me lightheaded and high, like some rogue chemical was coursing through my veins. In a flash and quicksilver of movement, he growled again, a rough, dire rumble and then we shifted, coming together, our bodies arching to join, to connect in a smooth sweet pleasurable pain.

"Finally," he hissed as he buried himself in me. He was larger than I'd ever had and fit me securely, filled me up with the strength of his body and the deep, pleasurable jarring of him inside me. We moved together, breaths moistening our faces, him stretched out over me, his hands on either side of my head. He stared at me and I could only manage to blink back. His mouth went to my neck, suckling.

"Bane." My whisper was breathy and weak, and I disregarded how desperately I shook, how the sensation of him inside me, over me, should have made me scared, should have filled me with guilt. It didn't,

I wouldn't let it, and with each juddering movement, each plunge, I shuddered, my skin humming with sensation, with the inexorable feel of him reaching up within me, piercing me completely. Yet, I needed more. I pushed on his shoulders, making him frown, then kissed him, tracing my fingertips over his skin.

I didn't have to speak, to demand. Bane followed my lead, went down onto his back easily when I moved over him, smiling, happy, giddy when my knees went to his hips and I slid on top of him.

Eyes rounded, he obeyed my silent command, not hastening to grab my hips, his fingers pressing into my waist, sitting up to fasten his mouth to my breast. The room filled with noises—the rhythmic creaking of the wood floor, my harsh whines and Bane's low growl, assimilating to form a liquid song, the sound of life, of inevitability. When he reached a hand to my breast, his fingers shook, grazing my ribs, and I saw the low glow of red light swirling over my body. The heat coiled beneath me, rose to crest through my knees, up my torso until it exploded below my stomach, a dulcet, aching stab that had me pulling away from his mouth and leaning my head back as I cried out, racked by wave after wave of searing heat. I could feel Bane's smile on my chest as he rested his forehead against my collarbone, the sensation only helping along the complete satisfaction of my finish.

Boneless in his arms, I fell on the rug, with Bane's impatient hands pulling my hips, settling me over him again so that my back arched, just touched his leg as he sat in front of me, my weight centered over his lap, him still hard, pushing up deep inside of me. His movements continued, and I could hear our echoing heartbeats, thundering in time with one another and the smell of us, thick and feverish as we moved together. Bane's attentions went back to my stomach, holding me at the waist while pushing me up and down on his cock, so that he could rub his lips over the flat plane of my skin, across my ribs, near my breast, to pay tribute to the small birthmark next to my left nipple.

With a kiss, small and gentle, I squeezed tight around him, desperate to feel him slip out of control and Bane jerked, roaring as his head fell back and I watched him shudder under me. He held firm to my body, pushing down on my shoulders. His body tensed and convulsed as he filled me up, straining, shuddering to completion. Slowly he relaxed and, staring back at me, that fierce, red light faded as Bane's breath slowed, fanning along my skin to kiss me.

"Better," he said, his face buried in my neck. "So much better than the daydream."

# SEVENTEEN

THERE IN THE LULL OF BUZZING, NAKED SKIN AND THE COOL comfort of Bane's arm heavy against my back, the cabin grew quiet. We were inside a bubble of our own making—one that protected us from what lay beyond those walls. As long as we did not move, as long as we kept to the silence and the soothing hum of our limbs tangled together, then nothing would dissolve that bubble.

I had wanted him, it seemed, always. Just then, I had him. My hips still ached. My womb was full and swollen and deliciously used. Bane had cornered and caught every available sensation I tried to hold back; he'd shaken loose the hold I had on my own control. Letting him know my thoughts, the raw emotions, had not been my plan, and still he took them, wrangled them loose until he caught sense of what I'd felt wrapped around his body.

We weren't sleeping. Breaths too labored, too cautious came and went as I rested on top of him, his palm firm and steady on my lower back. For a moment I thought pretending would suffice. Not speaking, not breathing too quickly might make Bane believe I'd drifted off, that our time in the cabin could be prolonged.

I didn't want the spell to weaken. I didn't want the bubble to burst.

"All things end, Jani."

He curled that large arm tighter around my waist, a possessive, comforting movement that I wanted to resent. I couldn't. It felt too good.

"Stop reading my mind." My body still hummed, was still stretched and languid. I wanted the moment, to live inside it, keep it between my fingers.

"Not your mind," he said. "Emotions." Bane moved his fingers up my back, brushing the ends of my hair between his knuckles. "I can't read your mind."

"I disagree." When Bane looked down, eyebrows pinched together, I smiled. "Anyone that touches me like the way you did has to be a mind reader." The crystal glint in his eyes and the brilliant blue flecks danced in the firelight.

"Emotion, little witch. It's the best compass." He sighed, kissing my shoulder.

We'd leave soon and the thought wrenched my insides, coiled knots in the center, making a dull ache spread into my chest. To be, just there, comfortable, as though it was usual for Bane to hold me, as though it wasn't some disruption of our reality, was a kind of bliss I'd only daydreamed about. And so, apparently, did he—or thought he had.

The quiet room, the warm, sweet scent of our bodies all stirred something elemental, something that could match the lines' power. Something that could level its reach.

*I'll always want you.* He'd sworn that ten years ago. It'd been a vow I imagined he'd forgotten and laying there, thinking of that day, I wondered if some part of him remembered making that promise.

Whatever Bane thought, whatever he remembered about the past got cast aside by the slow movement of his fingers over my skin, by the long, liquid feel of his tongue against my shoulder, down the slope of my breasts when he kissed me there.

"You taste like jasmine," he said, moving over me, mouth open against my hip, hand gripping, fingers sliding inside me.

Bane tasted me again, his body strong over me, his slow, soft words reminding me that he wove spells with a touch, that he could shift the tides with a kiss timed perfectly. And when he lifted me, settled me over his lap again, urged me on top of him to take and take and take, that sweet, quiet fragile bubble protecting us expanded. We clamored for taste and touch, swimming in sensation—Bane sitting up, guiding me, my fingers tugging on the wavy strands of his hair, him thick and large, pulsing and deep inside me until I could only cry out. Then Bane atop me, arms shaking as he stared down, his body massive, his breath heavy, was all the sensation that mattered in the world.

But time spun quickly; it sped us toward an end we knew we couldn't avoid. No matter how long we stayed there—Bane still inside me, me clinging to his shoulders—reality would come knocking, insisting, reminding us that our obligations had already been set.

Still he held me like I was precious, like just moving away from me meant a goodbye he didn't want to speak, and I could only inhale, etch the smell and feel of him right in that moment to the sharper points in my memory. "We could run away," I said, knowing that would never be an option.

"Where would we run?" Bane would play a while, humor me while we fantasized.

"The beach. Some place remote." I smiled against his chest when he pulled me close. "Some place where I can walk around naked, roll around in the sand with nothing on."

"Wouldn't mind that." He moved his fingers down to cup my ass. "You with white sand dusting all over your plump nipples." He demonstrated, holding my breasts in his hand, testing the weight. "I could invent other things...things I've imagined for years."

"Like what?" I asked, sliding up his body.

Bane pulled on my waist, gliding his hands up my ribs. "You on my mouth, wrapped around me, holding me, gripping me... Gods, Jani, do you know how you looked to me back then?" When I shook my head, Bane got a little lost in the memory. That small unfocused stare of his shifted, and his voice took on something akin to wonder. "You nodding off in class, you staring at me like you were both scared and turned on and utterly at a loss how to deal with any of that? All of those months came to a head in that classroom when you kissed me." He snapped his fingers. "One minute I'm thinking about what you'd taste like, the next there you are, answering a call I didn't make and I'd never felt anything like it. I'd never wanted something so much and then wanted it even more after I'd had it. I want it again, Jani. Fuck, how I want it again."

"Bane..."

"No, don't make excuses. I know what's in your head." He followed when I shuffled to my feet, reaching for me as I disengaged. "Why is it you? Why is it always you, Jani? What is it about you that keeps me wanting you?"

"I don't...it doesn't matter." My shirt caught on my elbow when I lifted it over my head and Bane held me still, trapping me against the wall when I refused to look at him. "Your coven...they won't care about anything between us. Your uncle..."

He silenced me then, large hands covering my face, his forehead against mine. "I don't care what they want."

He smelled so good, his skin was so hot, all that delicious sensation distracted me, tempted me not to walk away. "Bane, I'm not going to let you sacrifice the future of your coven, of the Cove, for me."

"Why?" he said, looking down at me with one hand pressed against the wall. "I didn't ask for this. None of it. I never wanted for any of this to be my responsibility."

"It doesn't matter if you wanted it or not. It's here. You can't walk away." I hated the truth of the moment, how he closed his eyes, how he looked so eager to ignore the reality of our lives. The Elam was still missing. The Cove was still threatened, and Bane and I had spent the better part of the night forgetting about our mission. It wasn't fair, but then what the hell is?

"I would," he said, voice still soft. "I'd walk away in a second if I could have you."

"You can't..."

The quick rap of knuckles on the door interrupted me, and I frowned when Bane walked away. He moved his head toward the handle, then worked his jaw again, his shoulders falling.

"It's my uncle," he told me, nodding for me to finish dressing.

"Wonderful." The bubble disintegrated in my hurry to shimmy into my jeans and the disappearance of all of Bane's lovely inked skin when he covered it with his shirt.

"He isn't alone." Bane tilted his head, seeming to pick up another signature on the other side of the rattling door.

"What?" But I didn't need to ask who Mr. Grant had with him. I'd know that energy anywhere and grunted as Bane swung open the door, my shoulders falling when his uncle and my father walked inside.

"Nice sleep over?" Mr. Grant asked, moving his gaze around the room as though he looked for some evidence of our activities.

"Is there a problem?" Bane said, fastening his belt as his uncle and Papa walked further into the tiny cabin.

"Change in plans," my father said, casting a side-long glance at how close Bane stood next to me. I hadn't even picked up on it but didn't let my father's judgmental look make me self-conscious.

"Beckerman is calling in higher ranks. He caught wind of Cari's attack." Grant spoke to Bane, barely glancing my way when I folded my arms to combat the chill in the air. The wizard managed one long, slow look over at me before he returned his attention to Bane. "We need you in the Cove to help distract the mortals before the state troopers and feds are called in."

"Papa, can't you—"

"No, *mon petit*. I'm over my head with this one," my father said, interrupting me. "Ivy wants answers and is beginning to resist the compulsion charms. We can't manage to convince him that things aren't as they seem. Whoever stole the Elam is leveling up." Papa paused, squinting as he watched the way Bane moved his hand to my lower back. "Someone set Batty's bar on fire last night and it spread through the town. They're targeting our family, Jani, and the Grant's."

That hand on my back smoothed over my exposed skin and I swear I there was the smallest buzz of energy moving from Bane's fingertips, but then Mr. Grant spoke, giving Bane a look that seemed baiting, possibly a bit judgmental, and he crossed his arms, taking that small warmth from me.

"You're to come with me and help with the mortals," Grant said, slapping Bane on the shoulder. "Lundi will go with Jani toward the Elam on the trail."

How did this happen? Two minutes before he was inside me. Three minutes before that we were in our own world free from obligation and responsibility and the people who loved to control us. We had spent the night forgetting, just for a little while, about who we were and what we wanted. It was a small reprieve from the expectations that clouded our lives, not something to repeat, but as Bane dressed and we busied ourselves with preparing to leave, and his stare lingered on me, the trace of heat that always followed it warmed the longer he watched me.

"Your fiancée is worried about you," Grant said, and I caught Bane's low grunt as they moved toward the door. "And she is still recovering from her injuries, though you haven't asked as to her well-being." Then Bane stopped to look at me and there was something in that expression that told me goodbye was the last thing on his mind. It lasted only a second, but it seemed significant, something I'd store away like all my frayed memories.

Behind the closing door, Bane and Grant's voices trailed off into the distance as Papa and I prepared to leave. "What were you thinking?" my father asked me.

For a few seconds, my gaze unfocused at that closed door, another small reprieve I wanted to keep before reality crashed back on my shoulders. "Don't start with the interrogations. It's not the time."

When I shuffled my bag over my shoulder and headed toward the exit, my father stopped me, grabbing my arm. "Does he know?"

"What?"

The pressure on my arm wasn't tight, but was constrictive as Papa stared down at me. "By the Gods, Janiver, you didn't tell him, did you? About the block? Did you remove it?"

He thought I was careless. My father thought I was selfish and irresponsible, and that little stunt at eighteen had haunted me for ten years. Removing the block would have been a mistake, no matter how badly I wanted to do it. But it wouldn't remove the danger from the situation. It wouldn't restore the Elam and it would only make Bane hate me sooner. That was coming, but I wouldn't hurry it along. "Don't be stupid. Of course I didn't."

Something in my father's gaze eased the tension in my chest. Papa would never understand wanting to let the old ways go. He'd never understand that we still had to hide from the mortals. But even I knew what was at stake. We were all in danger, and I saw that emotion shifting my father's expression, making that hard frown dim.

Sometimes we see outside of ourselves. Sometimes there are moments so profound that it's like we're watching them from another vantage point, from someone else's body. That's how the next few minutes played out to me.

There was no forethought to what happened next. There was no preparation.

Papa stood in front of me, blocking my view of the door. He stared down at me. The cabin itself was small, the area around it filling with the noises of the woods and the animals and insects that went on living and being without any commentary from us. And the lines, the taunting, loud lines that Bane had managed to block from me somewhat still sung low and sweet, teasing, taunting so that it became part of the environmental elements that kept my attention distracted.

"You are my daughter and I love you. It is wholly unfair what you've been forced into, but we are to remain loyal to the Cove, always. Especially now, and it simply isn't time for you to make confessions."

"Which is why I didn't open my mouth." Papa released me and I stepped back, ready to get on the trail and forget everything that had happened in this cabin. "I told you that."

"You know I would never..."

Our words kept us distracted from the rustle of feet outside of the cabin.

"Papa, leave it." I glared at him, closing my eyes before the practiced monologue came out. It's the same one I gave him time and again over the years.

Distracted from the creak of the door opening.

"I didn't tell Bane about spelling his memory ten years ago. I didn't tell him a damn thing about us melding."

Distracted from Bane walking through that door, and not prepared for that rough, heavy wave of anger that shot across the cabin and landed straight in the center of my chest.

"What did you say?" Bane's question came out like the crack of a whip—disbelieving, mimicking the anger and pain that brightened his face as he stood in front of me.

"Listen, Iles..." Papa started, but Bane shook his head, silencing my father immediately. One nod toward the door and Bane dismissed him —a silent demand that he leave us alone. Papa was honor bound. We all were. He'd protect me, but he'd obey Bane for who he'd become. But he wouldn't let anyone hurt me.

"I will not have you harm my daughter."

Bane blinked, seeming astounded that Papa wouldn't cave to him.

"Papa, it's okay." When I shook my head, my father finally stepped back, watching the wizard as he stared at me, seeing, like me, that quiet fury reddening his skin.

It took several moments for my father to leave the cabin, a few more for me to work up the nerve to turn and face Bane, and when I did, his raw fury threatened to topple me.

"We melded?" His voice was calm. Too calm, and that rush of energy from his body rose, threatening to slam into me as I stepped back. "And you blocked my memory of it?" When I didn't answer, Bane took a step, one slow tap of his boot along the floor before he pinned me against the wall with his large hands on either side of my face. "The truth. Now."

"We don't have time for this."

My distraction didn't work. Nothing would. Bane had been lied to. Bane had been betrayed. It had been necessary, but the look in his eyes, that wide astonishment, the disgust I saw there hurt worse than walking away from him had.

"We claimed each other," he said, his voice small and bullet hard. Next to my head, Bane curled one hand into a fist and the small pulse of energy from it crackled against the wall. "All this time it was us."

"I didn't have a choice, Bane. It's not how things should have played out."

He didn't buy it, not if that frown meant anything. Bane shook his head as he watched me, but his eyes had gone dull, dispassionate. "You let them convince you to change my memories? You'd do that? To me?"

"It was for the good of the Cove."

He slammed his fist against the wall and small bits of wood splintered into my hair. "Bullshit, Jani. That's...that's bullshit."

I wished I could erase that expression from his face. I wished I could have seeped into his mind and laid another block, layered something sweet, something real over the truth. But I couldn't. Even if I had the power, Bane would have never let me inside his head. Not anymore.

"Show me," he said, his expression severe. "Show me now."

"I...can't...the block..."

"To hell with the block." He grabbed my hand, digging his fingers into my palm, ignoring the yelp of pain I released as he stripped the mental block away. My head pounded, my vision clouded as though I'd been momentarily blinded. Weight and agony converged into my mind as he pushed apart the barrier with no finesse, no ease at all, and then I slumped against the wall, crying out, my neck and head splitting from the pain. Bane frowned, his anger and guilt glinting in his eyes like tears.

Now there was no barrier between me and the lines. There was no hindrance protecting me from its raw power.

Now I could show Bane everything.

"Show me," he said again, dropping my hand, his lips shaking like he was on the verge of screaming or crying and could not decide which he preferred.

My hands shook when I reached for him, but I inhaled, praying for strength I wasn't sure I had before I touched Bane's temples, retracing that day, shifting through his mind to find the old block I'd planted ten years before. It was locked behind decades of runes and incantations. There were wards and protections I skirted, lyric and spells I'd never heard of, and disregarded in my effort to find the complicated knot of hidden memory I fastened deep in his subconscious. Bane shuddered, releasing a low moan when I found it and tugged at the gossamer strands to fracture it apart.

And then, like dominoes falling, the memory unfolded.

*He kissed me, taking and taking until I could not breathe. It was an overwhelming, unbelievable moment and I prayed for the endlessness, for the seconds to twist and stretch and never stop. Bane was large and beautiful and tasted like something that would fill me completely. I was greedy for each touch, each taste, and my heart became something that sped and pumped like I had just run a race and needed the extra blood flow.*

*"Jani," he said again, eager to have me backed up to the wall with his mouth nibbling against my neck. "Jani. Damn, what you do to me."*

*"Please...please don't stop..." And he didn't and that thick, warm tongue drew circles into my skin, his hands gripping and pulling, and for once I was needed, wanted more than I could have ever imagined.*

*"Touch me," he said, moaning, happy when I obliged.*

*And I did, just then, my nails down his neck, over his chest, my teeth skimming across the wide contours of his chest. He seemed to really like my fingertips against his hard nipples and my lips and tongue wetting down the center of his throat. There was a heat, some sort of spell cast between our bodies, a hum that mirrored the heartbeat of the earth, the faint, but constant purr of the ley lines pulsing through the Cove. That's what zipped around the room, the sensation foreign to anyone mortal. Bane tilted me back, his large, strong hands holding me, my head as he smoothed his mouth and nose down my neck, in the valley of my breasts and my hips moved, grinding against him, making our centers touch. Just then I felt it, him, long and hard and gloriously hot through my thin shorts.*

*We had let ourselves go on too far. There was too much touching, too many months of pent up attraction that we could not see the light flickering through our limbs or hear the slow thump of each other's hearts beating beneath our skin. Bane's low, hurried groan of pleasure, my eager, needy moans grew louder, stronger until that great whip of electricity between us moved hard and easy through our touching bodies.*

*"Shit," he said, stilling completely when I slowed my hips so that my center rode his straining cock. "I...shit, Jani..."*

*And just then, I knew Bane would stop me. He wouldn't let me have the only thing I wanted before I left Crimson Cove. He'd let me have a taste, but only a brief one.*

*"It's okay," I told him, already stuffing down my disappointment. "It's fine."*

*But as I tried to disengage from him and step away to retrieve my bag, Bane pulled me against his chest with his large arm hooked around my waist. "It's not fucking fine," he said, burying his nose in my hair. "It's not fine that I have to sell myself to some girl I don't know because your coven is..."*

*"Poor?"*

*He held me tighter, surer, as though his touch would erase reality from the moment. He wouldn't marry for love. He'd marry for power, and my coven was small, too young to have any real clout. There was no way I would ever be suited for Bane.*

*But that didn't make me want him any less, and it didn't stop him from spreading his fingers over my stomach, along my hips. "Right now I don't really care about anything but the way you feel against me."*

*I leaned back, resting my head on his shoulder as I scrubbed my fingers through his hair. "Gods, neither do I."*

*That growl did something to me, had my body clenching and pulsing, and I couldn't help but arch against him, kissing him again, desperate, eager and then, it happened again.*

*That quick, smooth light, the flow of magic from the lines, the red pulse of energy, our skin firing sharp, bright, and I shuddered. Suddenly I was being opened up completely, and in a blur of heat and energy, my nexus unfastened, colliding like a hammer with Bane's, and he and I both laughed joyously from the thrill of it, from the notion that this had been waiting for us for years. This had been what we were meant to do, to be, from the beginning.*

*"I claim you," he said, but it wasn't his voice. It sounded foreign, unreal.*

*"And I claim you," I mimicked, not sure why I sounded so sure, so ethereal.*

*And then, with Bane holding me tight, with our nexuses melding together, merging, in the red glow of togetherness, the door flew open and I was being dragged away, torn from his arms, the sensation of Bane's energy, his warmth slipping further and further away from me.*

*"No! Don't take her!"*

*"No, son. Don't fight me." Carter Grant held Bane back as my father kept a tight arm around my waist. "Lundi, I told you this would happen. You promised. That was the only reason I let him stay in this damn class. You said you could control her pull."*

*"And I will, damn it, Carter. I will." Then my father was holding me, brushing his fingers over my temple, soothing. "Take the memory, Janiver, mon petit bebe. Take it from him so he will not suffer."*

*Bane's face was a mixture of shock and despair, and his uncle whispered continuously in his ear, words that sounded old, foreign. It had to be the only thing keeping Bane steady. "It's for the best, Janiver," Carter told me. But his smile was really a sneer, and the way he looked at me, looked through me, made my stomach twist.*

*"Janiver, please, mon pet. For the good of the Cove. Take his memories." My*

*father pulled me close, pressed his mouth against my ear so only I could hear him speak. "Stay with him and your life will not be your own."*

The door crashed open and Bane jerked back, my chest on fire as I blinked, my face wet and hot with tears.

"Bane! You must come now, son," Grant said, his face twisted up in a severe frown. He glared at me as he grabbed Bane's collar. "We've discovered the creature. We must go. Now."

"Who?" I said, wiping my face dry, but Grant ignored me, pulling Bane away from me toward the door.

"Bane." I tried moving after him, but stopped when Papa entered the cabin, holding me back as the wizard paused in the door, his head shaking.

"Finish the job, Miss Benoit," Bane told me, not looking directly at me. "The sooner you find the Elam, the soon you can leave. That's what you're best at."

I had another outside-of-myself moment. I floated above us, looking down as Bane glared, as his gaze finally moved around my features as though he would never see them again. I watched him, watched myself and could nearly make out the thick weight of tension that flitted between us. The heat, the anger, the rage all mixed and pulsed together with the lingering scent of sex and the memory of what we'd done in that room just a short time before. It was an intoxicating brew that made my head feel weighted and my heart heavy. When Bane stepped back, taking his gaze from my features and his warmth from the room, I came back to myself and jumped into that crumbling body as it fell to the floor.

My insides twisted and despite my anger at him, I let my father hold me. "My girl," he said, patting my back. "He is hurting, no doubt, and will hurt still more." I shook my head, looking at Papa's face, head turned as I tried to catch his meaning. He wiped my wet cheeks with his handkerchief, releasing a long exhale. "It is Malak. He has been turned. Ethan is dead at his hand and he's responsible for the other deaths as well."

# EIGHTEEN

"BREATHE, *MON PETITE*. YOU NEED ONLY TO BREATHE."

"How can I? What he did...Malak..."

My father's hands were soft, his fingers kneading on my shoulders, kind, and the touch made my limbs tense and my stomach tighten. "Stop...just please, don't touch me."

Blame needed to be assigned. I needed to find a villain that hadn't been sweet, kind to me when he was a boy running after his cousin, flattering me with obvious grins and wide-eyed stares.

Malak killed Wyatt.

He was a monster.

He decimated Freya.

My...sweet Freya.

"Please, Jani..."

Papa's voice went soft, the tone placating and light. There were the marks of an incantation in the cadence I recognized and when I jerked away from him, stepping back as we moved further away from the cabin, he held up his hands, eyes round and shocked.

"I wasn't trying to..."

"You were. Hera save you, Papa...you damn well were."

He didn't bother defending himself as I walked away, marching along the trail, pushing back my shock and the rage that boiled inside me at the news that Malak had been turned. That he had destroyed so many lives with his deception.

There would be time for vengeance and anger, but it wasn't now.

Now I had to find the Elam.

It began with a melody.

It was like a song I only half remembered. So clear, so haunting, and all I needed was to float toward it, feel it, touch it, hold that power in the palm of my hands. If I'd only reach the Elam, secure it, then I could be rid of the guilt flooding my mind. Restoring the Cove to the way things were before I came here would make things right. Bane would have his place in the coven leadership and my family would no longer have to struggle against the effect of the lies and damage Ronan had caused.

So I followed the simple, sweet song that called me forward as Papa and I left the cabin and the night behind us as it led me to the Elam.

"Something is off here, Jani, can't you feel it?"

"No," I told my father, too distracted by the song, by the pull of that energy as we climbed into the deepest part of the wood. "No, I don't feel anything but the Elam."

Distantly, I knew he was right. There was something off, something that did not fit together as it should. The air was too thin up there on the hill. The maples around us were too still. But I could no more give attention to the things that were not right than I could ignore that song pulling me close.

"Perhaps we should call…" Whatever my father's suggestion would be died quickly, silenced by the loud rattle of an explosion and billowing smoke that arose from the town. We couldn't see anything but the smoke rising, despite Papa dragging me near the ridge to look down into the valley toward the groves. There was nothing but the empty woods and the rustle of branches within them. "Fire?" he asked, already moving down the trail.

"Dunno. Probably." My skin was dry, itching as though the Elam knew we were walking away from it and protested by thinning the air even further. "Papa, we're close."

"*Wi,*" he said, but didn't look at me, keeping his attention on the empty ridge and the sirens that began to sound. "Probably just..."

"Go check it if you want. You can get a signal from the cabin. It's not that far away."

"And leave you on your own?"

"What's going to hurt me out here? I'm protected by the lines and anyone who wants me needs me so there's nothing to worry over. You said Malak was sent to kill me. He's in custody. He's no threat to me now. Besides, I can take care of myself. Go." I nodded toward the trail, knowing it wouldn't take much for my father to quell his curiosity. "I'll be fine."

Papa looked at me for a long time then. It reminded me of the day I arrived home after our mother died. He'd taken me on the trail because I was his daughter. He'd leave because he knew I could handle myself. Still, the frown he gave me was too stiff; the low lidded cast of his eyes was too apologetic. I'd never seen my father looking so ashamed.

"What?" I asked him, eager to put some distance behind me.

"Perhaps..." Papa stopped, glancing once more down the trail as he ran his fingers through his hair. "If the higher covens are in need...but I should not leave you..."

"They come first, Papa... This is your way." I waved him off, already walking away when he called after me.

"*Mon petit...*" But what Papa wanted to say, I never found out. Yet another explosion sounded behind him and he lowered his shoulders, nodding once before he ran down the trail toward the cabin. "I'll return," he said over his shoulder, but I knew he wouldn't. At least, I knew I wouldn't wait for him.

I was close to the Elam, and the further into the woods I walked, the louder that sweet song sounded.

The wood broke up then, just a few feet further and the pulse of the Elam grew even stronger. It was like pure energy, something that tinkled against my skin and made my flesh pimple. Sound went numb, and I could only make out the low hum around me as I walked close toward a small outcropping of trees circling a bare patch of grass, and there, lying in the center, all alone on the ground, was the Elam.

It pulsed and hummed the closer I walked toward it, singing sweetly, like a lover I'd forgotten I'd had and wanted again. I wanted to touch it, take it, keep it with me always. The stone was a brilliant turquoise shaped like a strong, fine tortoise, and it would fit perfect in the center of my hand. I just knew it would be smooth to the touch, warm as I held my open hand over the top of it. It was mine. Somehow, merely looking at it told me as such. All I had to do was pick it up, grip it once, and claim it. No one else would dare touch it once it was mine. Stretching my fingers towards it, I noticed the fine, small hairs on my arm standing up and a small brush of chill peppering around my wrist. Nearly there, nearly mine.

But, like most things I wanted, it was out of my reach. Suddenly I was on the ground with some smelly, heavy weight pinning my hands at my side. "Don't you damn well touch that thing."

* * *

"Damn, woman, don't you recognize a thrall when you see it?"

Until Hamill said it, I actually hadn't known the thrall for what it was. Feeling stupid, I stepped out of his grip, moving back into the wooded area of the forest and away from the Elam on the ground.

"That obvious and I missed it."

"It happens," Hamill said, leaning against a tree, winded. Almost perversely, he pulled a crumpled pack from his pocket and withdrew a cigarette; his long fingers were narrow and smudged at the tips, stained with tobacco. "You can't know what it is when it happens. Not always." He lit his cigarette, taking a long drag as he watched me. "Why'd you take off?"

"You threatened me." When he didn't react to my accusation, I kept explaining. "I might miss when something is enthralled, but I don't miss when someone hates me and my family and wants to do us harm." Feeling a little calmer, somewhat more relaxed, I stood in front of Hamill. "I wasn't going to stick around and wait for you to attack."

Hamill was cool then, smooth, taking his time with his cigarette, inhaling deep and releasing his smoke through his nose as though he needed a second to figure me out. "Don't recall threatening you."

"You said…"

"What I said was, 'If I could, I'd rip you all to pieces.' There's a difference to what I think should happen and what I'd actually do."

"Why?" Hamill didn't stop smoking, didn't even pause as I stepped closer. "What did we ever do to you?"

He took a second to spit on the ground next to my foot and when he spoke, his words were weighted, as though he hadn't gotten rid of all the phlegm in his throat. "Your father is responsible for my cousin being in jail." Hamill flicked his spent cigarette on the ground, stomping on it as he walked toward me. "Ronnie's a good shifter, just ran with the wrong crowd, and when he got pissed drunk and passed out at a fire—stuck in his wolf form—and then woke up to the cops asking questions, well, your father couldn't get him out of it. That's what he's supposed to do, isn't it? Get us out of tight spots?"

It was an assumption everyone made. My father's business was smoothing over messy situations to keep the mortals ignorant. It wasn't his job to cover up for idiots who couldn't control themselves. "No, Hamill, that's not what he does, and if your cousin was too stupid to keep away from mortals when he shifts or when he drinks, then he deserves to be in jail."

"Say that again, woman," Hamill said, darting toward me. There was a wicked shake to his hand and a small, wild glint in his eyes. "I fucking dare you."

"Calm yourself," I started, stretching my fingers in case Hamill came any closer, but before anything could happen, the shifter stiffened, then slumped to the ground at my feet with Joe Arvel standing over him, the butt of a revolver in his hand.

"Got tired of waiting."

It was a shock to see him, out there with no one around, away from the search parties, away from anyone I trusted. The thought lingered then, a little distant, that I should keep my edge, worry how and why Joe had just knocked Hamill to the ground. Maybe if the Elam's song hadn't sounded so sweet, kept me calm, my awareness would have been sharper. Still, I thought fleetingly that it was good to see Joe, he had a kind face, but I felt a strange shiver of alarm when I spotted the smudges and tears on his clothes and the soot and ash covering his knuckles.

"Joe?" I asked, nodding to his hands. "What happened?"

"Fire. Big one." He walked toward me, stepping over Hamill's inert body. I kept my attention on the gun in his hand. "Had to get your father away from you. Knew he wouldn't stay here if he thought more of the Cove was going up in flames."

"Why..." I walked backward, careful to keep enough distance between us that I'd be able to twist a hex at him if I needed to. "Why did you want Papa gone?"

The shifter looked genuinely surprised, tilting his head as though he needed a second to make certain I wasn't teasing him. "I needed you."

"Me? Whatever for?"

"To destroy the Elam."

He didn't wait for me to run off. Joe, in fact, seemed very determined to get on with the task at hand and, despite my fidgeting away from him, was still able to pull me out of the woods to sit near the Elam pulsing on the ground.

"You'll want explanations, I suppose." He sat across from me, leaning his arms on his knees. "That's alright. I'd want them too."

Around us the morning was dying but there was no activity from the animals or birds—not even insects—in this part of the forest. It gave the clearing an eerie, disturbed vibe that unsettled me more that I wanted to admit. "You did this? The spelling? The storm last night?" I waved my hand around the still sky and shook my head when Joe's smile stretched wide. "You stole the Elam?" He nodded. "You knocked Bane out?"

"Took help, but yeah. I did that." He moved closer and I hated the proud little glint that made his smile widen. "He's not so big and powerful if you've got the right hex."

"But you're a shifter."

A small shrug and Joe waved off my assessment. "Shifter part comes from my mother. The wizard bit comes from my father, though you'd never know it." At the mention of his father, that smile went cold and there was a curl on his top lip that made him look angry, bitter. "I look nothing like the Grants, do I?"

"You're a Grant?"

"The bastard son of Carter Grant." He picked at the sparse tufts of grass at his feet, then threw the small sprigs absent-mindedly on the ground. The curl of his lip exaggerated. "Rightful heir to the Grant coven."

"Bane's cousin."

Joe's nod was dismissive and he looked away from me, glancing only once at the Elam with something akin to longing in his eyes. That's how he'd done it, I realized. His own blood, but blood without skill was weak at best. He'd have needed Bane's blood to strengthen the hex and take the Elam.

"Mom was a poor, stupid shifter traveling through the Cove to her folk in Mississippi. One too many beers at Batty's and Grant convinced her to stay the weekend." He jerked his attention back to me and I could hear the resentment, the cool anger in his tone. "Guess he wasn't expecting me. None of them were, and they damn sure had no problem sweeping me under the rug when she died two years later. Your father really is very good at his job, isn't he?"

It made sense to me. My father was traditional to the core. Of course he'd do Grant's bidding, no matter if he could stomach what that job was personally. It was an old argument we'd never been able to settle. What's right verses what's necessary. Still, Joe mentioned my father with the same bitterness in his tone that he'd used speaking about Grant, and I hoped that his anger for both of them wasn't the same. They were very different men. "So this is revenge? All of this? To get back at Grant and my father?"

"This is beyond revenge, Jani." Joe's eyes were a little too wide and bloodshot. It gave him a frantic, desperate look. "You should know that. I need you."

"Me?"

"Who else would side with me, help me destroy the Cove, destroy the secret, but the only girl to escape the Grants?" Joe took to pacing then, walking around the Elam, behind me as he spoke like he couldn't keep himself still. "The only witch to walk away despite what they did to you."

"What did they do to me, Joe? My family..." I scrambled to my feet when he darted toward me, holding up my hands to keep him back. "They've done nothing wrong."

"No? Your father, my father, they didn't conceal the fact that you and Bane were meant to meld? They didn't try to keep you apart just to ensure the lines are strengthened?" When I said nothing, Joe shook his head, likely understanding that I had no idea what he was talking about. "Your own father didn't keep shifting your memories, shifting Bane's so you wouldn't remember all the times as kids you almost melded?"

"You have no idea what you're talking about."

"No? That's not what Ronan said. That's not what your twin told him."

"Ronan?"

I was stupid, pathetic, and got the impression Joe thought the same when he looked at me like that. Pity. It was written all over his face. "I needed an in, Jani. I needed someone who would help get you back here. Sabotaging the jobs your father did was easy enough. I needed you here because I knew no one else would help me. Well, until Sam, that is."

My head went woolen and clouded then. This, all of this, was like something out of a bad super villain comic. My twin? My brother? My own father stealthily sabotaging my life so that they could conceal the truth? My father in concert with Carter Grant didn't surprise me. Him working his hexes to conceal what the lines wanted for me and Bane was a theory that had bounced around in my head for years. The possibility that it could be true hurt like a bitch. But Mai and Sam knowing about it and remaining silent? That was too much to accept.

Joe continued to watch me and that same pitying frown exaggerated the longer he stared at me. I was sick. "Sam?"

"Big brother caught on early. Figured out what Ronan was doing, that he was helping me. Of course, he had no idea what my end game was. He thought I was interested in getting a little revenge on the Grants.

Thought I just wanted to come out to the Cove and take Bane's place." Joe looked around the wood, the stretch of acreage and territory that technically was his and I was *almost* sorry for him. "I do that, then Bane would be free to be with you. And after all your poor brother has gone through, who could blame him for wanting his little sister to be happy?"

Sam had undergone the most horrible tragedy. Losing his wife, his unborn child... I couldn't image what that pain was like, but would all that heartache make him betray the Cove? Everything we fought to protect? "I...I don't believe you."

"Why in the hell would I lie? There is no reason for me to lie, Jani. I want the Elam destroyed, but my magic isn't strong enough to contain it."

"But my father said you turned Malak. You had him do your bidding. You had him kill Freya and Wyatt."

"No!" Joe's voice carried over the roar of the Elam, his face turning pink. "That's not what I meant to happen. I wanted that idiot to find you, to take you. But something went...badly wrong when I turned him. It was...too much for him. He caught your scent and he attacked. Fool couldn't even tell witch from wizard when he transformed into the creature." Joe shook his head, his coloring draining. "I didn't mean... Freya was a mistake and Wyatt...was unavoidable. He already had your scent but couldn't discern between male and female prey. He wasn't supposed to kill. Not you. Not...Freya...and I didn't want that. It was on Malak, not me."

"But you turned him and left him to do your bidding. That *is* your fault!"

He stood closer, looking down at my hands as though he itched to touch my fingers. "He'll pay for what he did. And they'll all pay when you destroy the Elam." Again he looked at my fingers, biting his lip. "It wants you. Can't you hear it?" Joe stood behind me then and I stiffened my spine, uneasy with him so close. "Grant blood created it. Grant blood is attracted to you. It's calling you. It's gotta be you." Joe moved my hair off my shoulder and rested his hands on my neck. I could hear the Elam singing to me. Its call was overwhelming. "You help me destroy it and you can leave the Cove. Walk away like you always wanted, and Bane will be free to go with you once I take over the coven. Everyone gets what they want."

"My family..."

"Your family what?" he said, jerking me around to look up at him. "Your family who lied to you? Your family who changed your memories, kept you from what you wanted? Abandoned you? Help me, Jani, and you'll be free from them. All of them."

Joe wasn't wrong. Circe and Hera, if what he claimed was true, then everyone knew about what had been done to keep me and Bane apart. My parents had known and my father had made certain I stayed away from Bane. My brother, even my twin, had kept me in the dark likely because they thought it was for my own good. Looking at Joe, I understood his anger. He'd been betrayed, too. He'd been abandoned by his blood. We weren't that different when it came right down to it.

There must have been some resignation in my features, something that made Joe pick up on my hesitation because he came closer and let his voice lower, soften. "Your father cared more about the bloodlines and the Cove than his own daughter's happiness. Mine wouldn't even acknowledge me. They both need to pay, Jani. They both deserve a little vengeance."

There was too much sensation, too much happening too quickly for me to concentrate. The Elam hummed louder and it filled my head, clouded it from the smell of the woods, the honeysuckle... Sirens continued to wail and cry in the Cove below.

"All the lies, Jani. We can bury them in the past or bring them forward. The mortals would know about us. We'd be free to be who we are, whenever we want. No more hiding, no more lies, and your father and mine would be held accountable for all the things they tried to keep hidden."

Joe stood too close, becoming part of the crowding noise in my head that made it impossible to focus on anything for very long, but he was too impatient, too eager to have me agree to his manic, mad plan. When I didn't respond, when I kept my face covered in my hands as that noise grew louder and louder, the shifter lost his patience.

"Fine then, if you won't help me, then I'll have to persuade you." There was a rustle from the woods and one of the trackers I'd seen following us appeared, dragging a gagged but still struggling Mai behind him.

"Son of a bitch." As soon as I moved towards my sister, the burly tracker shook his head, sliding a knife from his belt to hold it against her throat.

Behind him came three more equally brutish minions. They congregated behind Joe and watched me, looking like they could easily thwart whatever hex I threw their way. Outmanned, but not outsmarted. Not just yet.

"Decision time, Jani." Joe stepped next to Mai, looking her over before he glanced back at me, and for a second his features returned to the sweet, charming man I'd met in Bane's kitchen. "I wasn't lying about how beautiful you two are. It really isn't fair."

Blinking once allowed me a second to take in a calm, focusing breath and catch another scent on the breeze, this one thicker than it had been just seconds before.

"No," I told Joe as I opened my eyes to look at him. "It's not fair at all, but then not much ever is."

"How do you mean?"

"You got left behind by Grant." I glanced at Mai, winking once and my twin grinned back at me. "I ended up in the middle of a plan that had nothing to do with me. Shit is unfair, but we adjust and we deal."

"I don't adjust." Joe grunted when I stepped toward the Elam.

"Maybe that's your problem. Conflict resolution, Joe. We all need a game plan when life throws a hurdle in our way."

"Oh? And what's yours?"

I stood, looping the leather cord the Elam was connected to between my fingers. "Back up, asshole."

# NINETEEN

IN FILMS, WHEN THE BIG BAD GETS A LITTLE TOO COCKY, THE HERO typically takes advantage. She uses their lapse of attention, the point when the villain thinks he's won, to draw her ace in the hole, to bring out the twist that shocks the bad guy and gives her the upper hand.

Joe wasn't Grendel and I wasn't Beowulf. He didn't look remotely like Mordred and I lacked the necessary *parts* to be King Arthur. But I did have something that the half-shifter, half-wizard was either too stupid or too unaware of to notice. Bane Iles could read me.

*"Decision time, Jani." Joe had said, getting a little too close to my sister for my liking.*

But my mind hadn't been on him or even her at the moment. It was otherwise entangled with Bane and the silent conversation he'd started with me just as Joe had produced Mai from the woods. The wizard was powerful, his concealment charm untraceable except for the small click of energy I felt whooshing around the wood. Joe wouldn't be able to detect it or the congregation surrounding us.

*We're here, Jani. I'd heard. We've got your back.*

That allowed me a moment of confidence, something that rarely happens, something that gave me the idea of distracting Joe while Bane and his crew circled us.

*"I wasn't lying about how beautiful you two are," Joe said, looking between me and my twin as Bane instructed his crew deeper into the woods, circling stealthily. "It really isn't fair."*

*"No. It's not fair at all, but then not much ever is."*

*Keep stalling. It's working.*

*"How do you mean?"*

I wouldn't think of the tone he used when he spoke to me. I didn't think of the hurt I'd caused him and how I could hear the hint of it even in my mind. Instead my focus went to Joe, to baiting him, distracting him so he would not notice my brother just a few feet behind him in the woods, or Trevor and Bane directly behind the tracker holding Mai.

*"You got left behind by Grant."* I glanced at Mai, winking once and my twin grinned back at me. *"I ended up in the middle of a plan that had nothing to do with me. Shit is unfair, but we adjust and we deal."*

*"I don't adjust."*

*When you're ready, tell him you're not alone. That's when we'll charge. Get Mai and get to the lines. We need you to get the Elam back to town before the feds arrive.*

*How the hell am I supposed to do that?* A quick glance over Joe's shoulder and I caught Bane's gaze. There was no warmth in that expression.

*Aren't you a witch? Ride the damn lines, Jani.*

*"Maybe that's your problem,"* I told Joe, avoiding the glare Bane gave me. *"Conflict resolution, Joe. We all need a game plan when life throws a hurdle in our way."*

*"Oh? And what's yours?"*

One glance at my twin and I knew she'd caught my hint. *Duck,* it said and *move quick.* We were twins. We knew each other better than we knew ourselves. It was all right there in a glance, and I knew it the second Mai's smile flirted on her lips.

*"Back up, asshole."*

One small grunt and Mai stepped back, twisting out of the tracker's grip just as Papa, Sam, Bane, and the rest of the covens emerged from the woods.

All was chaos, the wild rush of hexes and spells, bodies

transforming into animals—wolves and panthers, eagles and ravens all twisting from skin and bone to fur and feather—the small congregation of fighting building to a cacophony of violent sounds that gave me pause, had me stumbling as I dragged my twin away from the melee.

"What are we doing?" Mai screamed, dodging spell fire and leaping wolves as we ran from the fight.

"Getting to the lines and getting the Elam back to town."

But Mai stopped me, pulling out of my touch behind a large cropping of trees where Sam fought with a large tracker. His nose was bloody and there was a wide cut on his bottom lip, but my brother kept fighting.

"You can't ride the lines, Jani. They'll absorb you."

"We don't have a choice."

"You'll die!"

"I won't..."

"What's wrong?" Sam asked, rushing toward us as the fighting continued. "What do you need?"

"This crazy witch wants to ride the lines back to town."

Both my siblings stared at me, eyes wide, and I could feel the thick wave of fear coming from them. Around us the fighting continued and the Elam throbbed in my palm.

"It's the only way to stop the lines from flooding the town with magic. It's the only way to keep the mortals from knowing anything is wrong."

"They already know, Jani," Sam said, dodging a hex with a counter wave of his hand. "Beckerman has called in the feds and..."

"They aren't here yet. I can stop this."

"At what cost?" Sam shook his head and I could just make out the glassy flicker of his eyes in the mid-morning sunlight. "I never wanted any of this..."

"It doesn't matter what you wanted, Sammy. It's done. You helped Ronan..."

"You did what?" Mai asked, jerking on his arm so he had to look at her.

"Mai, it doesn't matter."

"I only wanted the truth to come out," he told Mai before glancing at me, "about you and Bane." He exchanged a glance with Mai and by her expression I knew for sure she'd kept the truth from me as well.

"It doesn't matter now." My siblings had done what they thought was best. They'd done what they could to shield me. None of that mattered anymore. Not when everything we'd fought so hard to protect was threatening to unravel. "Bane knows and he hates me for it."

"Oh, Jani..." Mai started, grabbing my hand, but I waved her off, not willing to let my emotions cloud my thoughts. That's not what I needed at the moment.

"This," I nodded toward the forest, in the direction of the lines just beyond the ridge, "is the only way to save the Cove. It's the only way to keep the mortals from finding out."

"Then I'll help you," Mai said, taking my hand.

"What? No!" Sam said, stepping between us.

But as she offered, I knew Mai was right. She could center me. She could be the peak of realization I needed so that the lines would not overtake me. She could tether me to who I was and how I wanted to remain.

When we stood, inching away from the fighting, Sam grabbed tight to my arm, twisting us both around. "I am damn well not going to lose both of my sisters for this fucking town."

"You won't, Samedi. We'll be fine." Mai kissed his cheek, taking my hand as we ran toward the line, letting the pulse and buzz of its song wash over us.

Behind us Sam called out a thousand warnings, then a thousand oaths when Joe sucker punched him in the jaw. One quick glance over my shoulder and I saw Sam tussling with Joe as he clamored toward us. Both men rolled around on the ground, arms flailing, fists flying, and then my brother went still.

"He's going to try to jump with us," Mai said, tightening her arm around my waist.

"Let the asshole try." Mai's skin was cool to the touch when I rested my palm against her wrist. In front of us the ley lines hummed like an electric fence and their energy signature glowed bright. We need only step into the streams that ran perpendicular to each other—one shooting toward town, the other moving toward the back of the ridge and into the groves.

"Beautiful," Mai said, resting her face against my shoulder. "So beautiful."

"Don't let it absorb you," I told my twin, pinching her hand when she hummed.

"Right. I've got you."

"You ready for this?" Mai nodded, gripping me tighter and we both stepped into the lines. But we weren't alone.

Just as the brilliant energy coated us like a second skin, Mai shouted, pulled back from me as Joe grabbed her arm.

# TWENTY

"Get off my sister!"

The tussle of strength was unbelievable. Joe shouldn't have had the power to battle me and Mai, not to mention the current that flowed from the lines, but he fought it, shooting hexes that looked dark, that the lines both absorbed and exaggerated the moment they left his fingertips.

"You idiot, you'll kill us all."

"Fine with me," he growled, shaking Mai like she weighed nothing. My sister kept reaching for me, but my fingers ached against the current vibrating from the Elam and the struggle it made to drop into the lines. "As long as that damn thing is destroyed in the process," he said, nodding toward the Elam.

Mai continued to struggle with Joe and it took all my focus to keep the Elam from bouncing out of my grip. All the time we were moving; around us, the forest slid past, a zip of trees and limbs and ground that became a big blur, the whiz of animals and rock all zooming past us as the line shot us forward on the surface of arcane energy. It was like walking on a half-erected stone bridge with pavers that slipped and tottered with each step you made.

"Nearly there, Mai," I shouted over my shoulder, glaring at Joe when he pulled my sister against his chest.

"You had better drop it before we reach the Cove." Joe slipped his arm around Mai's neck and she widened her eyes, immediately grabbing at his large arm to put her fingers between it and her neck.

"Stop it!"

"I'm not messing around, Janiver. Drop the fucking Elam or I will kill her."

"You wouldn't."

"Are you stupid?" He jerked Mai closer to emphasize his point. "You believed me when I said I didn't mean for Malak to kill Wyatt? Of course I did. That asshole overheard me talking to my trackers."

"Wyatt was a ..."

"Too damn nosy for his own good."

My throat closed up and magic ran like lava through in my limbs. "And Freya..."

Joe frowned, his features going tight. "Collateral damage. Wrong place. Wrong damn time."

When I moved forward, Joe tightened his grip on Mai and my sister winced. "Careful." He moved his gaze to my hands, to the glowing turquoise stone resting in my palm. "Now drop the Elam or I will choke the life out of your pretty twin."

Behind Joe the lines rippled and I knew someone else had hopped them, but my attention stayed on Mai's face, on the rounding of her eyes and the blue cast of her skin as Joe squeezed the breath from her.

"Please," I told him, making myself seem small, wishing he knew what this pain was, to have an impossible choice. "I can't choose between them."

"Then you will lose them both. Your sister and your town. Either way," Joe said dragging Mai closer as he stepped toward me, "the Elam will be destroyed."

It was so heavy in my hand. That beautiful stone, the small tortoise face blinking up at me, as though it could read me, see me, tell me how important I was, how pivotal it was that I restore it to its home. And then there was my twin, eyes wide, shining with fear as Joe choked her.

The choice should have been so simple. It should have been something I needn't give any thought to. My blood, my twin, she was what mattered most to me. But the Elam protected thousands. It kept us all safe. Millions more would be affected if it were destroyed. Life as we knew it, life as everyone knew it, could change. Disintegrate. Come to an end.

Who was I to make that choice?

"Save the Cove, Jani," Mai spit out, her voice hoarse, raspy, and I needed to only look at her expression, see that complete trust, that utter confidence in her eyes that she'd always shown me. I wouldn't lose that and I wouldn't let Joe take that from me.

"Fight like hell," I told my twin, grinning back at her before I jumped from the line and rolled right onto the ground just two blocks from the town center.

Mai would fight, I knew that. She was the scrappiest witch I knew. I heard the fight in her, that scream and shout of "you rotten bastard" she cried at Joe as I took off. I bypassed the quick looks I received from the mortals hovering around the silhouette of smoking structures that had once been Batty's and several other buildings but now looked like black, ashen skeletons.

A group of firemen glanced at me running away from the crowd, and a cop watched me as I dodged through traffic, but they all were overwhelmed by what they were already tasked with doing. I kept running, weaving around parked cars and numbed spectators, toward the gazebo in the town square, running along the small picket fence that secured the square and small courtyard.

"Hurry, Jani, he's right behind you!" I heard Mai shout and my breath came out easier as I jumped the picket fence, hoping the small crowd of mortals would pay more attention to the smoldering buildings than to me or Joe, whose heavy breathing I could hear behind me.

The gazebo came into view as I ran around two large cypress trees. Just feet from me and I'd be able to climb the trellis and refasten the Elam to the amulet that secured us. Grant blood would be handy just now, and it hit me that I would have to face Joe if I wanted to use his blood to secure the Elam back into place. I didn't need Bane's strength as Joe had. I had my own.

But I had not anticipated on his shifting, not with so many mortals around. Joe did, however, stripping off his shirt just as I stopped to face him in front of the gazebo, stepping back when all that expanse of olive skin transformed into inky black fur. Panther and massive. His square jaw smoothed out, elongated, and then recessed into powerful jaws, and the man's small capped teeth stretched and reformed into fine, deadly points that snapped at me the closer he came.

"Figures you'd be a giant pussy," I said, jumping when the panther growled and pounced toward me.

Behind me Mai was joined by Sam and Bane and a small crowd of curious mortals. To them, they'd see a wild animal, circling me. They couldn't make out the awareness in the creature's eyes or the calculating way he sized me up, like a villain anticipating his enemy's every move. Bane lifted his hand, shooting a concealment charm across the crowd and the mortals around us stood still, unmoving, frozen and unaware. I glanced over at my twin, at my brother, shaking my head when they both advanced.

*What are you doing?* Bane shouted inside my head, and I managed one quick jerk of my gaze at him before I smiled. *You watch my family's back.* And then I lifted my hands, throwing up a shield hex that would keep them back and leave Joe the panther and me to settle this without the intrusion of wizards.

He came fast and brutal, growling, snapping at me, and in the advance he caught the cord holding the Elam in his snapping mouth, twisting it around his tooth. Flinging his head back, Joe threw the Elam across the ground.

"No! I don't think so." I charged, toppling him as I jumped on his back with my arms around his neck. The big cat's growl and the rebuking sound vibrated against my hand as I gripped his throat. It sounded like the whip of lightning cracking across the sky.

"Jani! Please!" I heard Mai crying, but her words or Sam's cursing didn't do much to discourage me, and Bane pacing outside the perimeter of the shield only annoyed me.

"You cannot have it!" I shouted at the panther when he charged toward the Elam lying near the steps of the gazebo. My focus, my energy came quick and sharp with an effort borne of adrenaline and pure nerve, but still I hesitated, my fear holding me back.

*Open yourself completely,* Bane shouted in my head. *You can do this.*

*When I merely grunted, he added, Let me see the rest and I'll give you my strength. I want to see everything.*

*Fine,* I told him, closing my eyes to concentrate on the writhing cat in my grasp. *Just do it.*

Anger and fury filtered from Bane and landed straight into my chest. It fueled me. Centered me and left me even more raw and open to the lines. Stunned for a split second, Joe took advantage and threw me off his back. I sprawled there on the ground outside the gazebo, and when I looked up I saw the great black cat preparing to strike. I barely had time to think, to focus—I only had time to react.

The lines flooded into my skin, absorbing every pore, coating every cell and when my eyes flashed open and I caught the gaze of that big black cat, every bit of white energy and seeping power flowed right into him.

# TWENTY-ONE

HE'D FOUGHT TO THE END.

The lines shot out from me, flooded from me as the panther pounced, but there was too much pent-up magic, too much aggression and frustration from the lines to stop me from shooting hexes and spells and crippling injuries at the beast as it came at me.

"Leave, Joe," I warned, and still he continued, scratching at me with weak, ineffective grazes against my arms, my legs.

Every step he made, every charge was deflected, weakened by the force of the lines that pulsed and vibrated through me. They shot out wicked, old magic that the shifter could not take, that I, honestly, could barely manage to control. Perhaps I never really did control it.

He stopped fighting once I reached the Elam, and when I picked it up, when I managed to crawl toward the trellis with Joe's blood coating my fingers and smeared across that beautiful tortoise face, Joe stopped moving altogether.

"*Cumaisc*," I muttered, pushing the Elam back into the amulet.

The effect was immediate. Beyond the shield the Cove went still. The approaching mortals froze mid-trot. The firemen and emerging feds that slipped from their cars paused, eyes stopping in blinks, breaths held as the surge of magic waved over the town and the lines were once again tempered by the strength of the Elam.

Birds in midflight overhead went still, the water from the hoses stopped in mid-stream and all the mortals around us simply ceased doing whatever it was they were involved in, pausing where they stood. Wizards, witches, and shifters, however, watched it all unfold, caught the quick flow of magic tempered and resettled once again as the Elam fixed itself right and took in that ley line energy.

Papa looked around the crowd, nodding, before he moved away, likely heading back to see to Carter and sort out what came next. My sister smiled, shoulders lowering. My brother ran his hands over his fade, scrubbing the back of his neck, his features relaxing as Mai touched his arm. The tension left them quickly, easily, and I offered them both a smile of my own until I shifted my gaze to Bane and knew, with one glance, that he saw everything now.

It was all there shifting beyond the block he'd lowered, part of my memories. It came back in a flash and passed just as quickly.

*Bile rose quick in my throat and my father stumbled when I jerked against his hold. But he wasn't wrong. Some part of me knew that, saw it in the fear and frantic way Carter held Bane. There was desperation in the old wizard's features that I had never seen before.*

*And Bane. I could not take the fear working in his eyes. I could not let that shock, the horror that etched into his features settle too deeply. It was bliss when our nexuses melded. It had been safe and home and secure, but who was I to take all of that and leave none for anyone else? My home was wherever my family was. My safety, my happiness would come only when theirs did. Who was I to take that from them? From everyone in Crimson Cove?*

*"Don't be greedy,"* Carter said, letting Bane come to me.

*I glanced at the old wizard once, hating him, despising everything about him. "Leave us."*

*"Janiver..."*

*"Papa, if you want me to take his memories, I'll do it in private."* My father came to my side, stood next to Carter as both men glared at me. *"Leave us,"* I repeated, keeping my attention on Bane. Finally, they did.

*"Come here,"* I told Bane, and he obeyed, his head likely still compromised by whatever manipulative hex his uncle had done to him.

But Bane still kissed me, looping his arms around me, his mouth wide and eager against mine. For a few more moments, I let myself enjoy the taste and feel of him. He was mine, no matter what they'd make him do, who they'd make him marry, I would keep Bane in my heart, claim him. She, whoever she was to be, would never have him, not all of him.

And as he pulled me close, I flitted through the memory of the day, grabbing the mark of our melding, taking from him the touch and taste and feel of me against him.

There was a moment, small, microscopic, where Bane's hands fell away and I stayed close to his chest. It was like watching him wake up...slow, confused until he blinked, his expression shifting from worry to alarm and then reorganization when his gaze landed on my face.

He lowered his eyes, until they stopped on my hand resting on his chest. I could still taste him on my tongue. My scalp ached where he'd pulled on my hair. My mouth was still swollen from his kisses. And now I had to pretend that none of these things were real. I had to ignore them completely.

"Jani?" he asked, frowning when he looked back up at me. "What's happening?"

Hell, I'd never see him again, and I would not walk away completely without him remembering at least something about me.

"I'm sorry, Bane."

"For what?"

I exhaled, relaxing when he didn't try to fight off my hand on his face. "For this," I told him and kissed Bane. I poured into that kiss everything that I'd felt for nine months, everything I'd keep safe in my memory from the afternoon we'd spent together in that classroom.

He didn't fight me, didn't pull away, and I tried not to smile or think too much about how fiercely he kissed me back. I pulled away before Bane could reject me, taking three steps back with my gaze planted firmly on his features.

"What was that?" he asked, smirking.

"That," I said, picking up my bag from the floor, "was me saying 'have a good life, Bane Iles.'"

He frowned, disappointment and confusion keeping him immobile, and I turned and left him in that classroom, alone with only the scent of my perfume and the memory of one single kiss.

The movement around us shifted and my shield dropped as the

time sped back up. Before I could blink, before I could walk to Bane and explain why I'd let my father and his uncle convince me to take his memories, my sister and brother were at my side, hugging me, holding me, and Bane left the crowd as several Board of Coven members passed along explanations of a missing panther from the parish zoo as they left the town center.

Bane paused only for a second, glancing back at me, and I hated the expression on his face. It looked like anger. It looked like pain. It looked exactly like goodbye.

# TWENTY-TWO

THE HOUSE WAS A HUNDRED-YEAR-OLD VICTORIAN THAT SAT ON THE edge of Crimson Cove. Outside what had been my childhood bedroom on Lake Pontchartrain, the shoreline dipped close to Mandeville and dotted along the horizon. Even as October ended and the cool snap of fall brought the drop in temperatures and the holiday season, the Cove shone like something picturesque—a Thomas Kincaid wet dream of perfection that had nothing to do with good fortune and everything to do with the pixy dust and fey charms planted in the ground and along the Cove over two hundred years ago.

Charmed herbology or not, I'd always loved the view from my old bedroom window. That had not changed since I'd been gone.

"I wish you'd stay." Mai's voice carried from the door where she leaned against the frame. She looked pretty that morning, with her hair around her heart-shaped face and the light breeze from the window in front of me blowing her bangs against her forehead. My twin walked into the room, pulling her sweater tight around her thin waist, and reached for the opened window. "You don't have to worry about Papa. You can stay with me." Mai closed the window, locking it before she sat on the seat in front of the white frame. "I had the electricity turned back on and took it off the market."

"Not selling?"

She shook her head, shrugging when I smiled at her. "It's a nice little place, just big enough for me and, you know, anyone else who might come along."

"Anyone like..."

"No one in particular." But I caught her shy grin and heard her talking until three a.m. on her cell just outside the ledge that joined her room and mine. The name Lennon and a few giggles had flowed frequently from her mouth.

"You're a terrible liar, Mai. Just gods awful."

"It's not serious," she promised, stopping me when I tried walking away from that view. "And you didn't answer me. Stay with me. Don't go back to New York just yet."

She let me pat her hand but didn't stop me when I returned to the bed and the open suitcase sitting on top of it. "There's nothing for me here or there, sis."

"We're here."

"And you're wherever I need you, Mai." The bed shook when I sat on it and let my sister watch me fold and unfold my socks. "Me not being in the Cove doesn't stop me from having you or Sam in my life."

"And Papa?" Mai's voice was low when she asked that, as though she knew she shouldn't but still needed to. "He's your father, Jani, and he loves you."

"I'm not so sure about that." Almost on cue, the creak behind me at the door brought my attention away from socks to the old wizard who stood at the threshold with his hands deep in his pockets, looking between me and Mai.

Papa looked a good deal older that morning than he had when I'd returned less than two weeks before. He seemed to walk slower, take steps that were more cautious, and I didn't know if that had anything to do with the drunken phone calls or half-attempted visits Bane had made a few days after the Elam was restored. Bane had made threats, I'd heard a few myself and, according to Sam, they were all leveled at Papa.

"*Chérie*," Papa said to Mai, "let me speak to your sister for a little bit." And the little coward left me alone with the old wizard, not bothering to shoot an apologetic smile my way as she left. It didn't matter. I'd be gone in the morning and wouldn't have to bother with hearing his excuses again. They'd come, I knew, but I'd make certain this would be the last of them that darkened my ears.

"Say what you will."

"*Bebe*..."

"Don't bother with sweet talk, Papa. It won't work."

He stood next to me, not watching, not doing anything but keeping his gaze forward, like mine, on the horizon and the shoreline beyond the window.

"I have made many mistakes, Janiver." This wasn't new information and it wasn't something he hadn't already said to me. "Samedi, Mai, what they did to you, was for your protection."

"I know that, Papa." I could no more stay mad at my siblings than I could at Bane. All of them made efforts to protect me despite what I'd been convinced of doing. Sam wanted me with Bane. He wanted us both happy because he had known what that meant once. My brother had held something perfect, a few months of bliss that I would likely never get the chance to understand. He'd still wanted me to have a taste of that. "To see what that feels like," he'd told me the night before. "I wanted you to know what I still dream about every night."

Mai only kept what she knew from me because she knew how it would hurt me to know what our father had done my whole life, just to keep Carter Grant happy.

But my father, I could not forgive.

"You're angry with me, I know this. You may well keep that anger for a long time, *bebe*." His gaze was heavy on the top of my head but I wouldn't look at him. I wasn't sure I could keep from lashing out if I did. Instead of pushing the issue, my father sat behind me on the bed and the mattress dipped when he rested his elbows on his knees. "I came here trying to build a life, trying like hell to make something of myself. The only way I knew to do that was to serve the higher covens, to hide away the accidents our folk made from the mortals. I suppose I've grown so used to serving them, to doing their bidding that I forgot what it was not to agree when they ask too much."

"Even if it means your child's happiness?"

Papa turned to me then, quick, as though my question was an accusation he hadn't prepared for. It was a long while before he answered, before he moved at all, but finally the bed shook again and the springs creaked when he stood. "*Wi*," he said, sounding defeated. "Even then." He tapped his feet against the hardwood as he headed for the door, but Papa stopped short, just near the threshold. "One day, Janiver, I hope you forgive me."

"One day, Papa, I hope I won't need to."

When that door closed behind him, when I knew that Mai would leave me to my packing, that no one would bother trying to convince me not to leave, only then did I let the tears start and leave quiet tracks down my face. I came to the window seat wishing I could swim out into that lake, that the lines would still sing to me out there as loudly as they had just a week before. There was quick comfort in their song and the temptation it offered. But I had quieted the music by replacing the Elam, tempering the chaos the lines promised to bring. I missed it, that wild, raw energy. I missed the sweet crackle of its power as I climbed closer and closer toward it in the woods.

And gods how I missed Bane. His smell, his touch, that sweet, thick laugh of his. I missed him like an amputated limb, like something I always had but never really thought to appreciate until it was gone.

Since he'd shown up drunk and in a rage on my father's front stoop, only to have Sam and a few coven guards drag him off to parts unknown, I hadn't heard from him at all. Neither had anyone we knew.

Hamill, who apparently hadn't been a traitor after all but had been responsible for the sledgehammer in the store window, had taken, a bit begrudgingly, a position with my father's business, amends, Mai mentioned Papa saying, for the awful way Ronan had handled the Donaldson arrest. But even in the brief moments Hamill had passed me in the kitchen two nights ago, he hadn't mentioned Bane or what had become of him.

It wasn't until this morning, in fact, that I knew what the day would bring or why the town had gone so busy with activity.

"A wedding," I'd overheard Mai telling Sam as they sat down to breakfast. "Last minute." And then my sister saw me watching her, saw what must have been likely a bit of devastation on my features, because she darted to me, pulled me to her chest, and held me. "Oh, Jani," she said, "you are the only person I know who makes heartache look good."

I hadn't had a drink in weeks. Not since the night Mai and I watched Sam leading a drunken Bane away from my father's house. I thought maybe his behavior had more to do with Malak's punishment than with any betrayal he felt by my hand.

"Easton Williams will have his hand full," I'd told Mai when news had reached us of the coven's decision.

"Malak can't be blamed. Not if Joe changed him. Not if that bastard was controlling Malak to get to you."

"No," I'd told my twin, feeling sorry for the younger wizard. His life wouldn't be his own in the desert, and he'd have to learn to live as an outcast. His own coven would have nothing to do with him now that he was considered a mixed breed creature. No matter how high the coven, that power and wealth wouldn't save Malak now. "But to be in the desert working for that group..."

"It's better he leave than face the wrath of Freya's family. Selene was livid. Did you see her when Carter Grant told them Malak would only be banished?"

"I thought she'd claw his eyes out."

"I did too. It took Sam and Papa both to keep Selene from attacking the man." I'd almost been proud of the witch. She seemed uncaring that Grant was coven leader. Malak's punishment wasn't enough for her. If I was honest, it wasn't enough for me, but then I knew the wizard better than she did. I had to believe he'd never meant to hurt anyone.

But Freya...my sweet, silly friend still haunted me. I tried to drive out the memory of how she'd died, of what had been left of her, with thoughts of the life we'd lived together as girls. Gods, how we'd laughed, how I loved her. Her death, her loss was a wound that would never heal. I would never let it.

I understood Selene's rage. It lived it deep inside me even if I still held some small pity for Malak as well.

"He'll never be back... It's a fate worse than death to some," Mai said as a shudder worked through her arms.

"Nothing is worse than death." I wasn't sure about that, and we'd destroyed a bottle of Bourbon and I hadn't bothered with it since. It burned too much now.

When I looked away from the shoreline of Lake Pontchartrain, when the bells from St. Andreas sounded, ringing in another joined higher coven match, my stomach dropped and I thought I might vomit. We had not been invited, luckily. As the bells echoed around the Cove and the voices beyond this old Victorian laughed and congratulated each other and went on as though nothing was out of sync, as though my heart wasn't fracturing into minuscule pieces so vast, so varied that it had no hope of ever being repaired, I packed my bags and decided to leave. Not for the city where my nexus would be blocked from the sweet, constant heartbeat of the ley lines. Not for my sister's cottage on the outskirts of the Cove where on any given day I could happen upon the man my fractured heart wanted so desperately to claim over and over.

I packed my bags and made for the beach and the tiny cottage I renamed *L'Abri Reach*. The Shelter Reach.

# TWENTY-THREE

*"What, class, do you think Lord Byron meant when he said 'Be thou the rainbow in the storms of life. The evening beam that smiles the clouds away, and tints tomorrow with prophetic ray?'"*

No one had listened to Mr. Matthews all those years ago, and I only thought of it now because the beach in front of me was empty, because my thoughts were scattered between the coming nightfall and the silence that surrounded me. Biloxi at night, right along my beach, was soothing, calm, and lent itself to random thoughts.

I'd thought of Matthews because the Byron quote had slipped in among the random thoughts.

*"Jani? Any ideas?" Matthew had asked me.* It had been the wrong day to ask me about Byron. I never liked the poet or his work. I especially didn't like him when Bane kept glaring at Nicky Collins for asking me to borrow a pen.

*"Not really, Mr. Matthews," I'd answered, becoming increasingly interested in the doodle on my page and the loop that arched into the cursive B.*

*"No, Jani? You don't have an opinion about Byron's use of nature in his prose? Specifically storms..."*

*"His use of storms," I grumbled, making that B bigger, extending it until it formed a heart. "It's predictable. It holds no weight."*

*"Storms?"*

*"Storms do," I'd answered my teacher, glancing at him when he cleared his throat. "But he used rainbows. Storms, specific storms, would have been better. Thunder, midnight."*

*"Why thunder and midnight?"*

*I hadn't thought about my response. Just then Bane leaned on his arms, staring right at me as I spoke, heating up my skin with one glance. "It...it's when magic is the most potent."*

*That time I looked at Bane, returning his grin, getting a rare smile that made me feel a little drunk, punch drunk at least.*

*"Ah. I see what you mean. Magic, love..."*

Matthews had gone on and on, probing, questioning about Byron, and I'd spent the rest of the class period with my eyes closed, pretending to sleep just to burn the image of Bane's smile into my lids.

The lights from the dock down the beach flickered on, brought my attention away from my thoughts, away from the beach and the water that went on and on, stretching out into the Gulf. Sunset would bring with it kids on their Thanksgiving break, drinking, running along the beach, avoiding the cops cruising up and down the shoreline. I didn't need the noise or the hassle, and pulled my canvas sneakers from the makeshift seat on the sand. I took a moment to dust more of the sparkling white sand from my jeans and hoodie.

The temperatures hadn't been truly cool yet, and the holiday was turning out to be a mild one, one that I'd spend on my own, painting the molding and trim in the den of my newly purchased cottage.

I slipped through the gate, trailing sand behind me, and smiled at the last remaining fireflies that flew near the bird bath at the edge of the fence line. The cottage was old, built back when Craftsmen were cheap and everyone got a GI loan to purchase their first home. It had survived Katrina, though just barely, and needed a new roof, mending on the back fence, and the chippy yellow paint needed a fresh coat. The crow I ate to cash Bane's check was bitter, got stuck between my teeth, but I'd gobbled it down just to get this place and out of my father's debt. I needed to start again, be away from the Cove, from the past and the sins that wouldn't let me rest at night.

That's what I told myself—that this cottage would allow me to begin a new life. I'd douse myself in a lot of elbow grease and DIY sweat equity, and eventually I'd leave the Cove behind me. Someday I might actually believe it.

It was my mantra—that this cottage would be a new beginning—and I repeated it to myself as I stepped up onto the porch, as I opened the screen door, and as I put my key into the lock. "A new beginning..." And then, shifting my gaze to the movement at my right, that mantra got replaced with a loud, shrieking curse. "Mother fuc—"

"Jani! Wait! It's me," Bane said, throwing up a shield with his hands as my hex ripped right over his head.

"Are you crazy?" I screamed, slamming the screen door, my gaze flitting out onto the empty beach and down the sidewalk. "I could have..." He stepped into the light and I went mute. Just seeing his face, the dark circles under his eyes, still with beautiful blue irises, silenced me stupid. "What...what are you doing here?" I said, stepping back when he moved forward.

"I came to see you."

"Why?" I asked, not thinking.

Bane seemed not to expect that. He scratched his chin and lowered his shoulders, a defeated, tired movement. "Can I...can we go inside?"

I didn't think about how that might look. It didn't occur to me that if we were in the Cove and Bane, a newly married man, came into my home with no one else to chaperone, that there would be gossip and lots of it. But this wasn't the Cove, and I didn't care who talked. Hell, I didn't care if anyone was watching, period. At the moment the only thing I did care about was asking why he looked so tired and how the hell he knew where I'd be.

"Excuse the mess," I told him, stepping around half-empty paint cans and tarps smudged with gray and white paint. "I'm renovating," I explained, leading him inside.

I'd spent a majority of the past week sanding and cleaning, and had finally moved on to painting. I'd tackled the monstrosity of harvest gold in the kitchen and dining room and had started in on the boring beige walls of the den this morning. Bane followed me, his gaze moving around the room, squinting at the rubbish rags and dried paint brushes.

"You're doing this by hand?" he asked. I nodded, turning toward him by the large bay window at the front of the living room. "With no magic?" He frowned when I lifted my eyebrows, when instead of answering, I crossed my arms. His frown deepened. "But that will take you ages." I narrowed my eyes and he shook his head. "Why are you doing it the hard way?"

"Because it gives me time to think."

Bane nodded, once again looking around the room, idly scratching his chin as though he needed some mild distraction to help him think. "Well, if that's how you want to do it, I can respect that." He pointed toward the hallway. "How many bedrooms?"

"Two down here, two upstairs."

Bane nodded again, stepping away from me. "You'll need to go into town so we can fetch some trim to replace the rotten wood along the corner of the front porch and fencing material as well. I did some rebuilding in New Orleans after the storm. I know my way around a hammer and nails." He stepped toward the window, moving his head to get a better look at the garden. "There isn't a thing I know about weeds or planting, but I trained with a Scottish wizard five years back and he taught me fey magic for growing vegetables. Can't be that different to making your roses climb."

"Bane."

He kept watching the garden, along the back fence, mumbling to himself as he looked out onto the property. "If you want to do it without magic, it'll take more time, of course, and you might not be ready to open by spring..."

"Bane." He stepped back when I touched his arm, as though that slight graze of my fingers along his bicep burned him. "What are you talking about?"

"Helping you."

For a second I couldn't read the expression on his face, the way he lifted his eyebrows, how his mouth tightened and the muscles around it thinned out his bottom lip. Then Bane licked his lips, looking down at my hands before he looped my pinky with his. "I want to help you, as much as I can. I want..." He dropped my pinky to thread our fingers together. "I want to see if this melding, if you and me, if there's something there."

"I'm sorry?" A small wrinkle worked between his eyebrows when I released his hand and took a step back. "That's not going to happen."

I'd seen Bane Iles angry. I'd seen him turned on, amused, utterly livid. I had never seen him completely stunned, incapable of forming words. He was just then watching me, frown set, mouth tight. "Is it... are you laughing at me?" He tilted his head, his eyebrows set so stiff now wrinkles formed on his forehead. "You're...you're mocking me?"

"I would never," I swore, lifting my chin.

"But...you don't want..."

He couldn't be serious, despite that expression, despite his shock, there was no way Bane could actually expect me to take him in. Not after the bells I heard. "I would never want another woman's husband. No matter who he is."

His mouth moved, opening, closing as though something unspeakable, shocking passed from his mind but couldn't quite make it past his lips.

"Husband?" I nodded, stepping back when he moved forward. "Whose husband?"

"Um, Caridee's?"

"Who told you I got married?"

He ignored the glare I gave him and the quick slap of my hand against his arm when he reached for me. "Was I not supposed to know?"

"Janiver Benoit, please shut it."

"I will not, don't you dare..." But he was already kissing me, taking, keeping my resisting fists from his shoulders as I swung at him until I was against the wall and Bane's low whispered hex made my mouth stiff and motionless.

"Cut those eyes at me all you like, little witch. I don't care." He laughed when I glared at him, barely containing his amusement when a growl vibrated in my throat. "Hush now," he said, moving my face up just inches from his mouth. "I am no one's husband." Another glare, this one I was certain full of doubt, and Bane's smile widened. "On my father's grave, I'm not married." He leaned close, moving his fingers over my face. "I refused the arrangement. With Malak sent off to the desert as recompense for his crimes, my uncle had no choice but to find an alternative. Your father, it turns out, knew of a healer in from Barataria Bay, an old witch with magicks no one has used in decades. He'd mentioned her to my uncle before, but the old wizard had never been so desperate. He agreed to see her, then. Soon she convinced him she was powerful. He took all her treatments, allowed her to work all her charms and he was able to heal enough of the illness that he could produce an heir."

"He could..." I blinked, flaring my nostrils when Bane's words sunk in. "You're saying he can..."

"Before, the illness prevented him from...*performing*. Now, he can. So, he married Caridee himself. When it was made known that he'd fathered Joe illegitimately, he was only too eager to provide the coven with a true heir, one of his own making. And Cari, it seems, was all too happy to oblige. My uncle is very free with his wallet. She is already three weeks along. Their son will be the coven's leader when he comes of age." When I only blinked at him, eyes round, looking amazed, I was sure, Bane released the hex from my mouth. "It's your fault, you know? All of this."

"Mine? Why me?"

Bane sighed, holding my face still. "Because you're the only one I know that would point out how beautiful the sky is in the middle of a hurricane."

"That's not what I mean and you know it," I told him, moving my head away when he tried to kiss me.

But he would not be rebuffed, would not be delayed for very long, that much I could tell with how vigorously he held me, how his bright gaze moved over my face like he couldn't get enough of the sight of me.

"My whole life, someone told me what was expected of me. I had to marry a Rivers. I had to lead the coven. I had to protect our folk from the curious mortals and the shit they do to the world. All the expectations, Jani, and I thought you were the only one who didn't level any at me. But then..." I couldn't look at him, not even when he stood in front of me, challenging me with one of his stares, calling me a coward without uttering a word. Then my gaze went up and I met his, chin a little higher. "But then," he continued, "then you took away the only moment of my life where I didn't have expectations, where all I had to do was touch and taste and take. What that did to me, gods above. Your mouth was pure freedom. Your touch set my skin on fire. All that hope and heat right between my fingers and then you ripped it away."

"Bane, I'm sorry. I thought..." I looked down, still ashamed, before I exhaled. "I thought it was what you'd want."

"Why in the name of all the gods would I want to forget something that made me feel so alive?"

He held me so tight, not letting me budge even the smallest degree. "And it still matters? After all this time?"

"It matters always, Jani. I don't want expectations."

"But your family..."

"Will have to learn what disappointment is. I don't want a life with old wizards and witches comparing how many of their dead relatives were burned alive in Salem. I don't want some life that doesn't allow me to scream every once in a while."

He was higher coven. He had money and power and strength I never would. We'd never fit into each other's worlds. "You deserve a good mate. Someone..."

"I don't want a good mate. I just want you."

If I lived a thousand years, I'd never feel again what those four words meant to me. It was the first time I was completely claimed. The first time I knew someone could want me, could say they did and truly mean it. We struggle and fight. We try to grab what small pieces of happiness we manage to glimpse in this life and sometimes, if we're very, *very* lucky, some of those pieces land. Sometimes, they stick to us, become part of us.

Bane smiled at me, and I loved that expression, loved more the strong glint of the ley lines I sensed under his touch, the red energy that flirted against my skin.

"When you saw the memory, Bane, I saw the look on your face. I... I never want to put that look on your face again."

"You can't make that promise, Jani. None of us can." He moved the hair from my forehead, watching as the small strands fell into place as though he didn't want to miss a detail about me, and right then I knew without any doubts that I loved Bane Iles. "I can't promise that I won't put the same look on your face one day."

"So why would we bother if there's a chance we'll hurt each other?" Something shifted in Bane's expression then, something real, something that had me forgetting what I'd asked. I only knew that I wanted to keep that smile on his face, that I'd kiss him again and again to make sure it never left his mouth.

"Because, little witch, out of everyone in the world who will hurt me, you're the only one worth the pain."

And with my smile came his kiss, that slow, long movement that I'd come to love, the one I'd missed and craved and needed for ten long years. And as Bane kissed me, as he took me to the floor, devoured me completely right among my tarps and paint cans and dried out brushes, I knew he was worth whatever the future might bring.

Please Add Your Review!

Want to be the first to get a look at covers, sneak peeks and excerpts?
Join Eden's newsletter.

Want to hear all about her pre-orders?
Follow her on BookBub.

Interested in meeting fellow Saints & Sinners?
Come hang out with Eden and her exclusive reader group.

If you're looking for Eden elsewhere, she's always hanging out on social media. And she would love to hear from you!

www.edenbutler.com

**Want more from Eden Butler? Try her timeless love story, INFINITE US, and more at www.edenbutler.com**

\* \* \*

*Love is timeless...*

Nash Nation loves zeroes and ones, over-sized monitors, and late office hours. He's too busy taking over the world to make time for relationships—that is, until his new neighbor Willow O'Bryant barges into his life, and now Nash can't shake the feeling that this isn't the first time she's interrupted his world.

Then, the dreams start. And in the dreams—memories. Memories of a girl named Sookie who couldn't count on love or friendship, never mind forever. Memories of a library and a boy called Isaac and secrets made in private that destroyed his world.

The memories seem real, but who do they belong to? When Nash and Willow discover the truth, life as they know it unravels.

The bridge between this life and the next is shored up by blood and bone and memory. Sometimes, that bridge leads to the place we've always wanted to be.

\* \* \*

For books in the world of romance and speculative fiction that embody Innovation, Creativity, and Affordability, check out City Owl Press at www.cityowlpress.com.

# ACKNOWLEDGMENTS

Everything I know about magic (and fantasy fiction), I learned from really great books. I read many of them. I keep reading them and I'm not likely to stop. Some come from authors I hope I never meet (because sometimes the human people who write the stories we love can disappoint us), some come from people who I call my friends. Each story has laid the foundation, however inadvertently, to the writer I am today and tomorrow. To them I offer my most humble thanks.

I'd like to especially thank Sharon Browning, my first editor of this book. No one I've ever met can crawl inside a story and examine, adore, critique and explain it the way she does. I love you, Sharon, even though your Vikings beat my Saints this season (2020).

My fondest gratitude to Tina Moss, Yelena Casale, and the entire City Owl family for letting me breathe new life into this story. I love working with each of you and am so excited about the journey we're on together.

To the sisters of my heart, Marie, Sherry, Barbara, Sarah, and Kalpana, and my "Sweet" Team and betas, especially Trish Leger, Judy Lovely, Jennifer Holt, and Heather Weston-Confer, thank you all for your immense support and encouragement.

Thank you, as always, to my bints, especially Judy, Aymes, Allison, and Lisa for always reading and cheering me on, and to my beautiful nieces: Joy, Jenn, Kayla, and Juli for your constant love and support.

Thank you to each of my readers who are on this journey with me. Thank you for your opinions and advice, for coming out to see us at signings and supporting every event we are involved in. Thank you also to the writing community and the wonderful friends I've made within it including Heather McCorkle, JD Hollyfield, Chelle Bliss and Renita McKinney. You all mean the world to me.

Finally, thank you so much to my girls, Chelsey, Trin, Faith, Grace, to our sweet moon baby, Jax, and to my Himself, Chris, for always believing in me and for helping me live such a blessed and beautiful life. None of it would matter at all if it weren't for you.

# ALSO BY EDEN BUTLER

## THE SERENITY SERIES

Chasing Serenity

Behind the Pitch

Finding Serenity

Claiming Serenity

Catching Serenity

## THE THIN LOVE SERIES

Thin Love

My Beloved

Thick Love

Thick & Thin

## SAINTS & SINNERS SERIES

The Last Love of Luka Hale

Roughing the Kicker

Offsides

## GOD OF ROCK SERIES

Kneel

Beg

## STANDALONES

I've Seen You Naked and Didn't Laugh

Platform Four

Fall

Infinite Us

COLLABORATIONS

Nailed Down, Nailed Down Book One, with Chelle Bliss

Tied Down, Nailed Down Book Two, with Chelle Bliss

Kneel Down, Nailed Down Book Three, with Chelle Bliss

Stripped, Nailed Down Book Four, with Chelle Bliss

Santa, Baby, A Carelli Family Christmas Novella with Chelle Bliss

Find out more about Eden's books on her site www.edenbutler.com

# ABOUT THE AUTHOR

Eden Butler is a writer of contemporary, fantasy and romantic suspense novels and the nine-times great-granddaughter of an honest-to-God English pirate. This could explain her affinity for rule breaking and rum.

When she's not writing or wondering about her possibly Jack Sparrow-esque ancestor, Eden patiently waits for her Hogwarts letter, reads, and spends too much time in her garden perfecting her green thumb while waiting for the next New Orleans Saints Super Bowl win.

She is currently living under teenage rule alongside her husband in southeast Louisiana.

Please send help.

facebook.com/eden.butler.184
twitter.com/edenbutler_
instagram.com/edenbutlerwrites

# ABOUT THE PUBLISHER

City Owl Press is a cutting edge indie publishing company, bringing the world of romance and speculative fiction to discerning readers.

www.cityowlpress.com

www.ingramcontent.com/pod-product-compliance
Lightning Source LLC
Chambersburg PA
CBHW020829260626
47169CB00003B/900